Table of Contents

Cover Credit
Title Page
Copyright
Dedication
Introduction
About This Book
Chapter 1
Chapter 2
Chapter 3
Chapter 4
Chapter 5
Chapter 6
Chapter 7
Chapter 8
Chapter 9
Chapter 10
Chapter 11
Chapter 12
Chapter 13
Chapter 14
Chapter 15
Chapter 16
Chapter 17
Chapter 18
Chapter 19
Chapter 20
Chapter 21
Chapter 22
Chapter 23
Chapter 24
Chapter 25
Epilogue
From The Author
About The Author

Cover Credit

Christopher Coyle
darkandstormyknight.com

CARNAGE

BOOK 1

WHISPERS FROM THE BAYOU

By Sandra R Neeley

Copyright © 2018 SANDRA R NEELEY

All rights reserved.

Thank you for purchasing and/or downloading this book. It is the copyrighted property of the author, and may not be reproduced, copied and/or distributed for commercial or non-commercial purposes without express written permission from the author.

Your support and respect for the property of this author is appreciated. This book is a work of fiction and any resemblance to persons, living or dead, or places, events or locales, is purely coincidental. The characters are creations of the author's imagination and used fictitiously. The author acknowledges the trademarked status and trademarked ownership of all trademarks and word marks mentioned in this book.

For my dear friend, DeAnne Taylor.

You never fail to lift me up when I'm down, support me without me having to ask, and always make me smile. You are the kind of friend people pray for. I love you, oh-giver-of-names. I'm very thankful to be able to call you friend.

Whispers From the Bayou

The swamps of south Louisiana shelter all manner of creature, paranormal as well as natural wildlife. Whispers is a community of paranormal beings hidden deep within the most uninhabitable areas of the wetlands. All of its inhabitants — be they Vampires, Shifters, Gargoyles, Banshees, Ancients, Windigo, Mer-people or any other — came here for one reason; Sanctuary. The members of this community intentionally migrated here over time in an effort to escape humankind and their intolerant ways. Some species were hunted to the point of near extinction, those few who survived, now live here. They all have one rule, one unbreakable rule — no humans. No humans are allowed to know about their community. It's the only way they can all remain safely hidden away.

About This Book

Carnage

Whispers From the Bayou

Book 1

Raised by a father who curses the day she was born, Carolena finds herself in the swamps of south Louisiana under the guise of overseeing her father's investments. In truth, she is making every attempt to avoid forced marriage to any of the men he would have her shipped off to. She's always believed that her husband would love her, would give his very life just to hold her; not be a man who would marry her to claim her father's wealth. When she arrives in the deep-south, she catches the eye of a local backwoods family of brothers. The eldest, Bobby, decides that he is deserving of a step-up in life, takes her against her will to his hovel of a home at the edge of the swamps to be shared between himself and his brothers. Carolena — not the shrinking flower they think her to be, flees into the deepest, darkest, wildest portion of the swamps in an effort to escape the brothers and their plans for her. Death at the hands of the creatures in these wetlands is a better option, in her mind. Little does she know, she's also caught the eye of the most dangerous creature there, one of legend — of nightmares. He's watching her every move, admiring her bravery — and he's decided he's keeping her.

Carnage is a Gargoyle. He's also volatile, dangerous, unpredictable, and lonely. One evening minding his own business at the edge of the sanctuary he calls home, he spies a female. A human female, and she's running headlong into his swamps, with no regard for her own safety. Then he sees the reason; three men, and they're hot on her trail, torches in hand, hell bent on catching her before she can get away. He watches as they get closer and closer to her, easily following her trail. Carnage makes a snap decision that changes both their lives forever; he drops out of a tree right behind her, slaps one clawed hand over her mouth to keep her from screaming, wraps her in his huge arms and goes right back to the treetops. He shelters her while the men traverse the ground below, unable to determine why her trail disappeared. Carnage admires this little female — she was brave to run into the swamps alone. There are many creatures lying in wait for just such a meal. But she no longer has to worry about that, because now she's his. He only hopes that she doesn't fear him too much once she gets a good look at his blue-grey skin, his fangs and his horns. Because regardless of what she thinks, or the rules of his community — he's not giving her up.

Warning: Intended for mature audiences. This book contains explicit love scenes, lots of use of the "F" word (among others), some violence, and possibly some abuse both real and inferred that may be disturbing for some readers. If you are offended by these subjects, please do not buy this book.

Chapter 1

Early 1900's

Carolena ran as quickly as she could despite the tree limbs snatching at her hair and tearing her clothing. The night was black as pitch, which made the eerie glow of their torches easy to pick out in the distance. Her heart pounded in her chest, the adrenaline and fear a live thing in her breast. She plunged into the icy, muddy water of the bayou, scrambling up the opposite bank and into the thicket of trees and brambles. The woods were alive around her, but she had no time to worry about the creatures that may lay in wait for her — the men on her trail were much more dangerous. She ran headlong into the huge web of a banana spider and shrieked as the web wrapped around her. As she turned in a circle, swiping the thing from her hair and face, she whimpered aloud, "I don't deserve this!" She glanced over her shoulder at the glow of the torches following her path, one in particular out ahead of the others, hot on her trail. "Just leave me alone!" she rushed out in a harsh whisper. She could hear the splash of the man following her as he entered the bayou she'd just crossed; hopelessness suffused her, she'd never make it in time. Just as she gave up and sank to her knees on the wet, muddy ground, a clawed hand covered her mouth from behind and a huge arm wrapped around her middle at the same time, yanking her backward into a grove of ancient, moss-covered cypress trees that grew naturally in these swamps. She fought and would have fought harder had it not been for the soothing, shushing coo that was being muttered right at her ear. It was growly and barely discernible, but she was sure that she'd heard the word "Safe" mixed in with those garbled syllables. Suddenly, she realized she was being lifted into the air, held tight against the chest of whatever had her in its arms. Instinctively her hands gripped the dark grey flesh of the arm that held her securely, lest she be dropped to the ground from the treetop, which was where she was so obviously being taken.

Carnage watched the small female as she plunged fearlessly through the swamps he called home. There was not much more dangerous than he in these swamps, yet he feared. He feared for the safety of this little human. He did not like this emotion: Fear. It did not suit him. He was the bringer of fear, not the recipient. His eyes caught the flicker of flames as males followed her trail. He had but a moment to choose his path, one that would alter his life forever. He dropped down from his perch in the top of one of the largest cypress trees, landing silently behind her, pressing his hand tightly over her mouth to stop her from screaming and giving away their position. At the same time he wrapped his other arm around her waist, lifting her from her feet and holding her tightly against his chest. She began to fight, small human hands clawing at him. He pressed his fanged mouth against her ear, "Shhhhhh." She paused briefly in her struggle to free herself. He took that as encouragement and tried to say a few words to her. He was not gifted with speech. Only limited words had he mastered and even fewer of her language, but still he tried. When his growly attempt failed to calm her further, he tried one of the only words he knew that she might clearly understand, "Safe." Immediately she stilled. And with her fight momentarily halted, he took to the tree tops, as he held her tightly against him. She clutched him tightly where he held her as he took them higher into the trees. His brow wrinkled at the mixture of emotion he experienced at her touch. Pleasure was an unknown sensation for Carnage.

Bobby hurried through the trees and shrubs in his path, not even looking up. He didn't want to lose her trail. "Hurry the hell up! She can't be that far ahead," he shouted over his shoulder at the men following him.

He had to catch this little bitch. Her father had entrusted her care and safety to him while she was there overseeing his investment in two businesses located just outside the swamps. Only he'd not exactly held up his end of the bargain. He'd planned on doing his part, but the more he drank, and the more he watched her prancing around in those trousers that no woman ought to be wearing, and thought about how much he'd like that little piece of heaven beneath him; the more he decided that he deserved a step up in life. The like remarks coming from his brothers and her holier-than-thou attitude had him deciding that, yes, he deserved her. And once he'd had a taste, though it had only been a little taste and not quite all he'd wanted to sample, he'd been loathe to let her go. So, he'd kept her. Hell, it wasn't like he'd tortured her. He'd fed her. He'd allowed her to go outside from time to time. It'd only been a couple days, and she'd loved it. Well, he'd loved it.

Eventually she'd come around and be thankful that he'd picked her. Then he'd get to sample all she had to offer. Pretty much everybody in his family'd had to settle. He wasn't settling. He deserved more. All the women in his village vied for his attentions, and this one just needed to be reminded of how lucky she was. Only now the little bitch was on the run. He'd left her outside alone for just a second while he went inside to get her a drink, just like she'd asked. No sooner than he'd gone inside did she run for the swamp. And if she managed to get to safety and contact her father, Bobby would have hell to pay. The man was rich, rich as the devil himself, and he'd not stop until he'd made everyone pay for any indiscretion his precious daughter had endured. He had to catch her and force her to see things his way. He'd be a damn good husband. Well, at least 'til he got bored and moved on, but by then he'd have spent most of her money, so it wouldn't matter what she thought. "Come on, ya'll! She went through here!"

Carnage adjusted the woman in his arms and held her tighter. He'd taken them across several hundred feet through the tree tops. He stopped when he was sure the one they were hiding in was thick enough to keep anyone on the ground from seeing them. He squatted on a high limb, close to the trunk of the tree, using his muscular thigh as a perch to place his woman on. She was shaky, and she was shivering. He tried to remove his hand from around her waist to point out the men that were following her path, but she'd clutched at his arm. So instead, he'd removed his hand from her mouth and quickly pointed them out. Again he tried to communicate as he pointed at the torches obviously headed toward them in the dark, "Shhhhh."

She didn't speak, but she nodded her understanding. Then slowly she turned her head toward him. He froze, afraid that she'd scream when she saw him. He was not beautiful. He knew he was not beautiful, and he was okay with that. He'd never been beautiful. He was a scary son-of-a-bitch. It worked for him. His kind generally made their way by being scary sons-of-bitches. Originally they'd been hired to protect churches, castles, convents and the like, in exchange for food and shelter. But his Sovereign had begun to sell their services to any who asked; he'd become greedy for coin. Carnage and his brethren had been forced to act as guard and soldier to many who they should have been destroying instead. But they'd been ordered, so they followed those orders. But he'd hit his limit when they'd been instructed to hurt innocents. He was a monster, but he was not so much a monster that he would hurt women and children. He drew the line and refused to participate any further in the goings on of any who had questionable characters. His Sovereign had demanded his loyalty and acquiescence. They'd battled, with Carnage eventually walking away — after he'd destroyed his King. He'd wandered for centuries with more than a few of his brethren following from a safe distance. Carnage was a dangerous male — volatile, unpredictable. But since he'd destroyed their corrupt King, his brothers had no one else to follow, so they followed him. Over time some had retreated to outer lying lands of whatever country they'd been in to survive. But in years of late, here in the southern United States, it was the swamp he'd disappeared into, and the few remaining members of his brethren silently followed. And they were not the only ones. There was a vast population of lost souls here. Some had even been born here in this swamp. Others were like Carnage. He was a first generation. He was well over seven hundred years old and had come here seeking sanctuary after centuries of wandering.

The woman made to turn even further toward him, bringing his attention back to her. She was trying to see him with her peripheral vision, but he caught her chin in his clawed hand and gently turned her face back away from him. He knew eventually she'd see him, but right now, he needed her as calm as possible. She was being hunted, and if he hoped to save her, he needed her to cooperate, not scream and try to get away from him.

She shivered again, and he wished that he'd worn a shirt this night. At least he could have given it to her. He placed his hand on her arm and rubbed it up and down trying to warm her a bit. Then his attention was taken again by the men on the ground underneath the first tree that he'd lifted her from the ground and into.

"Here! This is exactly where her trail ends," Bobby said. "She's gotta be here somewhere; she can't just disappear." Bobby stalked back and forth, looking for any trace of her.

Billy, one of his brothers, said, "Here, I bet she went this way. Too much moss on the ground to show her footprints."

"Let's go," Bobby said, taking the lead in the direction that Billy indicated.

Carolena had watched the men searching for her. Holding her breath, praying they couldn't trace her. Common sense told her that she should also fear the creature that held her, but she just couldn't find it in herself to fear him, at least not more than those already chasing her. He was obviously not human — dark, bluish-grey skin, clawed hands, only a few growled words — but he'd saved her. And he'd been gentle with her so far, even trying to warm her skin when she shivered. He was absorbed in watching her pursuers and had not even placed his hand over her mouth again to keep her quiet. She turned a little and saw his face. She couldn't help her sharp intake of breath. He was the stuff of nightmares; rather than hair on his head, he had two heavy, dark-brown horns. They were thick and heavy at the base of each and grew almost straight up, gradually slimming, but with a slight twist to them, and making a complete loop halfway up, then each straightening again, ending in a deadly point at least a foot above his head. They had the appearance of dark, polished wood — even looking as though there was a wood grain to them. His ears were just below the base of his horns and protruded slightly from his head. He had a strong angular jaw, with high, chiseled cheek bones. His eyes were heavily hooded, and as he turned them on her, she saw that the pupils were a slate grey color. His nose, as he looked directly at her, was wide and thick. He had full, pouty lips, a darker grey than his skin, that had he been human would have been considered sensual. May still be considered sensual anyway, had it not been for the canine-like fangs of his bottom jaw peeking from between his lips. His neck was huge and muscular. The striations of his neck muscles straining as he held himself in check, waiting for her shriek of fear as she finally got her first good look at him. But nature intervened.

    Carolena was in awe of the creature that had saved her. She wasn't sure if she should scream, try to escape him, or just continue to be lost in her observation of him. She'd begun to breathe heavily, her mind telling her that creatures like this didn't truly exist. Surely the strain of the last few days had taken their toll and her mental stability had left her. Her foot felt heavy; then, she felt something pressing its way up her calf. She glanced down and saw a big Yellow-bellied Water Snake nosing its way up her leg. She could handle a lot of things, but snakes was not one of them. She squeaked and threw herself at the creature that had her perched on his thigh. She kicked her foot out, dislodging the serpent intruder, and scrambled up the male's thigh closer to his body, throwing her arms around his neck and trying to stand on the same thigh she'd previously sat on, all the while biting her lip and trying not to scream, so Bobby and his brothers wouldn't find her as they moved back and forth on the swamp floor beneath them.

    Carnage wrapped his arm around the female now wrapped around him, reached out with one hand and shooed the snake away from their hiding place. He waited 'til the snake slithered away, then patted Carolena's back. But rather than trying to dislodge her, he pulled her in closer. She held on to him tightly, pressing her face into his neck, and marveled at the calm and peacefulness that suffused her while in his arms. He sat on his bottom, leaned back against the tree trunk, and rubbed his cheek on her hair. "Safe," he grumbled at her again. She looked up briefly, searching for any sign of the snake behind her. Carnage pointed toward the lower branches of the trees. She nodded her understanding and returned to her position, now cradled in his lap, facing him, her body pressed against his warm, massive chest, her face pressed into his neck, his huge arms holding her tight, as they waited for Bobby and his brothers to tire of searching for her and return to their shack. She had no idea what was going to happen next, but she did know she was safer here than with the men below them. So she held fast to the beast that had saved her, waiting for a chance to climb down and make it to town. No, that was wrong she thought — he wasn't a beast. Gargoyle, that's what he was, a Gargoyle. She'd been saved and was being sheltered by a Gargoyle.

Chapter 2

In the wee hours of the morning, before the sun rose, Carolena became aware of movement. She opened her eyes and found darkness. Her body stiffened, and a huge, warm hand patted her back while a very, very deep voice grumbled "Safe" at her. She suddenly remembered where she was and who had her. She'd apparently fallen asleep in his arms while they waited for the men following her to give up and go home. And now he'd deemed it safe to move from their hiding place in the treetops, so he'd gathered her close and started his climb down.

Carnage knew the moment the little female awoke, her entire body stiffened in his arms. He patted her and told her again that she was safe. And she was safe — he'd never allow anything to hurt her. He'd decided, as he sat in that tree holding her while she slept, her soft breath tickling his chest as its warmth blew across his skin. He was not giving her up. She'd not screamed when she saw him, she'd not been afraid of him - well, not very afraid. He'd never had a woman not fear him. He'd never had a male not fear him — hell, most of his own kind feared him. So he'd made up his mind; he was keeping her. Not even Enthrall would be able to convince him to give her up.

"I'm sorry I fell asleep. It's been a while since I could sleep and not feel like I was letting my guard down. Did I sleep for long?" she asked as she watched the deep red hues of a soon-to-be-rising sun seeping at the edges of the dark sky.

Carnage, who was making a steady trek deeper into the swamp, looked at her and shook his head no. But in fact she'd slept for several hours. He'd not wanted to move her in case she wanted to leave him when she woke. So he'd held her as long as possible, until he'd had no choice but to disturb her slumber so that he could get them to safety before the sun came up. And even then, he'd hoped that he could somehow manage to get her to their stronghold before she would wake.

"I can walk, you know. I don't mind, and it's time I was on my way anyway," Carolena told him.

He gazed down at the woman who rode comfortably in his arms, not wanting to let her go. Again, he shook his head, and this time he tightened his arm underneath her and lifted his other hand from her to make an imitation of an "S" shape moving away from himself, and hissed through his teeth. He looked back at her to see if she got it.

She did. "Oh! Really? Well, then if you don't mind, I'd rather not walk. I don't like snakes. But, you're going the wrong way, I think. I need to go to town, so I can speak with the sheriff and see if he can help make arrangements to get me away from here."

Carnage did not meet her eyes, but he shook his head as he kept walking — deeper into the swamp.

"Really, I'll be okay now. You can put me down," Carolena said.

Still he didn't respond.

Carolena squirmed a little, trying to get down from his arms.

Carnage stopped walking, regarding her with consternation, his brows pulled down low over his eyes, trying to figure out what to do next. His female wanted to leave him. He did not want her to go.

"Can you show me the way out of here and back toward town?" she asked. "Of course, a way other than back toward those men. I need to get to town and file a report with the sheriff and ask for protection."

Carnage just stared at her for a moment, trying to figure out a way to keep her here other than force. He used his free hand to pat his own chest, "Ppprooo - tec," he managed to get out after a few tries.

"Yes, you did. And thank you," she said to him sincerely.

They seemed to be at an impasse, then Carnage had an idea. He figured after all he'd done in his long life, a little white lie to keep her with him a little longer wouldn't hurt. He was not above just taking her to his sleeping space, but he didn't want her to fear him. Carnage peered back over his shoulder, as though he was listening.

Carolena looked back over his shoulder as well.

Carnage tilted his head as though more intent on listening.

"What? Do you hear something?" she whispered.

"Shhhhhh," he growled out, then pointed in the direction they'd come.

He could feel her heartbeat speed up and felt a little bad for frightening her, but he couldn't convince her that he could take care of her if she wasn't with him. So he did what he had to to make her think she needed him.

"Safe," he whispered harshly again, just before he ducked into the thickest of undergrowth and started running at a jog. Using one hand to hold her against him, the other to press her head to his chest, shielding her from the branches whipping at them, he hurried her away from the supposed danger he'd heard.

Carolena didn't ask him anything else. Her rescuer seemed to be intent on keeping her away from Bobby and his brothers, and for now that was most important. She decided to try to pay attention to the path they took so that she could try to find her way out later once it was safer, and Bobby wasn't looking for her anymore.

After the better part of an hour, she realized he'd stepped onto a path and had been following it. Finally she asked, "Is it safer now?"

Carnage nodded, replaced his other hand beneath her, readjusting her, and never once broke stride.

The sun was just breaking through the night, enabling Carolena to better see around herself as they started to see signs of life in the swamp around them. Not wildlife, but established life. What appeared to be shelters could be seen and paths that had been cleared to ease travel along them.

"Do you live here?" Carolena asked him.

Carnage looked down at her, nodding his head yes.

"Can you tell me your name? I'd like to at least be able to call you by your name. Mine is Carolena."

He smiled at her, but didn't answer, nor did he shake his head yes or no, just smiled, his fangs peeking through his lips just a little more.

"Okay, then," she said. She was prepared to ask again, when he suddenly placed a finger on her lips, indicating she should again be quiet. Carolena stopped talking, and perked up, looking around for any trace of what he wanted to avoid. Carnage had stopped walking and without warning stepped off the path he'd been on. He changed direction, but before he'd taken more than a few steps, he'd stopped again and placed a finger at her lips, raising his eyebrows in question.

She nodded, letting him know that she'd be quiet, then he tucked her into his chest, ducked his body over hers and started through the thick, dense underbrush once more, making sure to avoid whatever habitation she'd seen signs of on the path they'd been following.

According to the position of the sun in the sky, they'd been walking for most of the morning before Carnage finally stepped out of the thick bushes and undergrowth onto another path. This one wasn't quite as well worn as the one they'd been on earlier, but still, it was a path nonetheless. He examined his surroundings, and, apparently satisfied with whatever he was seeing, began hurrying down the path. Carolena was looking around, trying to pay attention to where she was going so she could find her way back out eventually. She didn't plan on trying for a while yet; she knew that Bobby and his brothers would still be looking for her for quite some time. This creature had been kind to her, he'd saved her, and now he was taking her to his home, or so she assumed. She'd wait until he was occupied and make her way back the way they'd come, only she'd have to be sure to stay away from the shack that Bobby and his brothers called home. Surely the Gargoyle didn't plan on keeping her out here. He was just concerned about her safety. Just a day or two in the swamp and then back to town, so she could contact the authorities and let them know what Bobby had tried to do. She hoped that they'd take her word for it, but women didn't even have the right to vote yet. They were still struggling for every right they deserved, and sometimes a woman in a strange town complaining about mistreatment at the hands of local folk didn't get much credit for their attempt to have a wrong righted. If they didn't give credence to her complaints, that's when she'd call in her father. The man was an arrogant bastard, and honestly he'd just let her venture to the swamps of South Louisiana in an effort to prove to her that she couldn't make it on her own, that she needed a man to keep her safe and make decisions for her — but he was her father. Carolena had always loved nature, and the swamps and legends of them had fascinated her since she'd first read about them with her nanny when she was a child. She'd always wanted to experience them for herself, and her father investing in one of the local fisheries and a cotton mill had been the perfect excuse for her to insist she be allowed to travel to Louisiana and keep an eye on his holdings. He'd argued at first, but finally gave in, expecting her to contact him in tears to save her. She'd refused to reach out to him when Bobby had first starting harassing her, but in retrospect, maybe she should have, and she wouldn't be here now. Wherever here was.

    She was starting to get nervous, hoping that this beast wasn't going to do more harm to her than Bobby had. He just kept walking and shushing her. Carolena looked up at his face, and instead of feeling fear, she felt calm. She still didn't understand how she felt safe with him, but she did. And it wasn't just because he kept rasping it at her.

    Carnage ducking through an opening between two big trees had her breaking her reverie and again paying attention. He paused in front of what seemed to be a big tarp and placed her on her feet. He smiled at her again and drew back the tarp with one hand, indicating that she should enter. She peered inside and turned back to him, "Is this where you live?"

    Carnage nodded and swept his hand toward the space revealed when he pulled back the thick, heavy canvas covering.

    Carolena regarded him for a moment, "Are you going to take me back to town?"

Carnage met her eyes, his smile fell. Then he slowly nodded his head, one time.

"Are you sure?" she asked.

His lips pressed into a straight line, and he pointed at the shelter again. She took his mannerisms to mean he was losing patience, and she was quickly beginning to think that maybe this wasn't such a good idea. Carnage jabbed his finger toward his shelter again, and Carolena ducked under the edge of the tarp and walked into his space. He followed her in and dropped the tarp behind them.

It was shaded inside. Not completely dark, but shaded. All four walls were tarps, heavy, dark tarps, and the roof was, too. Carnage struck a match and suddenly the space was glowing with the warm light of an oil lamp. He looked around himself as though seeing his space for the first time, then back to her, hesitantly.

Carolena looked around; there was a chair, a table with the oil lamp on it, and one plate, one cup, one fork and one spoon. There was a ceramic pitcher, and a huge knife on the table, too, but it was more the type of knife you use when you are cleaning wild game. There was a mattress at the back of the space covered with one sheet folded and tucked tightly around it, and another laying across it. One lone pillow sat at the top of it. Nailed onto the tree where the tarp was attached, was a single shelf, and on that shelf were a couple of folded pieces of clothing. That was it, all he had. This male obviously lived a very solitary existence.

Carnage motioned with his hands, mimicking eating. He raised his eyebrows as though in question.

"No, thank you. I'm not hungry. I'm just really, really tired," Carolena told him.

He nodded his head and took her hand, leading her to the chair that sat by his table. He took a folded cloth from the back of the chair, poured a little water on it from the pitcher and reached for her hands. She held them in her lap, but he insisted, still reaching for them. "Safe," he said again. Hesitantly, she held them out to him, and he very carefully wiped each hand clean.

Then he removed her shoes and stockings. And, dropping to his knees, carefully bathed her feet.

She glanced down at her clothing, her trousers torn and muddy, her shirt not much better, and back up at him. He stood and went to the shelf nailed to the tree, taking an item from there, he came back to her and handed it to her. She unfolded the item and smiled when she realized that it was a shirt, a very large shirt.

Carnage poured a little more water onto the cloth he'd been cleaning her with and motioned that she should take off her clothes. She looked down at herself again, then up at him, "I'm not taking my clothes off."

He nodded his head as though to say, yes, you are and again motioned for her to remove her clothes. Carolena crossed her arms across her chest and stood there. He glared at her; she stood unfazed. Carnage huffed at her.

Carolena said, "I am not taking my clothes off. I don't even know you. You can't expect me to undress and just stand here naked."

Carnage watched her for a moment and realized she was right. Though he was perfectly at ease with her, she didn't know him. She didn't know that he'd decided it was his personal responsibility to keep her safe, to provide for her, to keep her. And in order for her, a human, to trust him, he'd have to prove himself to her. He lifted his hand, the one holding the dampened cloth, and handed it to her. Then he turned his back to her and stood there waiting.

She knew exactly what he wanted her to do. And she was completely shocked that this male would turn his back to her and provide her with a bit of privacy while she changed her clothes. She dropped her trousers to the ground, removed her shirt, and quickly wiped herself down. Then she pulled his shirt on over her head. She checked to make sure she was suitably covered and said, "Okay, you can turn around now."

He turned and broke into a huge grin on seeing her wearing his shirt. His teeth were perfectly straight, beautifully white, with enlarged canines on top and bottom, with the bottom so long they were actually fangs.

Her smile stuttered a little as she looked at his smile.

Carnage quickly snapped his mouth shut, and muttered again, "Safe."

Carolena realized that she'd offended him, "I'm sorry. I didn't mean to... I just..." She decided to settle for the truth. "I've never seen anything, anyone like you. I'm just not sure what to think, what to say. I don't know what you want from me."

He nodded, but didn't make eye contact.

"Are you going to hurt me?" she asked.

Carnage immediately started shaking his head vigorously.

Carolena's eyes wandered around his shelter, "Am I a prisoner here?"

He shook his head a little less vigorously, then, "Pppprrroooooo - tec!" he said forcefully.

Carolena watched him for a moment longer, "Okay."

He seemed to be appeased for the moment, and Carolena didn't want to antagonize the intimidating creature any more.

Carnage suddenly moved toward her and swooped down, picking her up off her feet and turning all in the same motion. He took the few steps to his mattress, gently depositing Carolena onto it.

As Carolena tried to balance herself on his mattress, he reached for his top sheet, shaking it out and covering her with it. Then he stepped back, pressed his hands together and lay his face on them to mimic sleep.

Carolena watched him, "You want me to sleep?"

Carnage nodded.

He turned from her, gathered up her clothing, took his chair from the table and placed it facing the entrance to his place. He sat down, his back to her. She smiled to herself, realizing that she had her own personal body guard. She watched him for a little while, sitting there, guarding her while she rested. Yes, that's what I'll do, she thought. I'll just rest a little. She laid back and relaxed.

Not that much longer he heard her breathing even out; he peeked over his shoulder and smiled to himself when he saw her sleeping, her face peaceful. He stood, tucked her clothes under his arm and ducked out of his space.

Chapter 3

Carnage went to the stream that ran not too far from his resting space. He knelt by the stream and cleaned each smudge of dirt from her trousers and shirt. He held her trousers up and smiled after he'd cleaned them — he'd never seen a female wear trousers and loved that his did. He tossed them across his shoulder, then he took her stockings in his hands and rinsed them, too, in the cool, clean water. He didn't dunk her shoes in the water, but dribbled a little over them, so he could wipe them clean. Only once he was completely satisfied that his female's clothes were clean did he take a moment to clean himself before his return to his resting space.

Fully cleaned and refreshed, he entered his space and carefully draped her clothes across his chair so that they'd begin to dry. He saw that he didn't have enough room to hang both her trousers and her shirt, so he took his clothes from the shelf and hung her shirt from that, leaving the trousers across the back of his chair, and stacked his own clothes neatly on the table. He'd have to make Carolena her own shelf to keep her clothing on. Carnage turned, looking at the solitary dishes and utensils on the table as well. He'd have to get more dishes for her to use, too. Carnage walked over to the mattress she now slept on and smiled down at her. He'd never had his own female before. He had to be sure to take good care of her so that she'd want to stay with him. With that thought in mind, he turned to leave again, this time taking up his hunting knife on his way out. He was going to hunt dinner for his female and gather wood to cook it over.

<<<<<<<>>>>>>>

"What now, Troy? I don't have time for your daily bitch session today," Enthrall grouched at Destroy.

"You should pay more attention to my suggestions. They are not bitch sessions, I just think you could do a better job than you do," Destroy told Enthrall.

"Yes, I am aware," Enthrall answered in a bored tone, "What do you want this time, Troy?"

"Forget it. I was going to do you a favor and tell you that one of your males has stolen a human female. But you don't appreciate me. So never mind," Destroy told him haughtily, his chin in the air.

Enthrall wasted no time ghosting to where Destroy stood. He knew the male hated it, and it would throw him off his confident attitude, so he did it more than he should, but this time it was more than that. Humans were forbidden in their community. It was rule number one. No fucking humans.

"Bullshit!" Enthrall snapped just inches from Destroy's face, his fangs on full display. Enthrall was the leader of Whispers — the community where they all resided. He was their leader, their judge and their jury. They all lived by his rules because he kept them all safe. He managed to secure for them all they needed and kept a glamour in place to keep their community from being stumbled upon by accident. He was also hell on wheels when pissed off, but he was fair. They feared him. They respected him. He was by far the oldest of the creatures that had sought refuge at Whispers. There were those who were more 'nature' than creature, those that they called the Ancients, but they'd just always been there, as opposed to having sought refuge. There was no way of calculating their ages. They just existed, coming and going as they pleased. But of those who chose to be a part of Whispers, they recognized Enthrall as their leader. It had actually been his own refuge before he started welcoming others in, and then the community started to grow.

Destroy took a step back, "Get out of my face, Vampire!" he hissed threateningly, his voice low and deadly.

Enthrall took a step toward Destroy, putting himself right back where he was in relation to Destroy before he'd stepped back.

"Do not come into my home, pretend to deliver some bit of new information, then think you can walk away without finishing your story. And if you use that threatening tone with me again, you will have no doubt that you've made a mistake, *Troy*," Enthrall said in a deceptively calm voice, with emphasis on Troy.

"My name is Destroy. Not Troy," Destroy said.

"I know exactly who the fuck you are. Now tell me why you disturb my peace this day with your stories of a stolen female."

Destroy had thought to bring this new piece of information to Enthrall, maybe score some points with him. He personally hated Enthrall and all he represented. Destroy believed that he should be their leader. But there was a problem with that: Destroy was young, as far as Goyles went. Had he been human, he'd have been called an upstart; he was full of piss and vinegar. Nothing but attitude, resenting any form of authority. Destroy liked the finer things in life and hated living in the swamps, but the few times he'd left to strike out on his own, Enthrall had had to go rescue him, which just added to his resentment of the Vampire. And Destroy was full of testosterone, always watching the females in the community. He needed an outlet for his own needs and resented any male who had his own female. And even more resented any female who had no male and would have nothing to do with him. But it was his own damn fault. You did not just decide you should be respected and get it. It had to be earned. That was the part Destroy didn't get. He thought because he was a Goyle, the others should respect him. They didn't; his attitude grated on most. In truth he wasn't a bad male, just irritating as all get out in his arrogance. So Enthrall tried to be patient with him, give him time to come into his own and possibly gain some respect. Enthrall knew well that Destroy wanted to be the leader of Whispers. What Destroy didn't understand was that being leader also meant being protector, and sometimes when needed, provider among other things.

Maybe one day Destroy could grow into a worthy male. But today wasn't that day.

"Speak. NOW!" Enthrall barked.

Realizing that this meeting wasn't going as planned, Destroy decided he'd better come clean, "I saw him down at the freshwater stream. He was washing out a female's clothes. He even took care to clean her shoes. Then he went back to his place. I followed, waited outside, listening, watching."

"Of course you did," Enthrall drawled at him.

"He has no right to have a female! And besides, she's human. So that means that he can't keep her. Right?" Destroy demanded.

And therein was the whole truth of his visit to Enthrall that day. Destroy resented that another may have his own female and he was doing whatever he could to ruin it.

"How do you know for sure that she is human?" Enthrall asked.

"Because I waited until he left again, like he was going hunting, and then I snuck in. There she was, a little human all wrapped up in his sheets, sleeping. Human just as sure as you please."

"Are you sure?" Enthralled pressed.

"Absolutely!" Destroy insisted.

"Who brought her here? Whose home was she in?" Enthrall demanded.

The slow, sinister smile that crept across Destroy's face told Enthrall which male it was before he said it.

"Carnage. Carnage stole a human female and brought her here. Against your rules. And now she's sleeping in his bed," he finished as he smiled sardonically.

"Fuck!" Enthrall mumbled as he dragged a hand down his face. He hated confronting Carnage. Carnage was dangerous. He was unpredictable and volatile. But he was also a very good male. He was the reason the Goyle population had broken apart and scattered. He'd taken out his King, his Sovereign, as they'd called him, when he began to abuse his own people. The Gargoyles had borne their Sovereign's orders in silence, carrying out his decrees, so that he received payment in exchange for their services. But at some point, his lack of character had begun to place his Gargoyles in questionable circumstances, and when asked to slaughter humans and force others into slavery, Carnage had snapped. They'd battled, and Carnage had been the victor. He was a male of high morals, and all he really wanted now was to be left alone and live out his life in peace. If anyone fucked with him, he handled it swiftly. Rarely had Enthrall had to confront him. He knew what the rules were. Enthrall had made sure that he knew and understood what the consequences were when he'd first asked for sanctuary.

Carnage respected Enthrall, and Enthrall respected Carnage. They had an understanding. But if he'd truly taken a human for his own and brought her to Whispers, then Enthrall had a huge problem.

Enthrall turned and started out of his house, headed toward the shanty that Carnage called home.

He'd not gone far before he realized that Destroy was right behind him.

"Go away, Destroy," Enthrall said.

"I'm making sure all the rules are followed. You can't make rules for all of us and not make Carnage follow them, too," Destroy retorted.

Enthrall stopped in his tracks, turning on his heel to regard Destroy up close and personal. He tilted his head slightly, looking at him curiously, "What are you insinuating, Troy?"

"My name is Destroy! Why do you insist on calling me Troy?" Destroy yelled.

Enthrall smiled at him, "Because you love it so, Troy."

Destroy snarled, and Enthrall laughed, "Go away, I have man's business to tend to. The petty jealousy of little boys does not have a place here."

While Destroy stood in place seething, Enthrall ghosted from the front of his own home to the small shanty in the woods near the edge of the clear stream where Carnage lived.

The first thing he noticed when he arrived was that Carnage was not there. He approached the opening in the tarps and pulled one edge back. When he did, the sunlight fell across the dirt floor of the covered space and onto the mattress where a female did indeed sleep. Enthrall sighed. He'd still been holding out hope that Destroy had been trying to start trouble, and there would not be a human female there when he arrived. Naturally, he had no such luck.

He approached the mattress. "Female. You must wake."

She did not respond. He knew she was alive; he could hear her heartbeat, her breath.

Enthrall leaned over and gently touched her shoulder, "Female, you must wake," he said a little louder.

Carolena began to stir.

Again, "Please wake, miss. I must speak with you."

She opened her eyes and looked around, momentarily startled. Then she remembered she was in the Gargoyle's home.

Enthrall waited patiently while she regained her bearings. When her eyes finally fell on him, she pulled back, scooting away from him across the mattress, holding the sheet up in front of her.

Enthrall hurried to reassure her, "All is well. You are safe here. Do not fear me. I've come to see how you came to be here."

She just stared at him, her eyes wide. Then he realized — his eyes glowed in the dark. And while it was daylight out, he was in the shaded interior of Carnage's shanty, so he had no doubt that his eyes were somewhat alight.

He blinked and sighed again. He wanted to kick Carnage's ass for bringing her here, putting him in this position, and everyone in their community at risk.

He decided to try to be polite for now. There was no reason for her to know that her fate was sealed. She'd have to be terminated. He could not allow her to leave here. Every supernatural being in Whispers depended on him for their safety in this sanctuary, and he could not risk them over one inconsequential human female.

He smiled, trying for sincerity, after all it wasn't her fault, "Let us begin again. I am Enthrall. I rule over Whispers. I was told that you'd been brought here, and I came to see if the rumor was true. I can see that it is. Here you are," he smiled again.

She forced a small smile back at him, "Hello. I'm Carolena."

"Hello, Carolena. Would you tell me how you came to be here?" Enthrall asked.

She lifted a hand, indicating the front of the tarps, "He, the, well, I don't know his name. But he saved me. And then he brought me here." She looked around the small space, not wanting to believe that she'd been left alone with a male she didn't know.

"What did he look like?" Enthralled asked.

"Umm," she hesitated. It was clear this male wasn't human either. But she wasn't sure she should talk about her Goyle, regardless.

"He was tall, grey eyes, bald," now she was really stretching it, trying not to mention his skin or his horns.

"Ah, you must mean Carnage," Enthrall told her.

"Carnage?" she asked, shocked. "His name is Carnage? Wonderful, just perfect. Saved by a nightmare named Carnage," she mumbled quietly to herself.

Enthrall smiled, genuinely. He was impressed that the human had not lost her wits altogether, her sarcasm was well intact.

"Does your grey-eyed, bald savior also have dark grey skin and pointed horns?" Enthrall asked in all seriousness.

Carolena nodded, "He does," she answered truthfully.

"And are his horns curled half way up in a complete loop before ending in a point?" he further inquired.

"Yes," she answered.

"Then, he is indeed Carnage."

She said nothing, just watched this new male named Enthrall.

"Please, if you would be so kind, rise and accompany me to my home. We must decide what to do with you, and it's much safer in my home than it is here."

"It is?" Carolena asked.

"Yes, Carolena, it is. Carnage, while well intentioned, is very volatile and unpredictable. If you stay here, I cannot guarantee your safety. Please come with me; we'll return to my home and get you situated there until I can find a way to resolve all this. You can tell me what Carnage saved you from. Then you can have a proper meal and bath. We'll proceed from there."

"So you think that I should just get up and go with you despite not knowing who you are or if you're telling me the truth. How do I know you're not lying to me?"

Enthrall smiled at her; she had spunk — he liked it. He had no patience for wilting flowers of a female. "You do not know that I am not lying to you. But, neither did you know if Carnage would eat you, or feed you, and you came here with him."

"That's not entirely true, he saved me. If he wanted to hurt me, he would not have saved me," she retorted.

"And that, my dear Carolena, is not entirely true. Perhaps he planned to make a dinner of you, and that is why he saved you."

She sat where she was, looking at Enthrall.

He pressed the uncertainty he'd created, "Perhaps he's out now looking for firewood to cook you over."

"He is not!" she insisted.

He smiled again; this one was not stupid. He sighed and gently shoved his hands into the pockets of his slacks, shrugging, "No, he is not. But, the truth remains. You should not be here. Your skin is covered with insect bites, you're asleep on a mattress on the ground inside a bunch of tarps strung together with ropes. This is no place for you. Come. Let's get you settled in my home. We'll talk. I promise not to hurt you this day, and I have no doubt that Carnage will come for you the moment he realizes that you are no longer here."

She looked down at her arms where she had not realized that she was constantly scratching at the mosquito bites that now lined them on every inch of exposed skin. She made her decision, "Very well, I'll come with you."

She stood and stepped off the mattress. Enthrall moved back to allow her access to her clothing. She reached for it and realized it was wet.

"Oh, my pants are wet!" she exclaimed.

Enthrall shook his head, this was going to be tougher than he'd thought. Carnage had already started taking care of this female. He'd brought her here, washed her clothes, and put her to sleep in his bed.

"It's all well, Carolena. I will find you something more to wear at my home. Come, let us go before Carnage comes back. He does so have a horrible temper."

She peeked over her shoulder at the opening in the tarps, "Really?"

"Yes, really," Enthrall answered as he approached her.

She took a step back, and he responded, "Come now, I've already promised not to harm you this day. I must touch you to take you back home."

He placed his arm about her waist, and before she could pull away, he said, "Hold tight. We'll be there in a moment."

"What are you?" she asked on a whisper as he tightened his grip on her waist.

He smiled charmingly down at her and said as though it was no big deal, "Vampire."

Her eyes got huge, and just as she would have pulled away, the ground fell out from beneath her, and she had the sensation of swirling through the darkness with cool wind breezing past her at the same time she felt she was falling.

Suddenly she was standing in a living room, very formal Victorian furniture set about, and Enthrall was stepping back from her. "Welcome to my home, Carolena," he said as he let her go.

Chapter 4

Carnage returned to his sleeping space, happy. Anxious to cook the rabbit he'd caught for his female. His Carolena, she'd said her name was. It was a beautiful name, as was she. He was very pleased with his female. And that did surprise him. He'd not ever wanted one before. Oh, he'd been intimate with several over the years, but one of his own never interested him. They were a lot of trouble and distraction. And he didn't need either. But things were different now, and this one made him feel strange. Pleasantly strange, but still strange. He'd been drawn to her the moment he saw her. He decided not to ponder it any longer; she was his — that was all. He'd decided, and he liked taking care of her.

He pulled back the tarp and stepped into his shanty. His eyes jumping to where she was sleeping on his mattress and his breath left him. A sense of dread filled him and his suddenly numb fingers dropped the rabbit as he stalked closer to where he'd left her sleeping in his bed. He snatched up the sheet, shaking it out as though she could be hiding in it. She was not there. His heart lurched, his adrenaline pumped, his lips pulled back in a snarl. Did she leave him? Did she run away? He hurried to the table, took the oil lamp in hand and swung it low to the ground to get a better look at her tracks. NO! She did not leave him; she was taken! There next to her tiny footprint was another set of larger prints. Ones that he readily recognized. Ones that belonged to Enthrall. He let out a roar that caused most of the wildlife near his home to scatter and immediately go silent. He was going for Enthrall; he was going to get his female back. And if Enthrall had hurt her, he'd destroy Enthrall just as he'd destroyed his own Sovereign. He stomped out of his shanty, roaring and snarling with every step he took. Enthrall was going to regret coming into his home and stealing his female — if Enthrall survived.

<<<<<<<>>>>>>>

No sooner had Enthrall steadied Carolena on her feet in his living room than his front door opened, and Destroy stomped through it. "You see? I told you! You said I was just jealous, but I was not! I was protecting us."

Enthrall placed his hands on his hips, looking down at his own shoes, shaking his head. Sometimes he wished he was alone. With no one else. No community, no other supernaturals, no jealous as fuck, self-serving Gargoyle to have to deal with. "I didn't hear a knock, Troy," Enthrall said, slowly turning and raising his eyes to Destroy.

Destroy, realizing he'd just stormed right into Enthrall's home, stuttered his progress a bit, "Yeah, well, sorry. I was excited to see your response and meet the female." Then, not being a stupid Gargoyle, he walked back over to the front door, rapped his knuckles against it, and smiled sheepishly at Enthrall.

Carolena stood there, stunned into silence. She watched the interactions of this new Goyle with Enthrall. It seemed to her that this new Goyle was more human-like than her Carnage, but still; this one put her on edge. She stood, watching them and did not realize that she was staring until Destroy spoke to her.

"Hello, female. I am Destroy," he told her proudly as he puffed his chest out.

Carolena snapped to attention, realizing that this Goyle spoke. She didn't answer, but she inclined her head in greeting. "Allow me to apologize for Carnage. He is my people, but he is savage — far from civilized. I apologize if he frightened you with his behavior," and he bowed deeply to her.

Carolena raised an eyebrow as she watched him. Enthrall took over the conversation at that moment, "Carolena, this is Destroy. He is, as you can see, a Gargoyle, just as Carnage is." He glanced sideways at Destroy, who was obviously trying to charm this human woman. "The only difference is that as dangerous as you may think Carnage is, Destroy is worse!"

"I am much more safe than Carnage! I am a gentleman!" Destroy objected, a fury clearly present behind his eyes.

Carolena didn't address Destroy; it was obvious to her that he was a manipulative male, regardless of his species. Instead, she spoke to Enthrall. "Are there many of you here?" she asked, genuinely interested.

Enthrall considered not answering her, but as her fate had already been sealed, it really wouldn't hurt to answer her questions. "Yes, there are many of us here. We became tired of hiding in your human world. Afraid of the fear of discovery and the attacks that could come with it. I found this place centuries ago. It was already inhabited from time-to-time by Ancients, but they allowed me sanctuary. Gradually, I found more souls, lost, with no place to rest. I invited them here; we created a community and live here in peace."

"Is it just Vampires and Gargoyles?" Carolena asked quietly, "And how do you move about in the sunshine?"

Enthrall turned his head just so and regarded her thoughtfully.

"I'm sorry, I didn't mean to pry. I'm just surprised that no one has ever discovered you. And shouldn't you be ashes from the sunlight?" She looked back and forth from Destroy to Enthrall, "And I'm curious. I never dreamed creatures such as yourselves existed. Well, I dreamed it, I just never thought it was real."

Enthrall regarded her for a moment longer before answering, "No, we are not just Vampires and Gargoyles; there are more peoples here than you ever dreamed existed. We all have one thing in common; we just want to be left alone. And do not believe every tale you hear, little human — I will not burst into flame should sunlight shine upon me, nor will Gargoyles turn to stone with the dawn. We are perfectly capable of moving about at any time of the day."

"Peoples?" Carolena asked.

"Yes, we are all just people. Different shapes, sizes, colors, habits and sometimes powers, but we are all, in some form or fashion, people," Enthrall answered. "Make no mistake about it, some of us are very, very dangerous." He smiled at her, coldly. "And the one thing not allowed here is human people. I keep a glamour around our land, the swamps, our community. It keeps us shrouded, it makes humans nervous, makes them want to move away from the area as soon as possible. Prevents them from wandering into our territory."

"What happens when they do find you?" Carolena asked.

"They never have," Enthrall answered, "until you."

"And if they do, they can't ever be allowed to leave; the safety of all of us depends on the secrecy of our existence," Destroy added.

Enthrall snapped his eyes to Destroy's exasperatedly, causing Destroy to clamp his mouth shut.

Carolena's heartbeat sped up, her sharp intake of breath letting them know that she picked up on the unspoken threat that Destroy had voiced. She wasn't exactly sure if they'd hurt her, or just never allow her freedom, but one thing was for sure, she should never have been brought here. Now she was stuck. She looked nervously from Enthrall to Destroy. Enthrall spoke to her first, "I promised you safety this day, Carolena. I will not harm you. But you are correct in deducing that you should not be here. Humans are not allowed in our settlement. Carnage has broken a cardinal rule. This cannot go unaddressed."

In the distance, a vicious roar sounded. Timbers could be heard splintering, and the very ground shook with each stomp coming in their direction. Carolena's head turned toward the noise fast approaching the house she now stood in, faced with two very dangerous males.

"Ah, it seems Carnage has discovered your whereabouts," Enthrall said.

Enthrall bowed slightly to her, "Please excuse me, I must tend to him before he causes complete unrest." He turned and walked out of his living room, leaving her alone with Destroy.

"Fear not, little human, I will protect you from Carnage," he said as he stepped closer to her. Carolena quickly backed up, staying away from this new Gargoyle.

Destroy smiled at her in a sinister way, "You are wise to fear us, human, but I will not hurt you — much. Only if you like it…" he grinned, showing all his teeth, fangs almost as large as Carnage's.

"No, thank you. I do not need protecting," she answered, trying to appear calm.

"Of course, you do," he countered.

Carolena decided that conversation with this Goyle was not something she wanted to pursue any further. At his next step toward her, she darted around him and through the front door just in time to see Carnage smashing his way out of the woods, full-blown roar on his lips, eyes immediately locking onto hers.

He threw his head back and roared, "Miiiinnne!" never once slowing his steps as he approached.

"Carolena, you should go back inside," Enthrall told her.

"No. I don't fear Carnage, and besides, Destroy is in there," she answered.

"Destroy, get out of my home! NOW!" Enthrall snarled.

Destroy, responding to Enthrall's demand, walked quickly out onto the porch. "I could take her and run," he said to Enthrall, as they watched Carnage coming steadily toward them.

"You will not touch her. She stays here," Enthrall snapped.

<<<<<<<>>>>>>>

Carnage marched steadily toward Enthrall's home. His fury rising with each step. His fear, yes fear, rising in his chest as each moment passed. He was afraid that Enthrall had harmed his female, simply because she was human. He hurried as best he could, but when one was as large as Carnage, it was not easy to hurry. Especially not in thick, overgrown woods. His own shelter was intentionally in the most thick, imposing areas of wild growth in this swamp. He'd have to thin it a bit, clear a path for his female to follow when she wanted to move about. And that thought brought him back to the realization that Enthrall had his female. He started running, as quickly as he could, crashing through the trees, splintering them as he went, a constant growing roar reflecting the fear in his heart.

As he crashed through the last of the trees and into the clearing that Enthrall's home was built in, his fear momentarily ebbed. He saw Enthrall standing on his porch, waiting for him. And just then, his female, his Carolena, stepped from Enthrall's front door to stand beside Enthrall. His fury again shot through the clouds when Destroy stepped onto the porch, and he took up a position directly behind Carolena, possessively — as though she were his. Carnage roared anew and increased his steps toward where they waited.

When he was but a few feet from the porch, Enthrall went down the steps to meet him. "Carnage! Stop where you are!"

Carnage only roared again, shaking his head in denial, and continued on, Carolena his singular focus.

"Carnage! You need to stop!" Enthrall tried again, moving to stand directly in the path that Carnage seemed to be following.

Carnage moved his focus from Carolena to Enthrall, snarling, "Mine!" as he tried to go round the Vampire who now stood planted firmly in his path.

"She is not yours! She is a human. And you sealed her fate when you brought her here! Stand down! Now! This is all your fault. You knew better!" Enthrall yelled at him.

Carnage came to a sudden halt, eyes locked on Enthrall's eyes. He'd never wished to have words as much as now. He stood his ground, struggling for the words he needed, "No. Huuurrrrrtttt." He managed to garble out, while shoving his pointed finger in Carolena's direction.

"I have to protect our people, Carnage. She can't just be allowed to walk away," Enthrall said sadly. Then, "You created this situation. Not me."

Destroy chose that moment to put his arm around Carolena's shoulders and speak quietly to her. Carnage snapped. He shoved Enthrall aside and stormed the porch where Carolena stood. He grabbed Carolena with one hand and wrapped the other around Destroy's throat. Roaring, "Minnne!" while lifting Destroy off his feet at the same time he shoved Carolena behind himself. Destroy started fighting to get free, roaring back at Carnage. The struggle toppled several of the rockers and the glass coffee table that Enthrall kept on his porch for relaxing. Enthrall rushed the porch, taking Carolena's hand and pushing her toward the steps and away from the battling Gargoyles. She took his hint and hurried out of the way, standing far enough from the porch to watch safely.

Enthrall then stepped between the snarling Goyles, calling on his own strength to force them both to stop, his throat emitting a high-pitched sound that only supernaturals could hear. Both Goyles hunched in on themselves; Carnage dropped Destroy. Both immediately covered their ears in an effort to stop the sudden piercing pain. Only when it was obvious both were hurting did Enthrall stop.

When Destroy recovered first, which was expected because he was the more humanesque of the two, and made to go around Carnage to where Carolena stood in the yard, Enthralled snarled, "You go near her, and I'll let him have you. I will not stop him."

Destroy froze, looking accusingly at Enthrall.

"Carnage was wrong to bring her here. That doesn't mean you get to keep her. She's not a pet."

"Then what are you going to do with her? You gonna kill her? Do it now! He shouldn't get to keep her at all!" Destroy shouted.

Carolena stepped back, realizing that being kept here against her will was not the worst thing that could happen. They meant to end her. To be sure that she could never tell of their existence. She let out a soft sob, as she again stepped back, looking around herself for an option, any other option to dying here. She was surprised to find that several of their "people" had gathered on the periphery to watch the show. She took in her surroundings, taking notice of each individual gathered there; then, suddenly, she was swept up in a strong pair of arms that she thankfully recognized.

Her Goyle, her Carnage, had rushed to her side and was holding her safely against his chest. He glared threateningly at the others gathered there, saying softly, but firmly, "Mine." Then he turned to Enthrall who had come back down his front porch steps and stood about ten feet from them, watching them curiously.

"Carnage, you need to put her down. Don't make this difficult. She can't stay with you," Enthrall said.

Carnage didn't answer, but snarled, low and deadly.

Carolena was scared. Very scared. She was afraid of what their plans for her were. She was afraid of the other Goyle, Destroy. And she didn't trust Enthrall. In spite of his civility and manners, it was his community and his rules that were a threat to her. But if he was at all truthful in his description of Carnage, Carnage wasn't safe either, despite the calm she felt when in his arms. She was frustrated and angry that she was in this situation. Carnage should have known the consequences of bringing her here. She squirmed in his arms, turning to him, she asked, "Did you know they'd hurt me if they found me here? Did you know this?"

He spared her a glance, but didn't answer, going back to his staring contest with Enthrall. Carolena took Carnage's face in her hands, forcing him to meet her eyes, "I said, did you know that they'd hurt me?" she asked calmly.

Carnage seemed to melt into her hands, his cheek rubbing softly against one of her hands where they cupped his jaw. She watched patiently, waiting while he struggled for words, "No. Huuurrtt," he said. "Saaaafffe." He smiled at her gently.

"Really? Because it seems like your people don't want me here. How can that be safe?" she asked. "And even if I manage to get away from here, how do I know they'll not come after me?"

His brows came down heavily over his eyes, his scowl clear, "Nooooo, go. Ssssssttaay," And he held her more tightly.

"She can't stay, Carnage. We have rules for a reason. No humans!" Destroy chimed in.

Carnage looked at Enthrall and Destroy, shrugged, and started walking. He was heading past Enthrall's house and away from his shelter in a direction that would eventually take him out of the swamps with his female safely in his arms.

Chapter 5

"Where are you going?" Enthrall asked.

Carnage didn't answer, just kept walking.

"You can't take her out of here! The whole point is that she now knows we are here! Your leaving with her is just as bad as letting her go. Either way, she's out there, knowing we are here!"

Carnage turned back toward Enthrall, "No. Hhhhhuuurrrrrttt!" he said again. Then he became positively terrifying, "Killllll! Tuuuussssshhhh mine!" Carnage snarled in his deadliest growl. His message was clear. You touch my female, you will die.

Carolena, still held tightly in Carnage's grasp, smoothed a hand over his chest at his threat to his own people over her safety. He took his snarl down a notch, afraid that he was frightening her.

But Carolena wasn't afraid of him any longer. Any doubts that she'd had, or that Enthrall had created in her mind, were now gone. She knew Carnage wouldn't hurt her. And he wouldn't allow anyone else to hurt her either. She wasn't sure how she felt about belonging to someone, something that wasn't even human, but she did know he wouldn't hurt her.

Enthrall had watched Carnage. He was indeed a volatile male, one that no one fully trusted because he was prone to emotional reactions. But, when this little human female touched him, he calmed. Even in the middle of a fully snarled death threat, he calmed at her touch. Hell, he'd conceded to their demands of her not belonging here and was prepared to walk out of here with her in his arms.

"Carnage, I'm going to tell you what I just told Destroy; she's not a stray pet. You can't just keep her. And now, since you brought her here, you can't just let her go either. She knows that we're here," Enthrall said.

"I won't tell anyone! I promise," Carolena said desperately.

Enthrall smiled at her sadly, "I'm sorry, Carolena. It's just not good enough. We can't take that chance."

He'd come to admire Carolena. She was thrown into a situation not of her making, but she'd not fallen apart, wasn't screaming and crying at finding out that creatures of nightmares actually existed. She was intelligent, and she was sarcastic, which he had a partiality to. He didn't want to kill her. Wasn't going to kill her. He just didn't know what to do with her now.

Enthrall ran his hands through his blonde hair. "Fuck," he muttered under his breath.

"Carnage, put her down. I give you my word I won't hurt her," he said.

"What?! You can't allow him to have her! It's not fair!" Destroy shouted.

Enthrall turned on Destroy, ghosted to right in front of him, nose pressed to Destroy's nose, "Shut up! Do not open your mouth again. Am I clear?" Enthrall's already pale skin had gone translucent, almost like marble, the nails on his fingers had elongated and become blade-like, and when satisfied that he'd made his point, turning back around to face Carnage and Carolena, his eyes were blood red and glowing, fangs on full display, so enlarged that he had trouble speaking around them.

"Again, I give you my word, she is under my protection. She will not come to harm. But you can't take her with you. I must consider all options, offer her a choice of some sorts. She has a right to choose how she'll stay with us. Though staying with us is not optional. It's a must."

Carnage didn't like that, "Mine!" he shouted.

Enthrall watched Carnage standing there, holding Carolena tightly to him as she scratched at her arms, and used the toes of one foot to scratch at the top of the other foot. He smiled slyly to himself.

"Carnage, you can't take her with you, even if she wanted to go. Look at her. Really look at her."

Carnage looked down at his female, and back up at Enthrall, puzzled.

"Look at her skin. The insects have bitten her. She's tired, she's dirty, and I'd bet she's hungry. Your shanty is fine for you. But not for a human, especially a female human. Let her stay here with me. I have the proper shelter for her. I'll watch over her. You cannot expect her to live in the conditions in which you live."

Carnage looked at Carolena, seeing for the first time the red marks on her soft skin, the marks where she'd been unconsciously clawing at the irritation on her own skin. He looked into her eyes and saw the fatigue there and listened to her stomach growl. Which wouldn't be happening if the Vampire bastard hadn't stolen his woman. He'd have already cooked her rabbit for her, and she'd have a full belly.

"Rrrraaaabbii," he said.

"What?" Enthrall asked.

"Rrrraaaabbii!" He tried again. Then he hopped a step or two trying to show them what he meant.

Carolena got it, "Rabbit. He's saying rabbit," she told them.

Carnage grinned huge, nodding his head, thrilled that his female understood him. Then he secured her in one arm while miming eating with the other hand.

"You caught her a rabbit? You were going to feed her rabbit?" Enthrall asked.

Carnage grinned again, puffing his chest out proudly, now that they knew he tried to feed his woman.

"Fine. But what about the bugs making a dinner out of her? What about the cold at night, the rain, the snakes, the spiders, the gators? Shall I go on? You cannot take her to live on the edge of the water as you do. The wild creatures can come right up to your shelter. If you're not there, they'll carry her away, or she'll become ill because of infection — you know what, never mind. Take her, I won't have to kill her. You'll do it through your own stubbornness."

Enthrall turned to walk back toward his home, hoping that his ploy would work.

Carnage looked down at his woman, looking up at him, waiting for his next move.

Enthrall was right. He didn't have a suitable place to take her. He needed to make her a safe home. He sprinted to catch up with Enthrall, growling his name to make him stop, "Trawll!!!!"

Enthrall turned, "What, Carnage? Aren't we done here?"

Carnage shook his head, no.

Slowly Carnage lowered Carolena to her feet. He took her hand in his and closely inspected her skin, already broken and red from the insect bites and her scratching. He smoothed his huge, clawed hand over her skin, then looked to Enthrall, making a noise similar to a hum, while lifting her hand and showing it to Enthrall, his eyebrows raised in question.

"Yes, I have something to put on them. I can take care of the bites and scratches."

Carnage looked at Carolena, indecision warring in his eyes. Finally he turned to Enthrall, "No. Tusshh. Mine," he struggled to get out.

Enthrall nodded his understanding, "I won't touch her, Carnage. I've promised to protect her."

Carnage reached over and tapped Enthrall's temple, then pointed at Carolena, then tapped Enthrall's temple again, "Mine."

"I know you've claimed her. But the final decision is hers, Carnage. I keep telling you, she's not a stray. You can't just find her and decide to keep her. She'll choose."

Carnage turned to Carolena, who was smiling at him, trying to ensure that she'd be safe with Enthrall. "Sssstttaaaay?" he asked her and pointed to Enthrall.

"Glad you thought to ask," she snarked at him, her eyes big as she smirked at them both.

Carnage glanced down, bashfully, then back up at her.

Enthrall couldn't believe it; the Goyle was actually embarrassed he hadn't asked her what she wanted.

"May I stay with you for a few days, Enthrall? I will earn my way, I will help out as much as you'll allow."

"Yes, please, do. I will welcome your company."

Carolena turned to Carnage, "I'm sorry, I just can't go back out there." She examined her own hands, "I'm being eaten alive."

Carnage nodded, then reached for her hand and pulled her toward Enthrall. When he got close enough that Carolena could touch Enthrall, Carnage laid her hand on Enthrall's chest. Then let her hand go, met her eyes, scowled at her, and slapped her hand away from Enthrall as though she was a naughty child. Carolena snatched her hand back, looking at Carnage as though he'd lost his mind.

Carnage reached for her hand again and placed it once more on Enthrall's chest. Then slapped it away again, which had Enthrall dissolving into peals of laughter. Carolena couldn't help herself; she laughed, too.

"What are you trying to say?" she asked Carnage, still chuckling.

Carnage reached for her hand, only this time she pulled it back to her chest refusing to touch Enthrall. Carnage grinned, nodding his head in approval. Then he struggled for the words, "Nnn, nnn, nooooo tush Trawll."

Carolena smiled at him; he was communicating the best way he could since he couldn't speak as much as the others. He used a combination of sounds, grunts, actions and mimes with the few words he could struggle through. He was trying to make sure that neither of them touched the other. He was still insistent that she was his, whether she'd agreed or not. And honestly, for right now, that was fine with her. If he claimed her, that meant she was safe from all the other males. For the moment anyway, until she made it known that she didn't belong to anyone, but that was a problem for another day. Right now, she needed shelter, safety and food. And they seemed to have worked that out for now.

"I won't touch him. Nor anyone else," she assured Carnage.

"And no one will touch her. She is safe from all advances, no matter from who, Carnage," Enthrall promised.

Enthrall swept an arm toward his home, Carolena started walking toward the porch. Enthrall made to follow her, but Carnage cut him off, falling into step between them.

"By all means, Carnage, won't you join us?" Enthrall drawled sarcastically.

Carnage nodded enthusiastically as he marched past Enthrall, following his Carolena toward the house.

Enthrall realized that no one had moved; all the others that had assembled to watch the fate of the human, still stood, watching Carnage and Carolena walk toward his home.

Enthrall addressed his people, "Go. Why are you all still standing there?" They watched him, curiously, not sure of what was happening here. The rule was no humans. And Enthrall, it appeared was breaking his own rule.

"Her name is Carolena. She is human, but she is not leaving here. We are all safe. We will determine how she will join us and contribute to our community over the next few days." He started to walk away and realized he needed to add one more bit of information. Turning back to them, he said, "She is under my protection." Carnage snarled loudly from across the way, "And Carnage's protection. He has made his desire to claim her clear. If you threaten her, there will be consequences." Then he turned and joined Carnage and Carolena where they waited on his porch.

Destroy was the last to leave the spectacle the human's presence had created. He watched everything, missed nothing, and grew more jealous by the moment. Carnage was little more than beast. He'd been the reason their own people had been scattered to the four corners of the earth, and he was the reason they had to hide like criminals. If he had his way, they'd be in control, and the humans would cower from them. But all of that aside, Carnage now had a human female, one that may very well become his mate. And Destroy was left alone, with nothing, no one. It just wasn't fair. His resentment was steadily growing, as was his idea to ensure that none of them got what they wanted. Except him. He would always get what he wanted; he would make sure of it.

Carolena followed Enthrall through his home as he showed her around. And Carnage followed her, following Enthrall. Carnage didn't like being in an enclosed space, but he needed to know where his female would be until he had a suitable place for her. Carnage's eyes nervously took in everything as he followed them around the small house. Enthrall showed them the extra bedroom where Carolena would sleep, and the bathroom that they'd share. He showed her the kitchen and the small office where he kept his books. She was especially excited when Enthrall told her that she could read any that she wanted.

Once the small tour was finished, she said, "If you don't mind, I'd like to take a bath." She'd been steadily scratching at her skin as she followed him through his house.

"Of course, Carolena. Here, let me show you," Enthrall answered. He showed her the hall closet where he stored the extra towels and linens. Then he went to the kitchen and came back with a handful of oatmeal. He started a bath and scattered the oatmeal into the water. "The oatmeal will take the sting out of the bites. Soak for a while; when you get out, I have some salve that we can put on the worst ones."

"Thank you. I know this wasn't exactly what you had planned. I appreciate your hospitality," she told Enthrall sincerely.

He didn't answer, but nodded and smiled sadly, pulling the door closed behind himself.

As soon as he was in the hall with Carnage, Carnage mimed eating and pointed down the hall.

Enthrall looked toward where he pointed, and back at Carnage, "What?"

Carnage patted his own chest, then mimed eating, then he hopped a few steps.

"You want to feed her the rabbit you caught for her," Enthrall said.

Carnage smiled broadly, nodding, yes.

"Determined to take care of her, aren't you?" Enthrall asked.

"'Es. Mine," Carnage answered.

"Fine, go get it. I expect she'll be a while. If she gets out before you return, I will tell her you're bringing her a late lunch."

Carnage turned to go but stopped, looking back to Enthrall with a scowl on his face. Before he could even say anything, Enthrall snapped at him, "I'm not touching her! The last thing I need is a human female to care for. Go!"

Carnage left the house, and Enthrall stood there, in his living room, wondering what the hell had happened. He'd been intent on having to end the woman, then seized the first available option to not have to harm her. It was not like him. He was very firm in his beliefs; things were black and white to him. It was how he so easily led such a wide variety of creatures. His decisions were fast and firm. There was no wavering, and everyone lived by the same rules. Until now. Now he'd allowed a human to join them. Well, taken her prisoner, actually. But he'd not killed her. She was here, in his own home, and he had a lovesick Gargoyle hanging around her insisting she was his. And that irritated the hell out of him. He so didn't need this. Enthrall listened as Carolena dropped Carnage's shirt to the floor and stepped into the bathwater. He could hear every rustle of fabric, every sigh, every ripple of water as she sank down into the tub. His body responded immediately, and didn't that just piss him off?

Chapter 6

Carolena sank down into the tub and sighed aloud. It had been a long, long time since she'd had a hot bath. Her head snapped up suddenly, realizing that she was in a hot bath, in a house that was far from electricity. She looked around the bathroom, no indication of electricity there. She sat up and leaned over the tub, saw the claw-footed supports of the tub and the floor beneath it, but that was it. Nothing else. She leaned forward, turning on the hot water again, and held her hand under it. It ran cold at first, but then, there it was, hot water. Though not as hot as before. She turned it off, puzzled, and sat back in the water. She wasn't sure how there was hot water in this bathroom, but there was. She was going to ask later, but for now, she was going to soak it up. Carolena's mind wandered to just a few hours ago when she'd run from Bobby and his brothers. No idea what was going to happen to her except that she couldn't stay there. Then snatched to safety by a creature she'd only ever read stories about, and taken to his home, where even more creatures lived. If she wasn't so sure she was sane, she'd have been deeply concerned about her own mind. Yet here she was. Carnage was sweet, but he wasn't human. None of them were. Which was why she had to get away. She'd have to bide her time until she could escape. Then she'd go back home and never, ever tell a soul what had happened. She wouldn't betray these people. They'd given her sanctuary. These people. She thought again of those that had stood on the periphery earlier, watching. There were so many different creatures, most of them male, but a few had females with them, and there had even been a few children. No matter how unusual, how strange they appeared, they all looked at her as though she was the strange one. And the families had stood together watching her as though she would be the one to disrupt their lives. She wouldn't do that. Not ever.

Some time later a soft knock sounded on the door. Carolena had dozed off and startled at the knock. Then there was another and a soft hum. She smiled, it must be Carnage. "Is that you, Carnage?"

He tapped twice on the door.

She pulled the stopper from the drain in the tub, and the water started draining. She stood, wrapped herself in a towel, and stepped out of the tub. She dried herself thoroughly, then wrapped the towel around her wet hair. Looking around, she realized that she had nothing to wear. "I don't have any clothes," she said to the door.

He made a grunting sound, and the doorknob starting turning slowly. She squealed and jumped to stand behind the door. "I said I have nothing to wear!"

Again, she got a grunt, then a huge grey hand appeared beyond the edge of the door, clasping her pants and her shirt. Gratefully, she reached for them, "Oh! Thank you, Carnage."

He hummed at her again, then pulled the door closed. What was that smell? She inhaled again and realized that it was dissipating just as quickly as she noticed it. Following her nose, she decided that it must be Carnage that smelled like that. And it made her stomach growl. She was starving! She hurriedly put her clothes on and left the bathroom in search of whatever had made him smell that way.

She found him standing in the living room, watching the hallway, waiting for her to come to him. As soon as she entered the room, he lit up — smiling hugely. "Hi. Thank you again for bringing my clothes."

Carnage nodded, then seemed to notice her sniffing the air. He smiled and pointed at the kitchen. She looked where he pointed and started walking that way. As she entered the kitchen, she found Enthrall placing steaming pieces of meat onto plates and spooning heaps of cooked mushrooms beside the meat. That was the heavenly smell she'd detected, the roasted meat and mushrooms.

"Well, there you are. I was starting to think you'd melted," Enthrall told her, smiling at her.

"Sorry, a hot bath is a luxury I've not lately had. Speaking of! How is there hot water? There's no electricity, right?"

Enthrall laughed, realizing immediately that this female came from a large city, and a family that was extremely well off. There were not many who had electricity or were familiar enough with it to know that hot water could be readily supplied through electrical heating. "No, there's not. Most of our people have never seen electricity. We are able to have hot water because we have metal water cisterns that we have installed on the tops of our houses. They are painted black to attract the sun to heat it, and screened on top to keep the insects out. We have a series of pipes that allow the water to flow through when the faucet is turned. Gravity does the rest. Turn it on, and gravity pulls it through the pipes. Some of us have wells that we draw clean water from, but all of us have water cisterns that we capture the rainwater in for use in bathing and cleaning with hot water."

"That's amazing. I'd have never thought of that. So simple, yet so effective," Carolena said.

"Yes, it is. Only problem is when it's the winter time, and hot water is scarce. It still warms from the sunlight, but not quite as warm as we're used to otherwise." Enthrall was secretly pleased that Carolena was sharp enough to wonder how they had hot water if they did not have electricity. But he was also a little worried, if she was used to living an easier life, how would she adapt to such a different lifestyle?

Carnage grunted at her, and when she turned, he was holding a chair out from the table for her. She regarded him curiously, surprised that he knew to do that, "Thank you, Carnage," she said as she took the seat he offered.

"The food smells wonderful, Enthrall, thank you for cooking. I'd have been happy with just a cold sandwich," she said.

Suddenly, Carnage was leaning over, right in front of her, vigorously shaking his head back and forth, alternately slapping his own chest and pointing at the food.

"You cooked?" she asked, trying not to smile at him desperate for her to know that he cooked for her.

He nodded, and Enthrall was chuckling, "Yes, he said he wanted to feed you. He made it a point to rush back home to get the rabbit he'd caught for your lunch. Then he cooked it and slid some mushrooms on the spit with it and cooked them, too."

Carnage nodded and took the plate that Enthrall held out to him. He placed it very, very carefully on the table, then slid it over to rest in front of her. Enthrall handed her a fork and sat down with his own plate as he handed Carnage a plate, too.

Carnage tore into the food with both hands, chewing noisily, as he ripped the meat from the bones with gusto.

Enthrall, accustomed to the more bestial side of some of his people, didn't give it a second thought. But Carnage noticed that Carolena was eating with her fork. He stopped mid-chew, watching her. He stood, reaching across the table for the untouched fork meant for him, still lying on the table. He picked it up and fumbled to hold it properly, then clumsily tried to use it to pick the remaining meat from the bones on his plate, snarling a little in frustration as he worked at it.

Carolena reached out, placing a hand over his, "Stop, Carnage. You don't need to try to be anything you're not. I don't care about proper use of forks or table manners. You are a good male. You saved me. Just be you."

Carnage looked at her, his heart in his own eyes. Then she took the fork from his hands, picked up the rabbit quarter still on his plate, and handed it to him. He took it from her hand gratefully, and when he put it to his mouth to take a bite, she smiled at him and went back to her own dinner.

Enthrall watched, spellbound. This was what he wanted. He wanted a woman, no matter her species, that made him feel that it was alright to be who he was. He was a monster in the eyes of most. He'd once been human, but that had been so long ago that even he sometimes forgot his origins. He watched Carolena eating the food placed before her, and the Gargoyle watching her between gnawing on his own rabbit bones, and wondered if there was any chance that this female may see him as a good male. He was lonely, and he'd not even realized it until he'd seen the little human showing Carnage that it was okay to be who he was. He rose to reach the pitcher of sarsaparilla tea he kept at the ready and pour them each a tall, cool glass. He kept a storage of the root for just this drink; it was his favorite. He would steep the root in a small amount of water to make a strong concentrated tea, then blend the cold water of the well with it to make a cool drink that tasted very similar to root beer.

Carnage picked up the glass and sniffed it, then, smiled and drank it down in one huge gulp. He smiled and slammed the glass down on the table, grunting at Enthrall, gesturing toward the glass.

Enthrall chuckled, "Yes, I will get you more. But try to make it last a little longer this time."

As he got up to fill Carnage's glass, he asked nonchalantly, "Carolena, you've said that Carnage saved you. What did he save you from?"

Carolena put her fork down, and clasped her hands in her lap, looking up at both the males sharing the table with her. Her lip started to tremble, remembering.

Carnage said, "Safe."

She met his eyes, nodding. Then she started talking, "I talked my father into allowing me to come to Louisiana under the guise of overseeing his investments. He'd just bought into a cotton mill and a fishery. He'd been trying to marry me off for the last year, but I didn't love any of the men he'd chosen. I told him that I'd come down here and keep an eye on his investments for a while. If I wasn't successful, I would come back and then I'd seriously consider any one he chose for a husband."

Carnage growled.

Absentmindedly, Carolena reached out and patted his hand as she continued speaking.

"His foreman was supposed to keep an eye on me, make sure I was safe while I was here. I know my father thought I couldn't do it. That's why he let me come. So I could fail, and he could eventually have his way without any argument from me. But his foreman, Bobby, decided that being foreman wasn't enough. He decided that I should be honored that he liked me — that I should choose him as husband. He started coming up with excuses to come to my room at the boarding house at unusual times. Then he told the lady running the boarding house that I'd been flirting with her husband. She put me out without even allowing me to defend myself. I had no choice but to stay in Bobby's home with him and his brothers. I'd thought of sending a telegram to my father, but I didn't." She lowered her head in shame, "I couldn't let him know that I was failing. But in retrospect, I should have. It would have been better than life at Bobby's."

"What did he do?" Enthrall demanded, a snarl in his voice.

Carolena looked up at him, surprised.

With a great effort, Enthrall reined in his own fury and encouraged her to continue.

She kept her eyes downcast as she continued, "He kept me locked up. Chained me to the bed post. He would touch me every chance he got. He made excuses to walk up on me while I was trying to get cleaned up. He'd crowd me into the corner, trying to kiss me. Shoving his hands under my shirt. He'd slip into the bed with me and rub himself against me until, until…" she stopped talking.

"I understand. Go on," Enthrall said.

"The night I ran, he'd told me, in front of his brothers, that he was going to put a baby in my belly, so my father would have to allow him to marry me. They were angry that they didn't get to marry me, so he told them that he'd share. There wasn't any reason to not share me; they shared everything else, so they'd share me. I decided that winning his trust was my best bet. I told him that if that was all he wanted, why didn't he just say so, I'd have given in a long time ago if I'd known he wanted to get married. I just thought he wanted sex." She lowered her head even more, "I let him kiss me. I let both his brothers kiss me. I pretended to like it so he'd think I wanted him and them. Later, as it got darker, I asked him if we could go outside for a little while, just the two of us first. He took me outside; he was kissing me, and I kissed him back. Then I started coughing, asked for a drink of water. The moment he went inside to get me water, I ran. I didn't know where I was going, or what would happen. Only that I couldn't stay there, and if I died, so be it, at least it would be on my own terms, not their prisoner, being raped by all of them. Just when I was about to give up, Carnage appeared. He wrapped me in his arms and took to the treetops. Kept me safe until they stopped looking, then brought me to his home." She raised her eyes to meet first Carnage's, which were filled with rage, then Enthrall's, which were equally angry. "And now here I am. Your prisoner."

"Carolena, you're not our prisoner, exactly. You just don't understand our laws. I can't allow you to leave here. And I can't kill you. Lord help me, but I can not take your life. So my only alternative is to keep you here. But you're free to walk around our community. You're free to choose who you do and don't want to associate with. You can do whatever you like. You just can't leave."

Carolena smiled sadly at Enthrall, nodding.

"Please understand. I'm between a rock and hard place. I have no choice. It's the best I can do at this point. You're here, you're safe. You just can't leave."

Carolena took a deep breath, looking around herself, then again at both males, "I do understand. And I thank you for choosing not to end me. And for the little freedom you can allow me. I'll try not to be any bother. I'll contribute in any way that I can. But I can't promise that I will ever feel like anything more than a prisoner."

Carnage, clearly upset by her admission, reached out his hand to her, wrapping her small hand in his own larger one. When she looked up at him, he started shaking his head no, then tapping his own chest. She watched to see what he was telling her. He pressed his hand to her heart, then to his own. Looking at her intently, begging her to understand. She thought she got it.

"I know. I care about you, too. You saved me, how could I not? I know you wanted me to be here. And I'll do my best not to disappoint. But this isn't my choice for my life, Carnage. I ran away because I refused to allow my father to decide my life for me. Now it seems, there's just a different male making choices for my life."

"Carolena —" Enthrall started.

"No, you don't know me. Yet you decided to give me a chance. I am aware of that, and I'm trying to find some middle ground here. It's an adjustment. I always thought I'd fall in love and marry a man that I adored, who adored me in turn. Now, it seems that will never happen."

Carnage immediately started shaking his head and pointing at his own chest again.

She nodded at him, "I need time, Carnage. Yes?"

Carnage nodded.

"I need time to decide what is best for me here. I don't want to choose unwisely. I don't want to make a choice that either of us will regret later. Can you give me some time?"

Carnage looked at her for a moment. An awkward moment, before nodding his agreement.

"Do you mind if I lie down for a while? I'm a bit overwhelmed with everything," Carolena asked.

"Of course not. Go ahead and get some rest," Enthrall told her.

"Thank you. I'll just clean these dishes, and then go lie down for a bit," she told them.

"No, I have this. You've had quite a shock over the last several days and now even more so. Go rest. I can get this and don't mind at all," Enthrall said.

She agreed, "Thank you."

Carolena stood, as did Carnage. She reached up on tiptoe, and when he leaned down for her, she kissed his jaw, "Thank you for saving me, Carnage." Then she went to her room, softly closing the door behind her.

Enthrall and Carnage stood side by side, as Carolena walked down the hall, watching her go. As soon as she closed her bedroom door, Carnage turned to Enthrall, lifted his lip as he snarled, "Mine."

"For now. But if she refuses you, it's her right."

Carnage slapped his own chest, then said once more, "MINE!" in a deep, growled voice before leaving the house with Enthrall standing there watching after him.

Chapter 7

Carolena spent the rest of the afternoon sleeping, while dreams of legendary creatures filled her head. Enthrall spent the afternoon walking Whispers. Making contact with as many people as he could to ensure they knew that all was still well under control. Carnage spent the afternoon sitting in the top of an ancient cypress tree, watching the comings and goings of a group of males beneath him, as he waited for dark. As the sun began to set, and the brothers settled in for the evening meal, he silently wished them good appetite, for it was the last meal they'd ever have.

Carolena woke to darkness. She sat up, trying to see around herself to no avail. But she could see light coming from under the door to her bedroom. She got up, slowly making her way to the door, pulling it gently open. "Enthrall?" she called. There was no answer, so she tried again, "Carnage? Are you here?"

The voice that answered gave her chills, "No. They are not here. But I am. I came calling earlier and found they'd left you alone. I decided to stay and protect you in their absence."

She knew that voice, she thought. "Destroy?"

"Yes!" he called back pleasantly, "How flattered I am that you remembered my voice, little human," he responded.

She really didn't want to be alone with him, but he knew she was awake now, what else could she do? "Well, you've got a nice voice," she told him as she headed up the hallway toward the light and the living room.

"As do you," he answered seductively.

She went to the kitchen, poured herself a small glass of Enthrall's sarsaparilla tea, and took a seat on Enthrall's wingback chair despite the fact that Destroy made room for her beside him on the couch.

"Where is everyone?" she asked conversationally, privately praying for their speedy return. She just didn't like Destroy. He put her on edge.

"Well, Enthrall is busy spreading good will, which is not a bad idea after the unrest he caused by accepting you into our community. Carnage, who knows. The male wanders often, from place to place, female to female — he could be anywhere," he told her.

She paused, her glass halfway to her mouth, "Oh, really?" she asked him pointedly.

"Oh, yes. He's quite popular with the females of most species. He's very talented in that arena, I'm told."

"Ah, I see. And you're here, why?" she asked, pinning him with a look that said, I know what you're up to.

"To watch over you, of course. It makes no sense to leave a female, human at that, alone in a place she is unfamiliar with, and quite frankly, not yet welcome in. So I have taken it upon myself to be your protector where others fall short."

"How kind of you," she drawled.

"Yes, I thought so," he answered.

Fortunately, or not, it had yet to be seen; there was a firm knock at the door. Carolena startled, but recovered quickly and rose to answer the door.

She pulled it open only to step back in surprise. Standing on the doorstep, barely discernible in the darkness of the night, was another Gargoyle, almost black in color. He inclined his head in greeting to her, but said not one word. He stepped inside, made eye contact with Destroy, and pointed outside.

Destroy quickly got up and headed toward the door. As Destroy passed Carolena, he said, "I'll keep watch from outside, little one. Don't worry, you'll still be safe."

He went through the door, and the dark-skinned Goyle sneered at him. Just as he spun on his heel to follow Destroy outside, she touched his arm. The male froze, looking down at her hand on his bicep before flashing his yellow eyes up to hers.

She smiled at him and very quietly said, "Thank you."

He, in a perfect British accent, said, "You are welcome."

He stepped through the doorway, but before pulling the door closed behind him, he said, "I shall keep watch until your male returns. You will be safe."

She smiled even bigger for him, and on a relieved sigh said, "Thank you, so much, ah..." realizing she didn't know his name, but definitely got a sense of safety from him.

"I am Murder. Fear not," then he pulled the door closed behind himself and took up the position of sentry, his back against the front door.

She said loudly enough for him to hear her through the closed door, "It's nice to meet you, Murder. I'm Carolena. Thank you, again."

He didn't respond, but she had no doubt he heard her. She took the oil lamp from the kitchen table, went to Enthrall's office, and chose a book. Went back to the living room, curled up on his settee, and settled in to read, knowing beyond the shadow of a doubt that she was safe here with Murder standing guard outside.

Off in the darkness, Destroy watched, infuriated that Murder would dare interrupt what may be his only chance to win over Carnage's female. But Murder was even more dangerous than Carnage. Murder was rumored to be in service to the Ancient that still kept presence here in the swamps in and around Whispers. And that Ancient, he was evil incarnate. That Ancient, no one wanted to incite. There was not an evil on this earth that could rival his when provoked. Yet somehow, Murder had gained his counsel, had become witness to his abilities, confidante to his secrets, and it was rumored could now summon him at will. Destroy looked back at Murder, now blocking the door to Enthrall's home. No, he would not provoke Murder. It was a sure death sentence.

Carnage sat in the treetop watching the men gorging themselves on food and drink. He forced himself to wait until after full darkness, his rage on a slow boil the entire time. By the time he dropped silently to the ground, he was a force of nature, intent on justice for his sweet Carolena. Unafraid, he walked directly toward them, knowing the moment they became aware of him. The caterwauling stopped, the dancing and hooting stopped, and they peered at him with terror in their eyes. Carnage smiled, only sorry he couldn't tell them why they would die this night. Two of the men attacked him as one; he punched straight through the face of the first one and had to shake the man off his fist to prepare to hit the next. The second man, screaming at the sight of his brother with a fist-sized hole through his head, stopped his effort to attack and was trying to shake the very dead man back to life. Carnage lifted him from the ground, by his neck as you would with a puppy, turned the still-shrieking man to face him, and roared as loudly as he could. The man was trembling, crying, begging for his life. Carnage took the time to say, "Car leeeenah, hurrtt." The man went from sniveling to babbling, "Naw, naw, it wasn't me! My brother, he did it! He hurt her! He's in the house, right there! Go get him!"

Carnage watched the man eagerly give up his brother so that he might live. He was disgusted. Any of them could have tried to stop what was happening, but they didn't. Carolena told him how they had been angry until their brother agreed to share her. None of them deserved to live. Without another thought, Carnage reached into the man's throat and removed his esophagus, wind pipe, and anything else he managed to get a hold of. Flesh tore, blood spurted everywhere, but he didn't care. They deserved to die a vicious death.

He dropped the second dead man into a heap on the ground and went in search of the last brother. Bobby, Carolena had said his name was. Carnage snatched the door opened so hard it came off the hinges. He stomped into the house, searched everywhere, but Bobby was nowhere to be found. Carnage roared his frustration as he marched back outside, intent on finding the missing brother. He stood in the yard, his face in the air, nose flaring, trying to scent the direction the male went, when a very familiar scent hit him.

He turned his head in the direction the scent came from, took a step in that direction, then another. Then he smiled slowly, deadly intent clear in his smile, as Enthrall ghosted to a place just a few feet from him, Bobby in his firm grasp.

Bobby was whining like a baby, sniveling.

"Carnage! How are you, my friend? I realized when you were gone too long where you must have gotten off to. I came to watch. I knew you wouldn't need help, but only wanted to see them get their due. I've explained to Bobby here that the biggest mistake of his life was to abuse our Carolena. I thought about ending him myself, but I don't wish to sully my palette with the stench of his blood. So, when he ran, I went after him and brought him back for you." Enthrall thrust Bobby forward toward Carnage, and Bobby began to actually wail.

Carnage snarled in his face, grabbed him by the throat with one hand, and brought him closer. Then he took one of Bobby's hands in his and slowly squeezed, crushing it. Bobby passed out from the pain. Carnage shook him awake. Once he'd regained consciousness, Carnage grabbed his other hand, crushing it, too. Again, Bobby passed out. Carnage looked at Enthrall and rolled his eyes. Enthrall laughed. "You know, men just aren't as much fun to torture as they once were. They're very weak nowadays."

Carnage grunted and shook the male awake again. Once awake and sobbing, Carnage grasped his crotch, squeezing until the snap and popping of broken pelvic bones could be heard, "Nooooo. Tuuusssshh, MINE!!!!!!!!!!!" he shouted in Bobby's dazed, barely conscious face.

Carnage dropped the man to the ground and began to walk away, not wanting to end his suffering, but allow it to go on indefinitely.

"Carnage, you can't leave him alive," Enthrall said, stopping Carnage in his tracks. He turned back to Enthrall, "He could tell of our existence," Enthrall explained.

Carnage walked back over to where Bobby lay moaning on the ground; he stomped on the man's crushed hand, causing him to scream. Carnage reached down, grasped hold of his tongue in his open mouth, and ripped it out — holding it out to Enthrall, who looked at him with a surprised expression.

"Well, that would take care of it," Enthrall said, waving away the tongue as Carnage tried to hand it to him.

Carnage tossed the tongue to the ground and walked calmly away toward the trees, his purpose for this night achieved.

Enthrall watched the man lying on the ground, slowly choking on his own blood. He took pity on him and slit his throat with his sharp nails before walking away to join Carnage on his return to Whispers.

<<<<<<<>>>>>>>

As Carnage and Enthrall emerged from the wooded path that led to Enthrall's home, they noticed two things. First, Murder stood guard at Enthrall's front door. Second, the inside of Enthrall's home was pitch black. Carnage rushed to get to the house, worried about Carolena. Enthrall simply ghosted into his home; it was quicker and much more efficient for him.

<<<<<<<>>>>>>>

Carolena sat in the same place on the settee. The oil lamp had burned out an hour before, and she had no idea where any additional oil was. She'd wrapped herself in the afghan that was folded on the back of the settee and waited. Carolena had peered through the window a time or two and could just make out the shape of Murder as he continued to watch over the house while she was alone. So she'd gone back to her place on the couch, knowing at the very least she was safe. She startled when suddenly Enthrall appeared before her. "Dammit, Enthrall! You scared the bejesus out of me!"

"Are you well? Why are you sitting in the dark? Why is Murder outside?" Enthrall pelted her with questions.

Before she could answer, the door flew open, and Carnage stalked inside, perfectly able to see in the dark. He rushed over to her and scooped her up, holding her close to himself, "Kay? Kay?" he asked over and over again.

"Yes, I'm fine. You can put me down, I'm fine," she answered.

"Carolena, what happened?" Enthrall asked as he struck a match in the kitchen to light the now refilled oil lamp.

Carnage nodded and pointed at Enthrall, as though to say, Yeah, what happened?

"I woke up alone. Only I wasn't alone; Destroy was here. He said he was watching over me while you were away." Then she remembered what Destroy had told her about Carnage and his wandering. She tried to get him to put her down again, "A little while later, Murder showed up. He made Destroy leave and stayed to protect me. He told me his name and that I should not fear; he'd stay until you came back."

Carnage spun and walked to the door, Carolena still in his arms. Murder still stood just outside the door, watching the goings on in the living room. Carnage stepped right up to him, clasping the dark male by the neck. His hand curled around Murder's neck, he pulled him close, pressing his horns to Murder's. Murder inclined his head once, said, "You are welcome," and turned to go. But before he did, he turned back to Carnage, "You should not leave your female alone. Destroy is not to be trusted." Then he bowed to Carolena and walked into the night.

Carnage grunted at Enthrall, who answered with his own grunt.

"Will somebody speak?" Carolena asked.

"I'm sorry we left you alone. I'm sorry I left you alone. I thought you'd be safe in my home. I will have to make sure that Destroy knows there are consequences for entering my home uninvited."

"You can't possibly babysit me 24 hours a day. If you could just show me where the lamp oil is and how to refill the lamp in case it gets dark, I'd appreciate it," she told him.

"I'll show you, but we'll do better," Enthrall said.

Carolena looked down at the hands holding her and realized that they were covered in blood. "Carnage? Where have you been? What have you done?" Then she realized that Enthrall's right hand was sticky with blood as well. "Where have the both of you been?"

Enthrall went straight to the kitchen sink, turning on the faucet and rinsing his hand clean, while barking at Carnage, "Put her down! You're ruining my afghan!"

Carnage snarled at Enthrall, but put Carolena on her feet, then looked down at himself. He'd been covered in arterial spray when he killed the brothers. And now the afghan that had been covering Carolena was almost as bloody as he was, but thankfully, none of it was on Carolena.

He pointed at Enthrall forcefully, then the floor just as forcefully.

Enthralled answered, "Yes, I'll stay here."

Carnage offered Carolena a shaky smile, then rushed out of the door. He was going to bathe in the stream near his sleeping space. He planned to come back when he was clean.

"Where is he going?" Carolena asked Enthrall.

"I'm guessing to get cleaned up," he answered.

"What did you two do tonight?" she asked.

"Let us just say that you are safe from Bobby and his brothers. They'll never threaten you or harm you again," he told her with a slight growl to his voice.

Carolena's mouth dropped open; she was shocked.

"Close your mouth, Carolena," he told her softly as he walked past her to retrieve the bloodied afghan from where Carnage had left it on the floor. She just gaped at him, so he reached out and gently placed one finger under her chin, closing her mouth.

"Come now, you can't be shocked. We are not human. We have our own brand of justice, and if someone we value is harmed, we react in a fashion only wild beasts could comprehend. Perhaps it's because we are at times more beast than person." His eyes wandered to the door that Carnage had recently left through, "Some of us more than others."

"You value me?" she quietly asked.

He stared her in the eye, but didn't answer — just went back to the kitchen, afghan in hand, to try to rinse away the blood.

Chapter 8

Carnage went straight to the stream that ran by his sleeping space. He shed his clothes and splashed into the cool, clean water. He swept handfuls of sand from the bottom of the stream and rubbed it together between his hands to scrub away the last of the blood clinging to his skin. He smoothed it over his chest, his face, even his horns. He wanted no trace of blood on him to remind his woman of the abuse she'd suffered at the hands of the men he'd removed from this earth tonight. When satisfied that he was thoroughly clean, he left the stream and returned to his shanty. He pulled back the tarp and went inside. Carnage could see in the dark, so didn't bother with the oil lamp on the table. He looked around at his meager possessions. He was not a creature that required much in life. A place to sleep, food to eat, and that was about it — he'd never needed more, nor wanted more. Until now. Now he had a female to care for, to provide for. She deserved all the lovely things he could find to give her. And he would give them to her. He heard movement behind himself and turned to scowl at whoever dared to invite themselves into his space. But no one entered his private space. Still he knew someone was there. He silently moved to the tarps that formed the front opening of his space and snatched back one edge. Standing there, silently waiting for permission, was Murder.

Carnage and Murder regarded one another for a moment before Carnage inclined his head in greeting and stood back offering Murder entry. Murder stepped through, looking around himself. He took notice of the few personal things that Carnage stored here. Then he said, "Your female cannot live here."

Carnage looked around again; then, he met Murder's eyes, shaking his head, no.

"You must build her a shelter, much like Enthrall's," Murder explained.

Carnage nodded his agreement.

"Enthrall cares for your female," Murder continued.

Carnage snapped his eyes to Murder's, narrowing them as they peered intently at him. Carnage lifted a hand, waved it at Murder as though to say, go on...

"I have seen him watch her, but she watches you. He is like us, lonely. If you do not claim her, he may," Murder explained.

Carnage snarled, pounding his own chest, and forcing out the word, "Mine!"

"Enthrall has said she has the right to choose. It is not like years past when a male could declare a female his, and it was done. You must win her heart, Carnage. She is not here by her own choosing, yet will not be allowed to leave us. Enthrall says she has a right to a choice. Give her something worth choosing. Not this space," Murder indicated the tarp-enclosed space.

Carnage walked over to the edge of the tarp, taking it in his hand and rubbing it between his fingers, thinking over Murder's words.

Murder watched him; he wanted to help his brother. He and Carnage were the most bestial of all the Goyles, partially because of their violent streaks, and partially because they shunned most all other creatures, including their own kind. They always instilled fear in most everything they came across; it was simply their nature, and it was very tiring. So they preferred their solitude, at least no one recoiled in horror at their appearance. Though self-imposed, it was a very lonely existence. But now, for whatever reason, fate had decided to give Carnage a chance at his own woman. She did not fear him, and after a brief startle, did not appear to fear Murder much either. On the contrary, once he'd made himself known to her, she'd checked to make sure he was still guarding her when Carnage was away. He liked the feeling of being wanted near. He'd decided then that if he could help Carnage win her over, he would.

"Come. I have something for you," Murder told Carnage, walking past him to exit his space.

Carnage, curious about what Murder may possibly have to offer him, followed.

<<<<<<<>>>>>>>

Enthrall finished rinsing the blood from his afghan and squeezed it out as best he could, wringing the water from it. He left it sitting in the sink and went to get cleaned up himself. Carolena took it from the sink and out onto the porch. She shook it out and draped it over the porch railing. She stood there for several minutes, looking around the surrounding yard and the trees in the distance, searching for any sign of Carnage coming back to her. With no sign of him at all, she went back inside. Enthrall was just coming into the living room, "Are you hungry?" he asked her.

"No, thank you. I'm fine," she answered.

"Think I'll have a bite to eat," he told her. Going into the kitchen he made himself a sandwich and then came back into the living room to sit with her while he ate.

She kept glancing out the window, watching for Carnage, and Enthrall noticed.

"He will be back," Enthrall said.

"Who?" Carolena asked, pretending she didn't know.

"Carnage. You keep watching for him," he said.

She thought about it and decided to stop pretending, "Do you think he's with one of his women?"

Enthrall choked on his sandwich, "What?!"

"His women, Destroy told me that Carnage wanders a lot, from one place to another, one woman to another. Do you think that is what is keeping him?" Carolena turned her attention toward the window again.

Enthrall, though he entertained thoughts of keeping her for himself, could not ignore the fact that there seemed to be some type of bond between Carnage and Carolena. She missed him when he was away, and it was no secret to anyone who spent more than two minutes with Carnage that he considered her his. All the "Mine" snarled at anyone who happened to look in her direction was impossible to mistake for anything other than his claim on her.

He could have used Destroy's lie to create more distance between Carnage and Carolena, but he was not that kind of male. He was honorable. He huffed out a laugh at himself — an honorable monster.

"What are you huffing at?" Carolena asked him.

He looked up at Carolena, "Nothing. Just a self-observation," then he plunged ahead before he had time to change his mind, "Destroy lied to you."

Carolena watched him, waiting for more, but said nothing.

"Carnage may wander, but not to women. He doesn't sleep much, he keeps to himself, and he wanders from place-to-place, seemingly never satisfied. But he does not have women."

Carolena looked at him, as though weighing the truth of his statement.

He pushed his plate aside and leaned forward, looking her in the eye, "Carolena, look at him. He's not the type of male to attract a bevy of females. He's brutish, he's volatile, he's reactive and not pleasantly so, and he's terrifying. And in case you haven't noticed, he's not the most gifted conversationalist. I'm not telling you he's never been with a female; what I'm saying is that he is far from the type of male that ladies are drawn to."

She thought about his words and did not like them. She felt the need to defend him. "He is perfectly capable of communicating!" she snapped.

Enthrall, intrigued that she meant to defend Carnage, played along, "If you are paying attention, yes."

"He is unique. He is strong and protective," she declared.

"That is certainly true — where you are concerned anyway," he agreed.

"It's true regardless; it comes so naturally to him that I can't believe that he's not protective by nature," she stated flatly.

"You are more correct than you know, little one," he conceded.

Carolena looked away from Enthrall to the windows once more, then, she said softly, "He's beautiful. He's got the most expressive eyes and lips that look as though he is always pouting. And he has magnificent horns. They are shiny, and twisty, and dark and, and...beautiful."

Enthrall said nothing, just watched her, thinking of Carnage and struggling to see him the way she described him.

She turned back to Enthrall, "He's special."

Enthrall nodded his agreement, "He is. He is a good male." He watched her for a moment longer before deciding to tell her.

"Did you know that his people are free because of him?"

She looked up at Enthrall, "No, I did not."

Enthrall smiled at her, "They are. His people had a King, a Sovereign they called him. He became greedy, no amount of money, jewels, females, was ever enough. He sold the services of his most dangerous soldiers, his males, to the highest bidder. They were made to carry out all form of illicit activity and to protect others doing so as well. One of the chieftains Carnage was leased to became incensed that his people did not give him more of their harvest, more of their meager earnings, and ordered the Goyles under his command to massacre them. Carnage refused to murder innocents. He rose up against the chieftain, killing him instead. And when his Sovereign came to find out why the chieftain was not making his regular payments, he attempted to punish Carnage for supposed crimes, demanding that Carnage bow in submission before him. Carnage refused. He attacked Carnage, brutally tearing his wings from his body. Even with the intense agony, Carnage refused to bow before him, firm in his belief that he had done the right thing in protecting the innocents he'd been ordered to slaughter. His Sovereign ordered his personal guard to end Carnage. As one they attacked him, and still he refused to stand down. Finally, having been summoned by another of their kind to intervene, Murder arrived. He saw what was happening and immediately joined the fight, fighting side-by-side with Carnage. Together they battled against all the others, and the Sovereign was killed. Some were outraged that their Sovereign was dead. But others of his brethren stood with him, Murder especially, wholeheartedly agreeing that their skills had been misused, and they, themselves, taken advantage of. Their people scattered; they wandered for years, not fitting in anywhere. Finally, Carnage wandered into Whispers. He requested sanctuary and has been here ever since. Murder followed him shortly after. Over the years, more of his kind have found us as well. But always, Carnage and Murder have remained distant, setting themselves apart from the rest."

Carolena listened quietly, learning all she could about Carnage. Finally when she realized that he was finished talking, she said, "See? I told you he was good. I just didn't know how good."

"Carolena, you must understand. He is good, but he is very dangerous. He is unpredictable. I told you earlier we were bestial. We all are. But he is more than most. He feels something, he reacts. He doesn't feel anything, it means nothing to him. He is ruled by his passions. There is no rhyme or reason. And that is why he is volatile. No matter how good he is, you are dealing with, basically, the equivalent of a wild beast. Do not forget that."

<<<<<<<>>>>>>

Murder was aware that Carnage was following him. So he intentionally went slowly, so that Carnage could keep up. He could not move as quickly as he once did. His lack of wings hindered him. Deeper into the swamps they went until there was almost no dry land left. Carnage had had to take to the treetops in order to follow Murder who flew just ahead of him, right above the trees.

Finally, up ahead, Carnage spied a structure made of wood, standing high above the water. Carnage made a couple of strategic leaps from the trees surrounding the structure, and a short time later landed on the deck of the building, where Murder stood waiting for him. His wings folded neatly against his back.

When Carnage finally came to a stop in front of him, Murder said, "You can have it."

Carnage looked at the structure. He pointed at the building they were standing on the deck of, eyebrows raised.

"Yes. This structure. You may have it. It is made of cypress wood. It will last a very, very long time. There are items inside that your female may like as well. You are welcome to it all."

Carnage forced open the door and went into the structure. He walked around, looking at all the items still inside.

"It was Lore's long ago. He deserted it when he failed to secure his female."

Carnage whipped his head around to pin Murder with an unbelieving stare.

Murder offered a sad smile, "It is true. Even Ancients have but one they are destined to love forever. He's followed her for centuries — lifetime after lifetime, and yet she always remains just out of his reach. He suffers in silence, watching from afar, never quite able to reach her. Just as he thinks he's got a chance, she disappears from this realm yet again."

Carnage watched his friend speak of the Ancient that most creatures feared, as though he were a heartsick male, not an evil entity.

Murder knew what Carnage thought of Lore; he knew what they all thought of Lore. He alone held the male's confidence and would not break it any more than he already had, not even for Carnage. So on a shrug he whispered, "An eternity of unrequited love can drive even the strongest of creatures insane."

Murder looked around the raised house, "I've maintained it. I come here to escape everyone and everything. But it would serve better as a home for your female. You may take the wood, the posts that support it above the water, all of it. Take it and move it further inland, where she'll be safer. Where she can take herself about as she chooses, and not be trapped here until you come for her."

Carnage looked around, a slow smile growing on his face. His eyes met Murder's and he grinned.

"So, I'll take that smile as a yes?" Murder asked.

Carnage nodded and walked over to the wall, knocking on the wood, getting a feel for how he could take it apart.

"Do you know where you want to rebuild it?" Murder asked.

Carnage thought about it for a moment, then smiled, nodding, "'Es!"

"Well, then, let us begin moving it. Shall we begin with the roof? It is made of sheets of tin. It will be easy to remove."

Standing out on the deck, Carnage waited while Murder used his wings to support himself above the tin roof as he removed the sheets one at a time. He'd hand them off to Carnage, who would then roll them and stand them to the side, and prepare to receive another.

They spent most of the night disassembling the house and moving the harvested building materials to the spot that Carnage had chosen. It was the perfect spot.

Carnage looked around at the stacks of cypress boards, beams, posts and tin, that now filled the area he planned to build Carolena's house in. He looked up into the trees and did not even flinch when Murder landed beside him, with the final load for the night. Murder followed his line of vision, then slapped Carnage on the shoulder, "It is a good place. It is perfect for her. You have chosen well, my friend."

Carnage turned to Murder, unable to contain his smile. "Than 'uu," he struggled to tell Murder how much he appreciated his generosity.

Murder waited patiently for Carnage to say what he was trying to say, "You are welcome, Carnage. We deserve good things. Both of us. And it is past time for you. If she sees the male you are, do not waste a moment." He took Carnage by the shoulders, pulling him a bit closer before saying, "Seize your happy, Carnage. With both hands, seize it and do not let go."

Chapter 9

Carolena finally gave up on Carnage coming back. She rose from the settee, took the oil lamp in hand and went to her bedroom. She set the lamp on her dresser, stripped out of her clothes and climbed under the covers. Her head knew that Enthrall had called out the lies that Destroy had told her, but her heart still wondered why Carnage didn't come back to check on her. She lay awake for what seemed like hours, awaiting his return, finally drifting off to sleep with thoughts of him prevalent in her mind.

She'd fought sleep for so long that once she did fall asleep, though troubled, she slept deeply. Unaware that in the wee hours of the morning, a very tired, but very satisfied Gargoyle slipped into bed behind her, rested an arm protectively across her waist and fell asleep with a smile on his face, his nose buried in her hair.

<<<<<<<>>>>>>

Carnage and Murder had finished working for the night. After thanking Murder again and agreeing to meet tomorrow to pick up where they left off, he went straight back to the stream near his old space and quickly bathed again. Then he hurried to Enthrall's home. He let himself in and moved quietly to Carolena's bedroom. He opened the door slowly and peered in. His woman was curled on her side, the quilt grasped in both hands, tucked under her chin. He approached her on tip-toe so as not to wake her; he felt his heart warm as he gazed down at her sleeping. He turned down the flame on the oil lamp she'd left on her dresser and crawled onto the bed behind her. Carolena moved and murmured in her sleep; he curled up behind her rumbling, "Safe," and she settled right down. Falling back to sleep easily with his arm across her waist and her Gargoyle spooned closely behind her.

<<<<<<<>>>>>>>

Carolena rolled to the middle of the double bed and stretched, moaning pleasurably in the sunlight streaming through her bedroom window. It had been a very, very long time since she'd had such a satisfying sleep. Ending her stretch, she left her arms splayed to each side of the bed, becoming acutely conscious of the fact that she was alone. Carnage was not there. Not that he should have been, but she'd almost expected him to come back to her last night. Maybe he was tired of the struggle he'd been fighting to keep her here, thought better of it, and was now stepping back. The thought made her heart hurt. Huffing, she sat up, threw back the quilt and got about starting her day. Anything to take her mind off her loneliness — perhaps she'd spend the morning with Enthrall. She pulled on her only clothes and made her way to the kitchen, planning to make breakfast for herself and Enthrall. But he'd been there before her. Left on the table was a plate with three biscuits smeared with jam and a cup of strong black, chicory-laced coffee. She knew it was futile, but tried anyway, "Enthrall?!" She waited a moment, and when the expected silence met her call, she took a dish cloth from the kitchen and laid it carefully over the biscuits. She had no desire to eat. She hated this. She'd begun to accept where she was, how she'd live. She'd become attached to Carnage, only now he was pulling away. He was never with her, content to leave her to own devices. She looked around. Sitting on a porch, watching life go by, was not in her nature. She was not going to sit here and wait for him to decide that he had a moment to throw her way. She stood, looked 'round herself, and marched down the stairs.

Adventure, that was what she needed, adventure. And she was not leaving a note. She was a grown woman; she needed no one's permission to explore her new home, and if they got a little nervous because they couldn't find her, that was their problem — not hers. Served them right anyway for treating her like an afterthought.

Carolena walked for hours. She wandered this way and that, admiring towering trees and flowers blazing in colors she never dreamed she'd find in nature. She wasn't even the slightest bit aware of how long she'd been gone until her stomach started growling. She paused, looked back where she came from, and realized that she was lost. She wasn't exactly sure where she was. Looking up into the sky, peeking through the tall trees, she could tell it was late afternoon. She looked back and forth, now completely unsure of what direction she came from. Her heart rate picked up. She was scared. She chose a direction and started that way hurriedly. The noises she made announcing her presence to all wildlife within a mile of her location. What she didn't realize was that she was being hunted.

<<<<<<<>>>>>>

Carnage arrived back at Enthrall's home, intent on spending a little time with Carolena. He'd been leaving in the mornings before she woke, and he didn't feel quite right about that. She needed to know that he was thinking of her. That he was only away from her because he was making things better for her. He remembered that Murder had said that Enthrall liked his female. He didn't like that, not one bit. It was most of the reason he'd come back to spend the day with her. As he came out of the trees and started across the yard toward where Enthrall sat on the porch, Enthrall stood, looking behind Carnage. Carnage stopped walking, turning to look behind himself, then back at Enthrall.

Enthrall called out, "Where's Carolena? Did she fall behind?"

Carnage's face pinched up in confusion, he shrugged, then it hit him. Carolena was not here. Enthrall thought that Carolena was with Carnage, and Carnage thought that Carolena was with Enthrall.

Carnage growled, hurrying across the yard to Enthrall, who was now hurrying across the yard to him.

Enthrall spoke, "Is she not with you?" his voice rising with worry.

Carnage shook his head, no. Then he started running. He ran past Enthrall and straight into Enthrall's home. He went to Carolena's room, scenting the air for any trace of a clue he may be able to pick up. Enthrall came in right behind him. "I've been home for hours. I assumed that she went with you today. I've not seen her all day, Carnage."

Carnage brushed past him and went to the bathroom, scenting again, then the kitchen. Her scent was everywhere, but nothing fresh. She'd been gone a while. Carnage let out a whine and snarl, rushing outside again, his nose held high, scenting. Searching for her. His stomach lurched, his heart pounded — there were too many things in these swamps that didn't care if she was his or not. She was dinner, plain and simple. If any of the wildlife that lived here naturally found her, and he was not there to protect her, she'd not survive. She'd be torn apart. He'd annihilate anything that threatened her; he only hoped he was in time. His slightly civilized nature slipped away, revealing the true Carnage. The Gargoyle that didn't think, the Gargoyle that was ruled by instinct was once again in control. Only this Gargoyle was much more dangerous than he'd ever been before. This Gargoyle was different. This Gargoyle loved. And Lord help the creature, any creature, that threatened that love.

Carnage grunted, snarling intermittently as he followed his nose across the yard. He detected just a hint of the shampoo Carolena used. Yes, there it was, just enough to show him which way she went. He inhaled deeply, no other scent, just hers. She'd wandered off alone. He growled, his chest rumbling deeply. If she was trying to run from him, he was going to find her and bring her back. And he was going to spank her ass when he found her. If he found her. His heart lurched; he had to find her. He wouldn't accept any less.

<<<<<<<>>>>>>>

Carolena plunged through a grove of trees and found herself almost knee deep in muck and mud. She'd begun to hear howls and yips and they were frightening to say the least. At first they were behind her; then, they seemed to be beside her on both sides. It was almost like they were herding her. Carolena didn't know if they were wolves, coyotes, or dogs, but they were certainly too close for comfort. She tried to pull her foot out of the muck and just barely managed to get it most of the way out before it sucked her foot back in. Carolena fell forward on her hands and tried to crawl out of the mud. She managed to get a few feet, looking behind herself and back down at her feet as she struggled to pull them one at a time from the muck sucking at her limbs. Carolena heard a soft growl and snapped her head around. Her eyes got huge, and her heart pounded; there in front of her was a large, scruffy-looking canine. She wasn't sure if it was a wolf or a coyote, but it was big, and it was no more than ten feet from her, watching her, head lowered, snarling. Carolena heard another growl to her right and slowly turned her head that way. There, too, was another, mimicking the stance of the first. Several more deep growls let her know she was surrounded. Carolena realized that they'd been hunting her. She let out a soft sob; she was so stupid! How could she think that she'd be okay by herself wandering around a swamp. The large dog in front of her seemed to be the leader; he gingerly put one paw in the mud and tested it. Luckily, his leg sank into the muck. He growled and snatched it back out. He started pacing the perimeter of the muck Carolena was in, being careful not to step into it. Well, then. He doesn't like the muck; I'm staying right here, Carolena thought to herself. She sent up a prayer that someone would notice she was missing. Again, she cursed her stupidness, but she did not move. She didn't want to provoke the pack of wild dogs in any way. Carolena held her position, waiting, praying.

<<<<<<<<>>>>>>>

Carnage rushed through the swamps, splashing through water, sludging through mud, not pausing for more than a moment to scent for his female again. As soon as he pinpointed her direction, he was off again, full speed once more on her trail. Enthrall on his heels, struggling to keep up. Enthrall couldn't ghost to Carolena. He didn't know where she was, so he had to trust that Carnage was onto her trail and follow along with him. He'd tried to ask Carnage if he was sure he was on the right trail, but in the state he was in, purely bestial, Carnage only roared at him and continued running. Carnage was growing frustrated; Carolena had been wandering in somewhat of a circle. They kept coming back to the same starting place. Carnage dropped to all fours, scenting the ground — his head popped up, he looked off in a direction that was so thick with foliage it was impossible to see through. Then he was on his feet, forcing his way through the dense overgrowth. Suddenly a scream pierced the air. Carnage froze, and Enthrall's skin raised in goosebumps. "Carnage, we have to hurry!" Enthrall said, but Carnage was already moving. He was full-out running toward the scream he'd heard. Then he heard another and another and the high-pitched snarling and yipping of the wild dogs that roamed the outskirts of the swamps. They were descendents of domesticated animals, but had never themselves been domesticated. They were vicious. They'd hunt and eat anything they could kill, animal or human alike. It made no difference to them. If it breathed, they'd hunt it. And lately, Enthrall had found kills that they'd made just for fun. They hadn't even eaten some of the animals they'd brought down. He'd been planning to organize a hunt to kill them before they threatened any of the children of Whispers, but it seems he'd not acted soon enough. If anything happened to Carolena, he'd never forgive himself, he thought, as he ran along behind Carnage, following the screams that had now gone silent.

<<<<<<<<>>>>>>>

Carolena had shifted in the muck, her hands and arms had gone numb, her knees aching to her bones where they were submerged in the wet, cold mud. Her movements caused the dog on her left to dart forward and try to bite her. She'd screamed and thrown herself backward away from its jaws, and fortunately the mud had made the dog return to the edge of the pit she'd been trapped in. When she'd thrown herself backward, it'd been too close to one of the new dogs that had joined them. She was now surrounded by five of them. The new dog had darted forward and nipped her upper arm before she could pull away and back into the center of the mud pit, where she now sat sobbing. Her muddy hand wrapped around her upper arm, blood seeping through her fingers as the dogs circled the pit, growing tired of waiting, yipping back and forth to each other. The dog that had nipped her arm put his paw into the mud and tested it. It didn't seem to mind the mud as much as the others. The dog placed another paw into the mud and seemingly satisfied that it wasn't too deep, stepped fully into it, never once taking his eyes from Carolena. The dog on her right, encouraged by his pack mate entering the mud, just jumped into the mud, all in without hesitation. That dog waded through the muck and pounced at Carolena who had struggled to her feet. It grabbed her clothing and was doing its best to drag her back down to their level. The dog to her left had also started toward her, causing her to try to shuffle backward away from it, while trying to free herself from the dog hanging onto her shirt sleeve. The leader of their pack had circled the pit and was now testing the mud, so it, too, could enter. She was screaming and sobbing, trying her best to stay upright, but the shaking and pulling of the dog on her left arm was too much, and now its teeth had reattached and were piercing her skin; it had her by the wrist. The dog tugged one more time, a strong, full-body tug, and she tilted forward, her head and neck thrown back, trying to keep from falling face first into the mud, leaving her throat a perfect target for the leader who had launched himself directly at her. This was it; she was going to die, mauled by wild dogs. She closed her eyes and lifted her free hand to try to keep the dog away from her throat and face, bracing herself for the impact — that never came.

Carnage burst through the trees and saw his Carolena, surrounded by a pack of wild dogs, one hanging onto her hand, another in the mud on the way toward her, and yet another just about to launch itself at her throat. He did not think. He launched his own body right between Carolena and the dog that had just left the bank of the mud pit. He timed it just right; he caught the dog in his hands just before it made contact with Carolena's throat. He let out a mighty roar, snarling and ripping the dog apart with his bare hands — claws sinking into its fur, blood spurting, both snarling.

Enthrall plunged into the pit, wrapping his own hands around the neck of the dog that held Carolena's arm in its teeth. He roared his own battle cry as he slowly squeezed the life out of it. Carolena sank to her knees in the mud, sobbing, in shock, unsure of what was happening other than Carnage and Enthrall had found her.

Carolena watched as a Carnage she didn't recognize ripped the dog limb from limb, tossing pieces of it here and there as he easily rose from the muck and went after the next dog. Excited by the blood being tossed around, the dogs, rather than run, had begun to devour the pieces of their pack mates as they were tossed haphazardly to and fro. Carnage was in a battle frenzy, all thought gone, only instinct, emotion, passion, ruled him now. Mindlessly he moved from one dog to the next, roaring, viciously tearing them apart, the only image in his mind that of Carolena surrounded by them, one of them with his teeth tearing her flesh, another moving through the air toward her throat, and he'd snarl anew, attacking already dead pieces of animal.

Enthrall had moved to Carolena immediately after killing the dog that had attacked her first. He'd helped her out of the mud and sat with her on the ground, trying to calm her shivers, soothing her, but even he could not look away from the beast that was Carnage.

"Can't we stop him?" Carolena asked Enthrall through tears.

Enthrall shook his head, "No. This is what I was trying to tell you. He is volatile; he acts on emotion. You were threatened; he's taking out every single thing he sees as a threat. Only then will his beast be satisfied."

Just as Carnage dispatched the last dog, Destroy descended into the middle of the chaos, the sounds having drawn his attention. Carnage still breathing heavily, roaring, beating his own chest, looking about for something else to kill, seized on Destroy. His face turned even more brutal, and he started toward Destroy, who at least had the sense to realize that this was not a good thing.

"Carnage," Destroy said.

But Carnage was too far gone, and just kept stalking toward Destroy.

"Carnage! It's me…" Destroy said.

Carnage threw his head back and roared, never stopping his advance toward Destroy.

Carolena started struggling to her feet. Enthrall tried to stop her, but she said, "I have to stop him. He'll kill Destroy."

"Son of a bitch," Enthrall mumbled under his breath. He knew she was right, but still wasn't sure about getting in front of a rampaging Carnage. "Stay right next to me. If he turns on either of us, I'll ghost us out of here."

Enthrall helped her toward Carnage, who was almost all the way to Destroy, Destroy having consistently backed away from Carnage as he advanced.

Carnage was beyond words, nothing but snarls and roars emitted from him.

Carolena tried several times to call him, but he didn't hear her, or wouldn't respond. She turned to Enthrall, "Can you drop me right in front of him, between them, and disappear quickly?"

"I'm not leaving you between two fighting Gargoyles!" Enthrall said.

"You have to. If it doesn't work, come right back and get me. But I think it'll work, please," she begged. "This is all my fault. I should never have gone off alone. I can't let him hurt Destroy."

Enthrall didn't like it, but really they had no choice. He hugged her close and ghosted to a point directly between the two Goyles who were now about fifteen feet apart. He materialized, squatting on the ground with Carolena in his arms. He looked up to be sure where he was placing her, then ghosted away.

Carnage hesitated in his stalking of Destroy; a female had been placed in front of him.

She spoke, "Carnage, I need you." She lifted her left arm where the dog had torn her flesh. The blood dripped from her hand onto the ground in front of her, "I'm hurting. I need you. You've killed all the dogs; there is no more threat. Please, please take me home."

Carnage stared at her, his head turning to the side, this was his female. And she was bleeding. His expression turned from one of destruction to one of concern, his brow furrowed, "Leenah" he forced through his now raw throat.

Carolena sobbed, relief flooding her. She saw out of the corner of her eye, Enthrall signaling Destroy, trying to make him fly away. Destroy looked back toward her. She did not take her eyes from Carnage, but she said, "I'll be okay."

Destroy nodded his head once, then looked to Enthrall and lifted into the air.

Carnage didn't even look at Destroy as he left them. He'd already knelt beside Carolena and was tearing the sleeves of her shirt away so that he could see the damage for himself. He checked her neck, her throat, her other arm, and legs before deciding for himself that she wouldn't die. Then he rose, with her in his arms, and started back toward Enthrall's home. Enthrall followed quietly along behind them.

<<<<<<<<>>>>>>>

As soon as they got back to Enthrall's home, Carnage took Carolena straight into the bathroom. There he stripped her down and placed her into the bathtub. He ran warm water and bathed her body, and her cuts and bites. He let the water out of the tub several times and refilled it, until he was sure that she was clean. Once he was satisfied that she was as clean as she could be, he lifted her from the tub and wrapped a towel around her. He carried her to her room where he dressed her in his large shirt she'd been using to sleep in.

Enthrall knocked on the door, "Carnage, I have some salve for her injuries. Can you bring her in the living room?"

Carnage didn't answer, but he lifted her from the bed and carried her down the hall to the living room. Once there, he sat her on the couch and watched as Enthrall offered him the salve to put on her bites.

Carnage shook his head; he still wasn't himself, and he wasn't sure he knew what to do with the medicine anyway.

"May I?" Enthrall asked.

Carnage nodded.

Enthrall applied the salve to Carolena's injuries, speaking softly to her, asking how she ended up there, what made her leave and go off on her own.

Carolena explained that she was irritated at being left alone. She felt like an afterthought and decided that she didn't need them. She was perfectly capable of taking care of herself and decided to go on an adventure.

"You weren't trying to leave us?" Enthrall asked.

"No," she answered, in tears. "I just wanted to teach you a lesson, to show you that I can take care of myself, that I don't need any of you."

Carnage was snarling low in his chest again.

Enthrall said, "Do you know that a moment later and you'd be dead?"

Carolena nodded.

"Do you know that you are lucky that Carnage recognized you and stopped stalking Destroy? Do you know that this could have been catastrophic for all of us? All because you decided that you wanted to teach us a lesson? Who do you think needs the lesson now, Carolena? Who?" Enthrall demanded.

"Me," she answered weakly.

"That's right, you! I told you Carnage was not like other males. I told you he was volatile because he was reactive to his own emotions. Maybe now you'll be a little more careful," he said, rising from his place on the couch, having finished tending her wounds.

"I will be, Enthrall. I'm sorry," she said.

"I'm sure you are," he said before he left them to go to his own room — he was truly shaken.

"I'm sorry, Carnage," she said to the Gargoyle sitting beside her, watching her intently for any sign of pain.

He didn't reply, but reached out a thumb to softly caress her cheekbone.

He lifted her and took her to her room, tucked her in bed, and climbed in behind her, holding her as she eventually fell into a much needed sleep.

Chapter 10

The next morning Carolena woke sore, but thankful to be alive. She was not alone again. She felt Carnage pressed tight against her back. As soon as he realized she was awake, he kissed her shoulder and sat up. Carnage examined her wrist and arm and reached for the salve that Enthrall had put near their bedside during the night. He'd told Carnage to apply it every couple of hours until the bruising faded, and the skin started to repair itself.

After Carnage put another coating of salve on her wounds, they got up and headed into the kitchen. Enthrall was just putting breakfast on the table and welcomed them.

"How did you sleep?" Enthrall asked.

"Well," Carolena answered, not looking him in the eye.

Carnage reached out for a slice of ham and grinned when Enthrall pretended he would slap his hand with the spatula.

Well, Enthrall thought, at least Carnage is back to pleasant Carnage.

They sat and shared breakfast, Carolena not meeting Enthrall's eyes no matter the conversation he tried to draw her into.

"Carolena, you cannot avoid me forever. Why won't you look at me?" Enthrall asked.

"I'm embarrassed. I'm ashamed of my behavior. I'm truly sorry for all the trouble I've caused," she answered, still looking at her plate.

"Perhaps it is for the best," Enthrall answered. "Look at me. Please?" he asked.

She looked up at him slowly.

"It could have ended even worse than it did. But we are all here, we are all alive. And we have all learned a valuable lesson.

Do not let it affect our friendship. If I'd lost you, I'd be as devastated as Carnage," he explained.

Carolena nodded.

"Nooooo, mooorrre, Leenah," Carnage said, pointing outside.

She knew what he was saying, 'Do not go out alone again.'

"He's right," Enthrall said. "You can't go off alone again. What if we hadn't found you in time."

He realized they sounded like they were chastising a child and tried to make up for it, "I'm not telling you that you can't go where you like. I'm just asking that until you are familiar with ALL of Whispers, please don't go alone. There are so many dangers out there. Just ask for an escort until then. You are, as you said, a grown woman. You can go wherever you like, just ask one of us to accompany you. At least until you know your way around better. Learn the areas to avoid, okay?" Enthrall asked.

"Okay. You're right. And don't worry, I don't plan to go off alone for a long time. I've learned my lesson," she said. She looked at Carnage out of the corner of her eye.

Carnage saw her. He took her hand in his very, very gently, "Nooooo hurrrrttt, Leenah," he said softly.

Carolena lifted his hand to her lips and kissed it. "I know. I never for one moment thought you'd hurt me."

Carnage smiled at her. He wouldn't. He could never hurt Carolena. She was the only living thing on earth that never had to fear him. He held his hunk of ham out for her to take a bite of. She really didn't want any, but knew he needed to know that she trusted him, so she leaned over and took a bite.

~~~~~~

Days went by, and her wounds healed well. No bruising and only a few little puncture scars. She'd spent most of the last days staying close to Enthrall's house. Carnage had returned to his habit of leaving before she woke in the morning, and came home late, if he came home at all during the night — sometimes she wasn't sure. She was lonely, and she was bored. This morning was no different. Carolena woke alone, yet again. She rolled over, looking at the empty spot behind her on the bed. Carnage was not there. She got up and dressed, and went to the kitchen. Enthrall had left a teapot, still simmering on low on the wooden stove, but he was gone, too. She poured herself a cup of tea and walked outside to sit on the porch, wondering how long she'd be alone today.

<<<<<<<>>>>>>

Destroy sat just out of sight, across the way, high up in the trees, watching for Carolena. He'd been warned by Enthrall not to enter his home again under any circumstances and he hadn't. So dropping in on her as he'd done before was not an option. He'd just have to wait for her to make herself available. He didn't want to hurt her. He just wanted to visit with her, thank her for intervening when Carnage wanted to kill him at the mud pit. Maybe make her see him for the amazing male that he was. He was lonely, very lonely. He'd had a secret dream for a long time. A dream that involved a woman who could see no male but him. He just wanted to be loved. Well, he wanted to run Whispers, too, but that was no more than a way to attract a woman in itself. People thought he was an ass, thought he was out to ruin everyone else's happy, and sometimes he was. But it was only because he just could not pass up any chance to try to win over any woman he came across. He didn't understand why they couldn't see all he had to offer. And if they didn't want him, then he really didn't care if he managed to scare them off. If the other males were worth a damn, Destroy wouldn't have been able to scare them off; they'd have stayed, regardless.

He knew that as he sat here this morning, watching Enthrall's home, he had a very good chance of speaking with Carolena. Enthrall had left earlier this morning, heading into town to pick up some supplies for some of the inhabitants of Whispers. And Carnage was gone as well. But since he couldn't go in, he had to sit and wait for her to come out. And as he watched, it was as though the fates smiled on him; the screen door opened, and she walked out onto the porch. She looked around a bit, then took a seat in one of the chairs that Enthrall kept there, sitting back and sipping at her tea. No more than ten seconds later, he was striding up the stairs toward her.

Carolena, lost in thought, didn't notice Destroy until he was almost upon her. She startled and sat up straight as she heard his footfalls on the porch steps.

"Good morning, Carolena," Destroy said warmly. "How are you faring today?"

"Morning, Destroy," she answered, wondering again, why he seemed to know when she was alone. "I'm okay."

"I shall sit with you this morning," he declared.

"Wonderful," she answered flatly.

He took a seat near to hers, knowing full well he made her uncomfortable.

"I do not wish to harm you. There is no reason to fear me. You saved me from Carnage's fury; I shall not forget that," he announced

Carolena raised her eyes to his, "It seems to me that it was you telling Enthrall to kill me the first night I arrived, when Carnage came here looking for me. And I saved you from Carnage because it was the right thing to do."

Destroy waved his hand in the air dismissively, "I did not mean for Enthrall to actually kill you. I was irritated and merely pushing for an end to the confrontation." Then he smiled at her, "And regardless of your reason, you did save me."

Carolena raised an eyebrow as she considered his words.

He added as an afterthought, "I knew that Carnage would not allow your death that first night, so no real risk there." Then he looked her in the eye, suddenly a very sincere male, "I am truly thankful for your intervention, Carolena."

Carolena watched him, she didn't answer, just nodded her head. She sat back in her chair and watched the birds flitting in the treetops and the squirrels playing chase at the base of the trees.

After a few moments of uncomfortable silence Destroy started speaking.

"Allow me to tell you of my life — it has been a wondrous journey!" he told her enthusiastically.

Since she gave no resistance, he began with his tales. She tried not to listen, but she found herself laughing and smiling in spite of herself. He told her of his life. Of his training and some of his travels, ending his story with an assignment of guarding an historic library, when a female happened upon his station on the roof. He'd been bored and had been distracted watching a young couple in love, engrossed in the act of lovemaking in the shadows across the common square. He'd become aroused just before a female had come out onto the roof. He froze, mimicking the stone his brethren were believed to be, and not wishing to give away the secret of their existence. The woman had wandered around the roof for a few moments, enjoying the uninhibited view of the stars, before turning her focus on to him. She approached him, standing on tiptoe to get a better look. He did not move, continuing to stare straight ahead. She ran her hands down his chest, and dragged her fingertips lightly across his abdomen as she circled him. She maintained her touch, her hand lightly brushing his skin as she made her way back around to the front of his person. There, she looked down at his private area, and her eyes grew wide when she saw the bulge apparent through his clothes. 'Now why would anyone put breeches on a statue?' she'd asked out loud. She smiled and her eyes lit up as she nibbled her lower lip. She checked to be sure that she was not watched; then, she slowly reached out and traced a single finger down the length of his manhood as it was outlined beneath his trousers. She smiled deviously and covered it with her hand, squeezing and sighing. He described how difficult it was to maintain his frozen posture.

She was lost in his story. She leaned forward, interested in spite of herself, "What did you do?"

"I stood there. She continued to caress me, then she said, 'What I would do to you if you were real!' and she stepped closer, standing on her toes again to get a better look at my face. She never once let go of my manhood, stroking me the whole time, then she said, 'It's almost as though I can see you breathing!'

Finally, I could take it no longer. I stopped holding my breath, I looked down at her, and I said, 'Of course you can see me breathing! And if you don't stop stroking me, you'll see more than me breathing! So, now, Here I am, real! What shall you do to me, little female?'" Destroy was smiling as he relayed his story.

Carolena was smiling as she watched him remembering, "Then what?" she asked, giggling.

"Then she screamed, twisted my manhood, and ran! I could not do more than double over and moan for more than 10 minutes! And not in a pleasurable way! She twisted me! And she lied! She did not want anything to do with me once she knew I was real!"

Carolena had dissolved into uncontrollable laughter, and holding her middle, shrieking with each new round of laughter.

Destroy started laughing at her laughing, and they both forgot to be on edge around each other. As the laughter died down, Carolena spoke.

"Destroy, you are very attractive when you are not trying to convince everyone of how amazing you are. You should let your guard down and smile more often."

Destroy, stunned by Carolena's comment, watched her for sincerity.

She realized that he was watching her, not knowing her motivation behind the comment. "I didn't mean to offend you. I only meant that as a compliment."

Destroy didn't respond, just sat smiling slightly as he watched her.

"Would you like some sarsaparilla tea?" Carolena offered.

Destroy inclined his head slightly, "Yes. Very much."

She rose, went into the house, left her teacup on the kitchen counter, and came back out with two large glasses filled with the sweet drink that they all enjoyed so much.

As they sipped their drinks and sat in companionable silence, Carolena finally asked, "Do you happen to know where everyone is?"

"Enthrall went into town. Carnage...I do not know. He left early this morning, but I didn't speak to him or follow him. I'm not sure where he went."

Carolena perked up at his information, "Carnage left early? He was here?" she sat up, excitedly.

"Did you not know? How could you not know he was here? He slept beside you all night," Destroy said unbelievingly.

"I...he wasn't...he, he wasn't here when I fell asleep. I assumed that he didn't come back to me last night," she admitted. She looked down at the glass in her hands as her voice faded away at the end of her admission.

Destroy watched her doubting herself. Doubting Carnage. Being not quite sure where she fit into this community, or if she even did, or could. He felt bad for adding to her insecurities.

He looked at the glass in his own hands while he quietly spoke to her, first looking around to make sure no one was within earshot. He did have a reputation to protect. "I've been watching Enthrall's home. Watching you. Carnage was here last night. He came back late, entered the house. I'd already been told by Enthrall not to enter his home without invitation, so I resented that Carnage could. After he didn't come out, I approached and peered in the windows. I saw him through your blinds; he put out your oil lamp and got in bed with you. I waited, but nothing else happened. He just held you and went to sleep."

Carolena's eyes were glued to Destroy as he spoke. Her heart beating stronger, happy with this new knowledge. "Are you sure?"

"I am sure," Destroy told her, feeling a little sad that the news that Carnage had slept beside her made her happy.

"Wait! Through my blinds? You watched him through my blinds? In my window?!" she asked, an outraged tone to her voice.

Destroy looked at her sheepishly before nodding, "Yes. I did. About two-thirds down, some of the slats are out of alignment. I can just see through them."

She watched him, her lips pursed.

He smiled at her charmingly, all his teeth on display, "You're going to fix the slats aren't you?"

"Indeed!" she told him.

"Damn," he said under his breath.

"But thank you for telling me that Carnage was here. I was feeling...lonely — forgotten a little, I guess. I didn't know he was here. I thought he'd not come back. I was thinking that maybe he was tired of having to fight for me to remain here."

Destroy didn't know what to say. Though he was somewhat manipulative, he did not know how to manipulate a woman much less soothe one. He was more the caveman type. "I cannot speak for him. I do not know what he thinks or why he does anything that he does. But I do know he was here last night."

Carolena nodded and offered him a shy smile.

"Are you happy here?" Destroy asked.

"I don't know, yet. I've not been here long enough," she answered in truth. "It is an adjustment. I spend a lot of time alone."

They sat in silence for a few moments more before he asked, "Will you choose Carnage?"

She looked at him, realizing that though she was happy that Carnage had come back to her last night, she still hadn't made a decision. "I don't know. I feel like I'm in a dream, and I'll wake at some point to my regular life. And all this will have been a fantasy," she said as she looked around herself.

"Though some may wish it, we are not fantasy. Since you are to remain here, it would be wise to try to enjoy our world. There is much to enjoy here. Many different people, many different sights and even legends that we ourselves are unsure of. It will be quite an adventure to live here with us. We are not all bad," he finished on a whisper, realizing that he was actively trying to sell her on their community.

She watched Destroy, trying to talk her into being happy in this place. She realized that he wasn't a bad male; he was just misunderstood. She decided he was most likely lonely, just like her. And the loneliness had made him bitter.

"What kinds of legends are you unsure of?" she asked, trying to keep the conversation going, and genuinely interested.

"Oh, all kinds. There's the Dragon tree, and the Will-o-the-Wisp or as they call it here — the Fi Follet, just to name a few. And then there are so many different types of people here that it's never boring. There is always some type of conflict," he grinned.

"Are you grinning because you start some of that conflict?" she asked, pretty sure she knew the answer already.

He shook his head, "No, not me. I never cause conflict." He smiled like a shark.

"What other kinds of people are here? They just look like people to me," she said, ignoring his dangerous smirk.

Thrilled that he was finally in the company of someone that wanted to converse with him, and seemed interested in what he had to say, he launched into all the information he carried inside, "Well, we are all supernaturals. Yet all a little different. We have Shifters of any kind you can imagine. And Water people — a couple of different kinds, some with gills and some without. One that must keep to the waters or he will dry up and blow away, and others that can take on the appearance of humans when they choose. A Rougarou, a Windigo, Faeries, a Banshee, and Witches, just to name a few. There's even a large fur-covered creature, but he keeps to himself, staying far away from any of us. I'm sure there are others that humans have no name for. But we all pretty much live in peace," he stopped speaking and looked around himself, whispering, "We even have an Ancient."

Carolena watched him and realized that he was hesitant to mention the Ancient. "What is an Ancient?" she asked.

"Shh! Don't say that out loud! You don't want to bring him to you! Or us!" he admonished.

She looked around herself, seeing no one lurking she changed the subject, "Okay, what about the Dragon tree? Can you tell me about the Dragon tree?"

"I'll do better than that! I'll show you!" he said like an excited little boy. Destroy stood, reaching his hand out to her.

She regarded his hand, outstretched, waiting for her to take it. She hesitated, not sure if she should trust Destroy or not and not sure if she should go off again without Carnage or Enthrall.

"I'm not sure I should go, Destroy. I caused so much trouble last time," she told him truthfully.

"I promise I'll only show you the tree. I won't do anything to frighten you. And I'll bring you straight back. I will not leave you alone for one moment. I know your male wants you to have an escort when you move about. I will protect you."

She looked at his hand for only a second longer, tired of sitting alone in Enthrall's home she took the opportunity, "Okay. I'd like to see the Dragon tree."

Chapter 11

Carnage and Murder worked for most of the morning. Another day or two like this morning and they should have everything moved to the new location he'd chosen for Carolena's home. Some of the more humanesque people lived nearby, and for the same reasons he'd chosen this location. When all the activity had started, they'd come to see what he was up to. Carnage had smiled when appropriate and inclined his head in greeting to any who found their way through the large grove of Eucalyptus trees he and Murder were working in. They'd been led there by following the noises he and Murder were making. Upon finding him assembling building materials, they knew at once that he was building a home there, but none seemed to mind. A few even offered to help and assisted him in stacking the materials as Murder dropped them off. Carnage and Murder had decided that it was faster for them to disassemble the home together all at once. When that was finished, Carnage would make one trip back to the build site carrying what he could; then, he'd wait for Murder to fly the rest of the building materials to him. Carnage would then further disassemble and stack them together in piles of like materials…all the beams together, the tin together, the runners for the walls together, the floor boards together, the precious windows together and out of the way so that they wouldn't get broken. He'd accidentally put one of the posts through one of the windows and shattered it. Now he'd have to find another to replace it. So he was much more careful with them now. He even had a small pile of the nails they'd managed to salvage, though he had no doubt he'd have to ask Enthrall to get him some more nails at some point. He'd need plaster, too, to finish the insides of the walls with. He looked around at all the items surrounding him, and the sticks he'd driven in the ground to mark the area he planned to build in. He'd laid out the area he wanted the home in first and had marked it out before he'd started organizing all his building materials. He hoped to start reassembling the house in the next few days.

He watched Murder as he landed a few feet away, arms full of wooden slats for the floor,"This is the last of the larger things. I left the furniture from inside the house just inside the wooded area not too far from where the house stood. I'll go back with a tarpaulin and cover it."

Carnage smiled, nodding his head. He looked off toward the direction Enthrall's home lay in.

"You missing your woman?" Murder asked.

Carnage nodded, "'Es."

"Then go to her. I'll go cover the few things that are left and you go to your woman. We'll start again tomorrow morning. Yes?"

Carnage grinned, nodding his head enthusiastically.

Murder laughed, clapping Carnage on the back, "Go then. We'll pick up where we are now, tomorrow."

Carnage wasted no time hightailing it out of there, making a beeline straight for Enthrall's home.

He jogged across the clearing, letting out a soft roar, more like a call to let Carolena know that he was near.

She didn't come out onto the porch, so he called again, a little louder — still no answer. Perhaps she was napping, he decided.

He hurried up onto the porch, but quietly opened the door. He looked around the living room, but saw no trace of her. He went to her bedroom, but again, she wasn't there. He peered into the bathroom, but the door was open, and no one was there. He went to Enthrall's bedroom door and knocked. There was no answer, so he opened the door and peeked inside — it was empty. No one was there either. Carnage walked back to the living room, and then he noticed the two glasses sitting on the counter top in the kitchen. Well, she'd been here. Carnage lifted one glass and sniffed it. Carolena, he could smell his Carolena and smiled before he tipped the glass up and sipped the rest of the sarsaparilla she'd left in her glass. He smiled, really loving the taste of that stuff. He made a mental note to get some for them to keep in their home when it was finished. Then he lifted the other glass and sniffed. His eyebrows slammed down over his eyes; he rumbled deep in his chest and brought the glass close to sniff it again. He full out snarled when he was sure what he was smelling. Destroy! Destroy had been here, and now they were both missing. He dropped the glass and ran from the house, roaring out his frustration that his female was again missing. And this time she was in more danger than she'd been the first time, at least in his opinion.

<<<<<<< >>>>>>>

Destroy watched Carolena as she marveled at the Dragon tree. To him it was common place, but to her it was a thing of wonder.

Trying to engage her in conversation again, he said, "It is truly a wonderment how it came to be." He stood with his hands on his hips looking up at the huge tree, which was shaped just like a giant Dragon head, resting on its chin on the ground. The rest of the Dragon's body was clearly visible in the remainder of the tree. The trunk was shaped like the body of the Dragon, with smaller trunks appearing to grow up next to the main one and curved as though they were the Dragon's legs. The main trunk of the tree stood a good fifty feet in height with a long curve that bent all the way over and was shaped into the likeness of a horned Dragon's head just before it touched the ground, appearing as though it was resting its chin on the dirt. Two more groups of branches grew up from the center of the main tree trunk, spreading out with many smaller branches and leaves on them, almost winglike in appearance.

"It is! It looks just like a Dragon," Carolena said as she reached out a hand to stroke the Dragon's face. "How did it grow like this?" she asked. "Did someone bend it and shape it as it grew?"

Destroy shook his head, "It is said that he was a Dragon who displeased the Ancients long ago. They cursed him to remain here forever, in this form, always waiting for his beloved to find him again and free him from this curse."

Carolena did not look away from the Dragon tree as Destroy spoke and kept a hand on it the entire time. "That's so sad. How will she know to find him here?" she asked.

He shrugged, "They cursed him to stand in the same place he stood when last they were together. He waits for her to remember him and come for him. Day after day, night after night, frozen in time. Waiting, for a love that may never remember him."

"I feel bad for him," she said quietly, "What could he have done that was so bad?" She reached a hand up, gently petting the tree's horns. "I'm sorry you're standing here all alone. I'll come back and visit you until your love comes for you." She lifted up on tiptoe and hugged the tree.

"Perhaps he loved the wrong person. Perhaps she belonged to another. Perhaps he was warned and didn't listen. There was a time that humans were forbidden to us. Any who refused to heed the warnings were punished. Maybe, if he's not actually a tree, which I'm sure is not the case," he looked disbelievingly at the tree, "they froze him, because if he was merely punished and got angry, he would be hard to contain or control." He shrugged his shoulders again, "So now he's a tree."

"I think he's a Dragon. And to be punished for loving another being is just unacceptable." She petted the Dragon's face, pressing her face against the rough tree bark.

"Do not get too close, Carolena. If he were alive, he may eat you!" Destroy teased.

Carolena laughed, "Do you know that is exactly what Enthrall threatened me with when he first met me?"

Destroy was surprised, "That he'd eat you?"

"No! That Carnage would eat me! I told him that I didn't believe it, so he gave up trying to convince me," she said.

Destroy smiled sadly, "Enthrall is certainly very interested in keeping you in his sight. I had not realized that he was inferring that you should be wary of Carnage."

Carolena turned toward Destroy, "I don't think he meant it that way. But he's also said several times that Carnage is reactive, emotionally. So I should be careful. I know very well what he means now — though I still doubt that Carnage would ever hurt me. I'm sure that Enthrall was just looking out for me."

Destroy said sarcastically. "I'm sure Enthrall had no ulterior motive at all."

"Do you think that he was trying to sway me away from Carnage?" she asked Destroy.

"I think that perhaps you have more options open to you than you know. Perhaps you should beware of all of us. Run far and fast and never look back," he said ominously.

She opened her mouth to answer, but came back with nothing, her mind swirling at all he'd just said.

With the mood changed, and Destroy's comments becoming cryptic and somewhat unnerving, she was glad when he suddenly said, "Say goodbye to your Dragon, Carolena. I best be getting you back before Enthrall sends out a search party that comes back with my head, or Carnage decides that I'm better off dead again," he told her.

She looked at Destroy, surprised at his comment, "Has Carnage tried to harm you before?"

Destroy smiled at Carolena, "Often."

"I wouldn't let him hurt you. You're not bad; you're just misunderstood," she said as she patted the tree before turning to follow him.

"Perhaps, perhaps not," he answered. It had not escaped his notice that Carolena had indeed told the Dragon tree goodbye when they left its presence.

"Do you think that the story is true?" he asked her.

"What story? The Dragon tree?" Carolena asked.

Destroy nodded.

"I'm not sure, but I'd like to think so. I mean, I never thought that you or any of these other creatures were real either, yet here I am and here you are. I loved to dream of such things when I was a child learning about all the legends and myths of the past." She smiled as she thought about it, "So, why not a Dragon tree, too?"

Destroy smiled with her, "I shall agree with you, then. Why not?"

As they finally made their way out of the woods and stepped onto the path leading to Enthrall's home, the sun was high in the sky, indicating that it was midday. "Are you hungry, Destroy? I'll make us a lunch when we get back to Enthrall's."

"I cannot enter his home, Carolena. Thank you for the thought, but I'll just get you home, then be on my way."

"Why can't you enter? You've done it before," she asked.

"I was warned that if I entered again without his express permission, I would be punished. And no, I do not wish to tell you of the punishment he threatened. It is enough to say that I do not wish to suffer it," he smiled at her.

They came around a turn in the path and found Carnage running straight toward them. He seemed as surprised to see them as they were to see him.

Carnage recovered quickly and snarled at Destroy, rushing toward them and snatching Carolena off her feet, throwing her over his shoulder. He jabbed a finger at Destroy and snarled again, "Mine!"

Destroy, unperturbed, jabbed a finger right back at him, "Not yet!"

Carnage, shocked by his response, stood looking at him for just long enough for Destroy to clarify his comment.

"She has not chosen you. She may not!" Destroy said matter-of-factly.

Carnage, with Carolena still draped over his shoulder, growled and started for Destroy.

Destroy smiled, slightly holding his hands out to the side, his fingers slightly curved as though in invitation.

Carolena broke the path of Carnage's thoughts when she spoke,"Can you put me down, please, Carnage?"

At the sound of her voice, he paused in his movement toward Destroy.

Carolena patted him on the back to get his attention as she dangled down his back, his arm locked over her thighs as he held her in place over his shoulder, "Carnage, put me down. You're hurting my stomach with your shoulder."

Carnage immediately placed her on her feet, running his hands over her stomach gently, mumbling concerned noises at her.

"I'm okay; it just hurt my stomach being bent over your shoulder," she told him.

"A concerned male would have been more careful with his female. If he really cared about her wellbeing, that is," Destroy snarked.

Carnage growled at Destroy and pinned him with a stare. Then he waved his hand out to indicate the woods, "Nooooo mooorre?"

She knew what he was indicating, "I didn't go alone. Destroy was with me, and I was very careful. I just wanted to see the Dragon tree."

But Carolena was having none of it; she was determined that they would act like civilized creatures for at least a little while, "Please, let's have a nice afternoon; stop the snarling. I did what you said, I had an escort," she said, patting his arm lovingly.

Destroy smirked at Carnage, "Yes, let's stop all the snarling."

She ignored the fact that Carnage was glaring at Destroy and launched right into pretending that all was fine, "We are on our way to Enthrall's for lunch; do you want to join us?" she asked.

Carnage looked down at her, nodded yes, then realized that she said she planned to feed Destroy, too. He swung around glaring at Destroy, who stood there smiling at him like the cat who'd caught the canary. Carnage lifted his lip, snarled and took one step toward Destroy, who tensed.

"Yes, Carnage, do join us for lunch," Destroy drawled at Carnage.

Carolena reached out and grasped Carnage by the wrist, as best she could, while at the same time she said, "Destroy, you stop baiting him. Or I'll not feed you, and I'll stop holding him back," Carolena said.

Destroy looked at Carolena, his mouth opened, as though shocked she would accuse him of any wrong doing, "Forgive me, sweet lady. I would never cause you unease intentionally," he said to Carolena with a sweeping bow. Then he focused on Carnage, "Please, Carnage, do join us for lunch. We shall have a fine meal together," smiling again at a very pissed off Carnage.

"Much better!" Carolena exclaimed, "Come along, now. Let's go see what Enthrall has to eat," Carolena said as she started walking.

Carnage fell into step behind her, taking up the whole path, intentionally preventing Destroy from being able to catch up to her.

Destroy walked along behind Carnage, knowing full well that he'd just told Carolena that he couldn't join her for lunch, but he'd be damned if he told Carnage the same thing. He was not as bad as everyone thought, but he was still a little shit and loved to stir it whenever he had the chance.

<<<<<<<>>>>>>>

Enthrall finished his shopping, as meager as it was in the little country town, and walked toward the edge of town with all his bags. Once he was assured that he was alone, he ghosted from the spot he stood in to the yard in front of his home. He took in the sight before him, blinked, and focused again. Sure enough, his kitchen table had been moved to the yard, and Destroy sat on one side, Carnage on the other, as Carolena served them both from a covered dish in the middle of the table. She'd made a fresh pitcher of sarsaparilla tea, and she poured them each a tall glass full before taking her seat and taking a bite of her own lunch. Each male ate heartily, but never stopped their staring contest.

Enthrall approached them, sitting at his table in the yard. "What the hell is going on here?"

Carolena smiled and stood to greet him, "Enthrall! There you are! I made lunch. Are you hungry?"

Destroy did not look away from Carnage's stare, but said, "I did not want to enter your home. You said I could not without your permission, but Carolena insisted I stay for lunch. So she had Carnage bring the table outside. With your permission, I will help move it back when we are done."

"Of course she did," Enthrall said under his breath.

"Yes! I did. And I made cornbread and cabbage with ham. Would you like some?" she asked.

Enthrall looked at the males glaring at each other and decided that not joining them wasn't an option; if he didn't, they may soon attack each other — again.

"Thank you, I will have some lunch," he answered, resignedly.

He took his seat, and she served his plate.

Carolena, having finished her own lunch, and having just served Enthrall's, sat back down and said without looking up, "You will both stop staring at each other, or this is the last time I will eat with either of you."

Both Gargoyles quickly looked down at their plates, instead of each other.

Enthrall laughed. "I can see that you have it all under control, little one."

Carolena smiled at him, "Yes, I do. Was there ever truly any doubt?"

"Yes! There was! Have you forgotten the nature of the two males you are dealing with?" he asked with raised voice.

"Three males," she said quietly, taking another sip of her tea.

"Pardon?" Enthrall asked.

"Three males," she said again. "One," she pointed at Carnage, "Two," she pointed at Destroy, "Three," and she pointed directly at Enthrall. "I'm dealing with three of you," she answered smugly.

"Really?" he said disbelievingly. "Well, you should at least show some appreciation for number three," he said, reaching down beside himself and then handing her one of his canvas bags across the table.

"For me?" she asked, taking the bag from him.

He inclined his head, "For you."

Carolena opened the bag, and her mouth opened in surprise. Slowly, she drew out a skirt, followed by two blouses and a pair of slacks. She reached back into the bag and brought out a smaller package wrapped in tissue paper. She looked at Enthrall questioningly.

He said, "Those are your delicates. I thought you'd prefer if they were wrapped for your privacy."

She held the package and the clothes to her chest, "Thank you, Enthrall," she said quietly, with tears in her eyes.

"It's not a big deal, Carolena. You needed clothes. I was able to go into town and get them for you," he told her.

Enthrall noticed the fury behind Carnage's eyes. He thought about it for a moment and realized that the Goyle wasn't angry that Carolena had new things. He was angry because he'd not thought to get them for her. And, in actuality, had no way other than to break into a store and steal them to get them for her. He did not want his friend to feel as though he couldn't provide for his own woman, and every indication Carolena had given was that she cared deeply for the Goyle, so he made an instant decision.

"Besides," Enthrall said, "Carnage asked me to pick them up for you. He can't exactly go into town himself and knew that I was going there today."

He met Carnage's eyes across the table and saw gratitude there. Carnage nodded his thanks, and Enthrall nodded back.

"Which reminds me," Enthrall continued, "I have to deliver these other items to the families that requested them. If there is anything else you'd like to have, please let me know. I'm going back tomorrow to pick up some food supplies."

"Thank you, again, Enthrall, and Carnage, too. Thank you so much for asking him to bring me some clothing." Carolena leaned over the table and kissed Carnage's cheek. Then she headed toward the house to put her new things away.

Enthrall walked away, his arms loaded down with necessities that he'd picked up for several families in Whispers that had asked for them the next time he went into town. As he was almost out of sight, he called over his shoulder, "Destroy, you may enter my home to put the table back, but do not over stay your welcome."

Chapter 12

Carnage put the chairs back in place around the table that Destroy had just carried back inside.

Carolena had just rejoined them as they stood glaring at each other from opposite sides of the kitchen. "Will you two stop that? There is no reason for it."

Carnage looked at her disbelievingly, mouth open, eyebrows lifted. He pointed at Destroy, then at Carolena, then threw his hands in the air, as though to say, really? Then he paced back and forth once or twice before stopping to glare at them both.

"What is the problem?" Carolena asked him.

He looked at her as though she was out of her mind, then roared, "MINE!" and waved his hand at Destroy as if to say, does he not know this? Then at her, inferring, do you not know this?

Destroy burst into laughter.

Carolena glared at Destroy herself before she spoke to Carnage.

"There is no reason for all this strife, Carnage. I was lonely today. You and Enthrall just disappeared and left me here alone. But Destroy came to visit."

Carnage rumbled, but Carolena rushed to finish, "He was nothing but a gentleman! There is no reason to be upset. He told me about the Dragon tree, and I wanted to see it. So he took me to see it. As soon as we realized what time it must be, he brought me straight home. You have no reason to be upset."

Destroy smiled at Carnage smugly.

Carnage lifted his lip at Destroy, displaying his huge canines.

Carolena stepped closer to Carnage, "Destroy is a friend. Do not be mean to my friends," she told him firmly.

Carnage shook his head, hard, and garbled, "russt!"

Carolena watched him, trying to figure out what he was saying.

Then he did it again, and suddenly she knew, he was telling her, "No trust. Do not trust Destroy."

She stepped closer to Carnage, shoulders back, her back straight, her chin held high, her jaw set, "Do not ever presume to tell me who I can and cannot be friends with. You may be able to dictate that I have no choice but to live my life here or die. But you can not dictate who I spend my time with. Destroy has been a perfect gentleman, he has talked with me when no one else would, he has taken me to see the places that I must now learn to call home. He has in no way acted in any manner that should make you feel threatened. Rather, he has tried to make me feel more at ease here. I have very few liberties left to me; do not ever make the mistake of thinking to take those from me as well. If you do, you will not like the outcome."

Destroy winced at her words, but Carnage didn't see it. He stood there, stunned, watching his woman defend Destroy to him. Listening to her tell him that Destroy talked with her, made her feel more welcome here. Which was something he could never do. He'd never be able to speak with her. She still stood before him, waiting for his reaction. She was actually quite brave, as brave as he'd thought her when he'd first seen her running into the swamp. He nodded at her to indicate he understood, dropped his eyes to his own feet, and walked out of Enthrall's home. Disappearing into the woods, he needed time to think. To figure out if he should even try to make her stay with him. Maybe he wasn't able to make her happy. And he loved her. He wanted her happy. Even if it wasn't him that made her happy.

<<<<<<<>>>>>>

Destroy and Carolena waited on the porch for more than an hour, but Carnage did not come back. Carolena was obviously upset that he'd left.

"He'll be back, Carolena," Destroy told her.

"I'm worried about him. I didn't mean to upset him, just wanted him to understand that we are friends," she told him.

"I know. And you were right. You didn't ask for this. And you're trying to make the most of it. As long as you stay here and abide by the rules, no one here has a right to tell you what you can and can't do," Destroy said.

"Then why did he leave?" she asked.

"Did you not hear yourself when you spoke to him?" Destroy asked gently.

"What do you mean? You just said I was right," Carolena said.

"You were, for the most part, but you didn't realize what you said. Probably because it's never been an issue to you. But it's always been an issue for him," Destroy tried to lead her to realize what the problem probably was.

Carolena's brow wrinkled, she was confused. She sat going over her words again and again. Then it hit her, "Ohhhhhh!"

"You figure it out?" Destroy asked.

"I told him that you talked to me and spent time with me, making me feel more at ease here," she said, true regret in her voice.

"He thinks I care that he can't speak to me! That I enjoy speaking with you, and that is something he can't give me," she said.

"That would be my guess," Destroy said.

She jumped up from her chair, heading down the porch steps, "I have to find him! I have to let him know that's not what I meant! How can he think that he doesn't talk to me? We communicate beautifully!" she exclaimed.

"NO! You cannot go wandering around this late in the afternoon. You don't know the area well enough, and it's going to get dark soon, and you know what happened last time." Destroy said.

"I don't care. I have to let him know that I didn't mean it that way. I don't care that he doesn't speak."

"You will not go traipsing off into these woods! It is not safe, Carolena!" Destroy shouted, surprised that he actually meant it. He didn't want her to get hurt or lost.

He'd reached for her hand to keep her from walking away from him, and she tugged her hand away from him, "Let me go, Destroy. I have to go after him."

He snarled a bit, "Stubborn woman," he mumbled under his breath. Then against his better judgment he said, "Let me go, I'll find him. I'll tell him to come back to you."

"Would you?!" Carolena asked, clasping her hands together.

"Yes, I'll try to find him," Destroy said, resigned to the fact that he was going to find a Gargoyle he didn't particularly care for, for a female he originally hoped to steal from said Gargoyle.

Destroy started across the yard and had a thought. He stopped halfway across, looking back at her. "Carolena?" he asked.

"Yes?" she answered from the bottom step, where she now sat, preparing to wait.

"Nobody's ever wanted to be my friend before. Thank you for that," Destroy said.

"Oh, Destroy, you're welcome. I'm glad we're friends," Carolena answered.

He started to walk away again, but paused, turning back to face her, slowly raising his eyes to hers, "You should know that you have other options. You do not have to choose Carnage. There are many males here that would jump at the chance to have their own female."

"But they don't know me, Destroy. Why would I want someone who wants me only because I'm a female. I want someone who loves me because of who I am in here," she said, patting her heart. "I want someone who knows me and wants me for who I am."

Destroy still stood there, looking at her from his position across the yard, "There are two other males here who know you."

Carolena looked at him, surprise in her expression.

Destroy continued, "Carnage is not your only option."

When she said nothing, he added more, having no idea where it came from, but being compelled to say it, he did not hold back.

"Or I can help you leave here if you want to run. I'll help you leave."

Carolena watched him, confusion warring through her, "Why would you do that?"

"Because you're my friend. You were nice to me." He hesitated, "You trusted me." He looked away from her briefly before looking back, "If you want to try to get away, I'll help you."

Carolena didn't answer right away, then slowly, she did the only thing she could; she gave him the truth, "I'm not sure what I want anymore, Destroy."

Destroy smiled resignedly, "Then I'll go find your male."

<<<<<<<>>>>>>>

Enthrall stood perfectly still about two hundred feet inside the tree line just past his house. He was headed there when the voices drifted to him on the wind. He stopped to listen, wanting to get a better feel for the relationship developing between Destroy and Carolena. He knew that she was becoming attached to Carnage, but wasn't sure what part Destroy played in her life. It seemed that Destroy was even more faceted than he thought — he was not just a jealous pain in the ass. The male was terribly lonely. He'd just thanked Carolena for being his friend. Enthrall was chastising himself for not realizing what one of his people needed, and he'd not been aware. He'd have to be sure to pay closer attention to the needs of the single people in his community. Maybe they weren't loners because they chose to be, maybe they were just alone. He took one step when he heard Destroy tell her that there were two other males that could be options to her future. He wasn't sure it was a good idea to tell her that, but damned if he didn't want to hear her answer. Unfortunately, he didn't get the chance. The next thing he heard was Destroy offer to help Carolena leave, and his blood pressure surged. He'd made it perfectly clear that she could never leave here! He'd promised all the people in his community that there was nothing to fear because she'd not be leaving. And here was Destroy undermining all the security he'd worked so hard to restore since Carolena's arrival in Whispers. His first instinct was to snatch the Goyle's head off his shoulders. But then he heard Carolena's hesitant reply. She didn't accept Destroy's offer. She said she didn't know what she wanted to do. Which meant that she may truly want to stay here. And if she did, he had no problem with that. He truly cared about the little human. And it was no secret that Carnage already thought of her as his. If she chose to stay with Carnage, he'd wish them well. If she chose to stay and be on her own, he may decide to pursue her himself. He ran his hands through his hair frustratedly. Destroy wasn't the only lonely inhabitant of Whispers. Yeah, he'd wait. He'd see what she chose to do. And if she tried to run, he'd bring her back forcibly. Then he'd banish Destroy forever. He had to maintain control over Whispers. He was the lawgiver, the law enforcer. He had no choice but to be both. Without laws and rules, stupid mistakes would be made, and they'd no longer have sanctuary here. Too many depended on him — he couldn't let them down. He'd have to keep a close eye on Carolena and Destroy.

<<<<<<<>>>>>>>

 Destroy walked the path that Carnage had taken, rather than flying. If he took to the air, he might miss his scent and his hiding spot. So he walked, scenting the whole way. It wasn't long before he found himself approaching the Eucalyptus grove. It was about two acres of Eucalyptus trees that had grown for years unhindered. Those of Whispers that were more humanesque and more susceptible to insect bites and irritations, made their homes here. That was because the insects avoided the Eucalyptus trees. The trees put off an oil and fragrance that made the insects steer clear of them. Destroy continued to follow Carnage's scent and was led right through the middle of the grove to the opposite edge. He had begun to hear hammer blows as he approached but didn't think much of it until he came upon a build site. Carnage was surrounded by stacks of building materials and was busy trying to assemble them into some semblance of something. Destroy stood, watching for a good five minutes before he realized what it was. Goyles didn't need protection from the bugs and pestilence in the swamps — their skin was tough. But humans did. Carnage was building a home for Carolena. "What makes you so sure she's going to pick you?" he called out.

Carnage startled, turning to him with a snarl. Glared at him for a moment, before returning to his work.

"You know, she may not. She may not choose any of us. She may decide that she wants to be alone," Destroy said.

Carnage looked up at the frame he was building, to his left and his right at the stacked lumber and tin. Destroy was right; she may not choose him. But at least she'd have a safe home to call her own.

Not turning around, he nodded, then went back to working.

"You're just going to keep building it anyway?" Destroy asked, then, "You're wasting your time if she doesn't choose you."

Carnage shook his head, turning around to look at Destroy. "Leeenah, safe," he said, gesturing behind himself at the frame he'd started.

Destroy just looked at him, then at the beginnings of the structure, realizing that Carnage wanted this female because he wanted *her*. Not because she was a female, but because of who she was. He really cared about *her*.

This is why being friends with someone was generally more trouble than it was worth, he thought. You had to try to remember to put them before yourself. This was a new thing for him, but he'd try. Carolena had been nice to him. He owed her at least this much — after all, he'd told her he'd go after Carnage.

"She wanted to come after you, but I convinced her to let me," Destroy said.

Carnage lifted an eyebrow, then just turned back to his work, trying to nail the support beams to the posts he'd already driven into the ground.

"You should go back and speak with her. If you don't, she's likely to head out into the woods alone and get herself lost again. Then we'll all have to search for her. It will be a big mess. Go speak with her," Destroy said.

Carnage glanced at him over his shoulder, but kept hammering.

"She gets what you're saying, even without words. Haven't you noticed?" Destroy remarked, losing patience with the whole situation.

Carnage stopped working and looked at Destroy.

"She does. She understands you better than most. Go talk to her." Then Destroy decided that this was not working. And honestly, he'd done what he'd said he would. He'd found Carnage and told him to go to Carolena. He'd fulfilled his promise. He was done. He looked at Carnage, shrugged, "Or not. Actually it's better if you don't. Gives the rest of us a chance. Make no mistake about it, Carnage. If you don't want her, there are others who do."

Carnage rumbled deep in his chest.

Destroy tilted his head as he regarded Carnage, "Well, I've fulfilled my promise to my new friend. I am done here," Destroy said as he spun on his heel, spread his wings, and took to the air.

Carnage watched Destroy as he disappeared from view. Destroy was an ass, but he was right. Carolena did seem to understand him. And if he didn't let her know that he cared for her every chance he got, someone else would.

He placed his hammer with a stack of nails he'd sorted, then headed back to Enthrall's house. He needed to speak with Carolena. He looked up at the sky, dusky as the sun began to set. He decided to hurry so that maybe he could share dinner with her again.

Chapter 13

Carnage emerged from the woods and found Carolena sitting on the steps of Enthrall's porch, staring in his general direction. The moment her eyes recognized him, she jumped up and ran to him. He smiled at her rushing to him. Carolena paused just before she got to him, and said, "I'm sorry, Carnage. I didn't mean that the way it sounded. I didn't mean to make you run away from me."

His smile got noticeably smaller, he nodded, and reached a hand out toward her. She took it without hesitation, him pulling her in for a hug.

"I like the way you talk," she said into his chest as he hugged her. "And I think we communicate very well. Don't you?" she asked, trying to look up at him though he still held her tight.

He released her just enough for her to angle her head up at him. When they made eye contact, he nodded. Then with one arm still around her, he used his other hand to pat his chest. He said, "Mine, Leenah," in his gravelly voice.

She smiled at him and cupped his jaw with her hand, but she said nothing. She wrapped her arms tighter around his waist and rested her head against his chest.

He held her head to his chest and tightened the arm around her waist. He knew she didn't agree with his statement, was acutely aware of it. But she was holding him, and if that was all he could get for now, he'd take it.

The stomping of her foot broke the mood, and he looked down to see why she was stomping her foot.

"Sorry — mosquitoes," she explained.

Carnage took her hand in his, and together they walked back to Enthrall's home. He walked her inside, and once inside she led him to the kitchen.

Carnage took a seat at the table as she made them cold, thick sliced beef sandwiches, making an extra for Enthrall for when he got home.

They ate in silence. When she got up to clean the dishes, Carnage wandered over to the couch she'd been seated on earlier in the day and picked up the book she'd left there. He looked at it, smiled at the picture imprinted on the front, but had no idea what the words said. He didn't know how to read. Finally she finished cleaning the kitchen and joined him on the couch. He handed it to her reverently and lifted his chin at her.

She looked at the book she now held and back at Carnage, "You want me to read it to you?" she asked.

He nodded yes, very enthusiastically.

She smiled and said, "Do you know what it's about?"

He smiled back and raised his hands above his head, curving his clawed fingers into hooks and snarling.

She laughed and said, "Yes! It is about monsters, beasts, creatures of legend. Are you a creature of legend?"

Carnage snorted repeatedly, she guessed that was his laughter, and then nodding, said, "'Es!" between even more snorts.

Carolena laughed, but didn't start reading.

Carnage gently nudged the book in her hands toward her and said, "Leenah saaay."

She marked her place with a dried pine needle she'd been using for just that purpose and turned to the first page. "Let's start at the beginning, okay?"

Carnage nodded and settled in to listen to her read him the story.

"It's called, 'La Belle et la Bete.' Do you know what that means?" Carolena asked.

Carnage smiled widely; he knew exactly what it meant. He'd spent a great deal of time in France and understood the language well. He nodded.

"It translates to, The Beauty and The Beast." She turned it over in her hands, admiring it, "It's more than one hundred fifty years old, published in 1740. It's always been one of my favorites. I was surprised to find it in Enthrall's library."

She looked up to find that Carnage had slipped from the couch onto the floor, where he now sat at her feet, his chin resting on his arm where it was draped relaxedly on the seat of the couch he had just occupied.

"You ready?" she asked, smiling at his eagerness.

He grinned at her and nodded, and she began.

<<<<<<<>>>>>>

Enthrall stepped softly as he made his way up the stairs of his porch. He didn't want to disturb anyone; Carnage inside, or Destroy who watched through the window, as Carolena read aloud from one of his books. He knew beyond a doubt that Destroy was aware of his arrival, but when he took a seat on the chair next to him, Destroy did not move, did not make a sound, or acknowledge him in any way. He was so caught up in the story that Carolena read, he did not want it to end. So Enthrall sat quietly, and himself listened. He knew the story well, but it was her voice that caught him up in her tale. She had a beautiful voice, clear, melodic, and she took on a different tone dependent on the character she was reading. Both Goyles were captivated, as was he.

She was three chapters in and stopped to clear her throat. Carnage jumped up from his spot on the floor and went into the kitchen. He filled a glass with cool water and rushed back to her, handing it to her. Carolena took it from him, smiling her thanks, and drank deeply from it. She licked her lips and drank again before handing the glass back to Carnage. He watched her with a pained expression on his face and reached to take the glass from her outstretched hand. "Are you okay, Carnage?"

He nodded, "'Es," he mumbled. He hurried to the kitchen, rearranging himself in his breeches as he went. Being this close to her, inhaling her scent, listening to her voice, and watching her lick her lips had him swollen and throbbing. He took a deep breath, let it out slowly, gulped down the remainder of her water before placing the glass in the sink, and took his place at her feet once again.

"More?" she asked him.

He nodded, but held his fingers up, pinching them almost together, but not quite, leaving a little space between them.

"Just a little?" she asked.

He nodded, smiling. See? He thought to himself; we can talk perfectly well.

Carolena read another chapter aloud to him and to Destroy and Enthrall who she'd noticed had recently joined them. When she got to the end of the chapter, she removed the pine needle from her earlier marked page and placed it in the last spot she'd read to them. There was no way she'd read the rest without them.

Just as she leaned over to place the book on the arm of the couch, Carnage touched her wrist. She paused, looking down at him.

He lifted his chin, raised his eyebrows, and gently touched the end of the pine needle where it stuck out of the book.

"I'm using it as a bookmark. I don't want to bend the pages. Books are very precious to me — they are treasures. So instead of bending the pages, I use this pine needle to mark my place. It's not exactly a great bookmark, but it's dried so it won't get any sap or discoloration on the pages."

Carnage nodded his understanding. He stood and shoved his hands in his trousers, waiting to see what they'd do next.

"I think I'll take a bath. Do you mind?" Carolena asked.

He groaned. The thought of her naked in a bath almost brought him to his knees.

"Would you rather me not?" she asked, surprised at his reaction.

He shook his head and began gently pushing her toward the bathroom.

"You sure?" she asked. "I heard you groan."

He stopped ushering her toward the bathroom and made a show of stretching his back, his arms above his head, letting out the same groan.

"Ohhh! I see, your back is sore. Well, next time sit beside me on the couch," she smiled as she headed to the bathroom. "I'm going to soak for a bit; I'll be out shortly," she told him.

Carnage nodded his agreement and stood where he was until she closed the door behind herself.

Once she'd closed the door and the water started pouring into the tub, he spun and went straight to the porch. He pulled the door opened and glared at both men who jumped to their feet to meet his arrival.

He said, "Mine!" and dared either to argue with him.

Enthrall grinned at him, "She reads beautifully, Carnage. We were just enjoying the story as you were. We didn't want to disturb either of you, so we listened from out here."

Carnage didn't respond, but his eyes moved to Destroy's eyes. Destroy said nothing, just looked at Carnage with a sardonic smile in place, as though daring him to say anything.

Carnage stared for a moment longer before starting down the steps.

"You going to work on your house?" Enthrall asked.

Carnage nodded, pausing and looking back at where both males stood on the porch.

"We'll stay with her while you go work," Destroy said.

Carnage thought of his Carolena, soaking in a warm bath, and the males on the porch listening to her read *him* a story. He stomped back toward the porch, up the stairs and stopped at the screen door. He faced them, pounded his chest and said, "Myyy Ppppprrroooooo - tec!" Then he went inside and planted himself outside the bathroom, and listened to the water splashing against the soft, sweet skin of his beautiful female. As his breeches became even tighter and the agony brought with his incessant swelling became even more unbearable.

<<<<<<<>>>>>>>

Out on the porch, Enthrall watched Carnage through the screen door, take up a position outside the bathroom door where Carolena now bathed.

He looked to Destroy, who was still standing next to him. "You know if you make any effort at all to get between them, he may kill you."

Destroy didn't look at Enthrall, just kept looking at the door behind where Carnage now stood. That door is where Carolena, the only female that had ever been kind to him, now lounged naked in a bath. What struck him as strange was that he didn't want to rush in and fuck her. He wanted her taken care of. He wanted her fed, and protected, and sheltered and safe. He wanted her happy.

Destroy met Enthrall's eyes, "Yes, I know. But if he doesn't do right by her, then he has no one to blame but himself. She deserves to be taken care of. If he won't do it, and do it the right way, someone else will."

Enthrall didn't answer at first — he was watching Destroy with new eyes; maybe this male was growing up. "True. And I'm sure I know a male who would be willing to step up," Enthrall said.

"As do I," answered Destroy meaningfully, just before he turned and walked away.

<<<<<<<>>>>>>>

"I don't give a damn what your excuses are!" shouted the man seated behind the huge mahogany desk in the very expensively decorated office. "Find my daughter! Find her now!" Abraham Ashlar shouted at the grimy man in front of him.

"I've tried, Mr. Ashlar! There is no trace. I've spoken with all my contacts. No one knows where she's gone."

"What did the woman at the boarding house say?!" Abraham demanded.

"She said that Ms. Ashlar left with no word, just disappeared without any explanation of where she was going," the man told him.

"And you believe that?" Abraham bellowed. "Idiots! I'm surrounded by idiots!"

Abraham got up and rounded his desk, causing the overweight, sweaty man on the other side to step back suddenly. Abraham eyed him disgustedly as he went by. He pulled open the door to his office and yelled through it to his secretary, "Ms. Staples! Make arrangements! I'll be going to look for my daughter myself!" Then he turned to the man still stinking up his office, "Get out! I'll find her myself."

"Uh, Mr. Ashlar, sir — I have expenses. I went out there on good faith..." the investigator started.

Abraham stalked toward the man, now whining about money and tossed a handful of bills at him, "Take it! Get out of my office."

The sweaty little man gathered up the bills from the floor and scurried out of the office, quickly slamming the door behind himself as he went.

Abraham went back to his desk, flopped into the huge leather chair behind it. He picked up the ledger he'd been reviewing and slung it across the room in frustration. He was going to have to go to Louisiana. He had no time for this, and it irritated him to no end. If his insolent daughter had done her duty by accepting any of the suitable choices he provided her for husband, he'd not have to be put out now. But naturally, she had to be difficult. She'd always been difficult. If not for the promise he'd made his dying wife, he'd have sent the girl to a boarding school years ago.

He sat back in his chair, his heart softening, only slightly though, at the thought of his wife. He'd adored his beloved wife. She'd been his soul. Then she'd taken her from him — the daughter he'd had to raise alone. He remembered the night the doctor had placed her into his hands. He'd marveled at the ability such a tiny creature had to thoroughly devastate his life. His wife had wanted a child more than anything, so he'd given her a child. Anything to make her smile. But as she came into the world, she'd caused so much bleeding that her mother couldn't survive. His wife's life was exchanged for the difficult, confounded, unconventional girl child he'd now have to raise alone. His wife begged him with her dying breath to take care of their baby, to ensure that she'd be happy, always. If not for that promise, he'd have most likely been even less of a presence in the girl's life then he was now. But he'd promised his beloved. So he'd hired her the best nannies, financed vacations that would provide her with culture, tutors that would educate her, and legions of staff that adored her. Once she came of age, he started the search in earnest for a husband who would take over. He wanted to be freed of his promise. He was done; he could no longer pretend to care for the child that had caused his wife to be taken from him. Only the damn girl wouldn't cooperate. She negotiated for a time away, to oversee his business, to experience the culture of the people of the southern United States that she'd learned to love from one of her first nannies. The woman had been a mulatto woman, from south Louisiana. His daughter had learned the legends and superstitions of the region through stories that she never tired of hearing. He was glad for her attention being elsewhere, but in retrospect, perhaps he should have limited her exposure to the woman. She did so seem to love the child, though. At any rate, that's where she was now or was supposed to be. In an effort to prove that she needed to give in and allow him to plan for her future, he'd let her go. Now she was missing. And he owed it to his beloved Clara to find her, bring her back home and ensure her security and well-being — then, he could wash his hands of her forever.

Chapter 14

Carolena smiled to herself as she slipped the soft, silky nightgown over her head. Enthrall had chosen a pretty green that complimented her eyes. She had hazel eyes that could appear either green or golden, depending on the color she wore. She ran a brush through her thick, wavy, brown hair 'til it shined. She pinched her cheeks 'til they pinked, then, she pulled her lips back, checking that there was no food caught in her teeth. Satisfied that she was presentable, she took a deep breath and opened the bathroom door. Carnage, who had been leaning on it, almost fell through it. He caught himself and turned around to better look at the vision that stepped from the bathroom. He let out a soft moan, his hand coming up to clutch his heart as he watched her wait for his reaction. He reached out a hand to touch her face, but just couldn't quite make himself touch her. His hand lingered in the air, coming close once, twice, before she finally took his hand in hers and placed it on her own cheek so that she could cuddle into his palm.

She raised her eyes to his and smiled at him again, before stepping into his arms and sighing deeply as he held her.

"Ready for bed?" she asked.

Carnage's eyebrows shot to the top of his forehead, surely she couldn't mean what he hoped.

She realized she'd caught him off guard, "I mean, I know you slept here last night. With me. And I thought that, hoped that, maybe you wouldn't mind staying here again. I slept so well with you here."

Carnage nodded, understanding now. He pointed to the bathroom, "Myy, keeen." She knew he was telling her that he wanted to get cleaned up first and nodded, "Okay. I'll wait," she said.

Carnage knew that Enthrall stood at the end of the hallway, still in the living room, but watching them. He turned to Enthrall and pointed toward the bathroom, an unspoken question in his eyes.

"Of course, Carnage. Go right ahead," Enthrall said.

Then Enthrall turned and hurried from his own home.

He made it as far as his own porch before ghosting away. He found himself in front of the little shack he sometimes used for fishing. It was far down the swamp, on a little finger of land that the locals called a barrier island. He strode from the open door of his little shanty to the edge of the water, where it lapped against the shore. When Carolena had stepped from his bathroom, her heart in her eyes, he'd almost swept her up and taken her with him, anywhere. He just wanted her so damn badly. But then he'd recognized that her eyes were only for Carnage. She'd waited, not saying a word for the huge male to give her any sign of approval. Then Carnage had respected him by asking permission to use his home and his bathroom, not just assuming it would be okay. He'd had to leave, immediately, or risk losing control. It wasn't that he was in love with Carolena. He wasn't. He was just so damn frustrated. The first female he'd met in decades that didn't fear what he was, and she was meant for another. It hurt. A lot. She was kind, and sweet, and full of courage and adventure. And he really believed he could love her. But he'd never take her from Carnage, not that anyone could. She may not have spoken the words yet, but he had no doubt that her decision was made. He threw his head back and screamed his frustration to the night. After a near full two minutes of constant scream, he dropped to his knees in the briny water at his feet. Breathing deep, and cursing the monster that he was. The fateful night of his rebirth into this life, another cause for misery. He knelt there, for how long he didn't know, before he gradually became aware that he was not alone. He raised his head, looking around. Then he saw it, a vague purplish haze to the fog permeating the edge of the small barrier island. He closed his eyes, inhaling the salty air into his lungs, preparing to face another.

Finally, he stood and backed up a few feet, before dropping onto his bottom onto the sand and wispy grasses that grew in it. "Hello, Lore. What brings you here?"

The fog seemed to gather and swirl, moments later the outline of a male formed just to his right, sitting beside him.

"A wail of anguish I could not ignore," Lore responded in a deep, rich baritone.

"There is no lost soul, ready to give up, here for you to court," Enthrall said, not unkindly.

Lore chuckled, the richness of his voice sweeping over Enthrall, "Even if I searched still for souls to harvest, I would not take yours, my friend," Lore said.

"Is that because I'm your friend, or because I'm not suitable for your realm?" Enthrall teased.

"It is yet to be seen," Lore countered.

They sat in silence for a while before Enthrall asked, "How do you do it, Lore?"

"How do I do what?"

"The years spent alone, the solitude, the loneliness," Enthrall answered.

Lore gazed out over the water, "I am accustomed to it. I lost my soul eons ago." He waved his hand above his head, "She wanders, ever searching, never finding me, though I am seldom less than a day behind her. Then just as I think this is the end of it, I reach for her and she vanishes."

Enthrall looked at Lore, really looked at him, his image flickering in and out of focus, but the pain in his eyes so clear to see. "I am sorry, Lore. It is easy to forget that some have much more to deal with than I."

Lore turned to Enthrall, his voice when he spoke, hoarse and gruff, "She can't see me, Enthrall," he said desperately. "No matter what I say, no matter what I do, I can't get her attention. We cannot be saved until she sees me!"

"I know. How can I help?" Enthrall asked, sincere in his offer.

"I cannot remain much longer. I have just lost her again in this lifetime. Now I must wait for her to return, watch in silence as she grows to womanhood, all the while hoping that she will see me in another. If she cannot, I may lose all hope. I am old. And I am tired, so tired."

"I'm sorry, Lore. Tell me, what can I do?" Enthrall reached instinctively for Lore, but his hand passed directly through the mist created image.

Lore looked directly at Enthrall, his eyes seemingly corporeal in his misty appearance, "Pray for us," he said as his image began to waver. Then, as he disappeared, his voice could be heard again, "Pray, Enthrall. For all of us."

Enthrall sat there, realizing that death had just asked him for prayers. His head shot up, and he looked around. His friend had never asked for prayers and always scoffed at those who did. Lore was one of the original four elements of the world, answering only to the great creator. He was a hedonist in every sense of the word, living for the sake of pleasure and satisfaction wherever and whenever he could find it. He'd never believed in any god or goddess, saying they were all invented by humans to worship him and his three siblings. They were not capable of understanding them, so they made up gods and goddesses to explain the things they couldn't understand. Once he was banished, and cursed for eternity to wander the earth in search of his own soul rebirthed time and again as his female, harvesting the souls of evils in order to survive, he gave up any pretense of faith in anything. Not even in himself. But something was amiss; here he was, asking for prayers. Realizing how out of character that was, Enthrall rose from the sand, and calling on his Catholic upbringing, whispered a few well-memorized, though seldom-spoken, prayers to the winds — for Lore, for Carnage and Carolena, for Destroy, and even for himself.

<<<<<<<>>>>>>

Carnage ran the water in the tub and quickly cleaned himself, not even bothering to plug the water to keep it from running right back out.

Once he was satisfied that he was clean, he dried himself and stood in front of the mirror, watching his reflection stare back at him. His smile slowly fell from his face. He was monstrous. How could his Leena ever want him. She was merely settling for him out of necessity. For the first time, he understood the words she'd spoken at dinner with Enthrall the other night. He wanted to be loved for himself, not settled for. He watched in the mirror as his hand reached up and traced a fingertip along one of his bottom fangs. There was no way she could possibly love him. He left the bathroom, planning to go straight out of the front door and hide away from her, but she blocked his path. Carolena stood in the hallway, just outside the bathroom door, much the same as he'd done when she'd first bathed here. When he opened the door, he was startled to find her waiting for him.

She lit up when he opened the door, her smile for only him. "I was waiting for you!" she told him excitedly.

He barely smiled and wouldn't meet her eyes.

Carolena knew that something had changed, "What's wrong? What has happened?"

Carnage shook his head, meaning nothing is wrong.

Carolena stepped closer, but he stepped back.

"Why are you pulling away? What is wrong?" she asked again.

Slowly, shakily, he raised his eyes to hers.

When their eyes finally met, she pleaded, "Please, tell me what's wrong."

While keeping his eyes on hers, he lifted one hand and opening his mouth so that his fangs could be seen, he traced the same fang with a single fingertip.

Carolena watched him.

Then he reached out, gently pulling her lips apart, and ran his finger down her chin, across her soft skin, where there'd be a fang if she had one, only she didn't.

Then she got it. He was telling her he was a monster, he had fangs.

He reached up and stroked one of his horns, then ran his hand over the top of her head, indicating that she had no horns.

She watched him, the tears slowly gathering in her eyes. He was telling her that he couldn't have her because they were too different.

She did the only thing she could. She slapped his hands away from her, shouting at him, "No! No, I will not accept that!"

He looked at her, startled at her outburst.

"You are telling me that because we are different, we can't be together. Well, you're wrong! And I will not accept it!"

He watched the little human, steadily growing more angry, and raised his hands in the air as though to ask, what do you want me to do?

"You've claimed me since the moment you saw me. You brought me here with the intention of making me yours. Don't deny it! I know you did!"

Carnage didn't deny it — he nodded slowly to let her know she was right.

"And now that I'm ready to claim you, you want to back out because you believe, what? That I'm not enough? That you're not enough?"

He didn't answer, only watched her in her fury — she was breathtaking.

"Well, too bad! I've decided! I've chosen you. I want you. No one else, just you!"

Carnage's mouth fell open; he was shocked. He lifted a hand and placed it on his chest; his eyebrows rose in question.

"Yes, you!"

He watched her for a moment longer before pointing toward Enthrall's bedroom, then back to Carolena.

Then it was her turn for her mouth to drop open, "Really? You want me to choose Enthrall? What is wrong with you? Next you're going to tell me to choose Destroy!"

Carnage was certainly not going to tell her to choose Destroy. He shook his head vigorously.

"Well, good. At least you haven't totally lost your mind."

He glanced again at Enthrall's closed bedroom door. The male would certainly be a better match for his Carolena than he, himself, would. He looked back at Carolena and jerked his head back when he found her only an inch from him. She reached up and grabbed his head in her hands, bringing it down closer to her. She locked eyes with him, "Mine!" she shouted at him.

His eyes got huge as he watched her, but she wasn't finished.

Now that his horns were within reach, she wrapped her hand around one of them so that he couldn't stand upright without pulling her off her feet. Then she threw her head back and screamed, "MINE!!!"

Then, she looked right back at him, locking her eyes on his, "Do you understand?" she asked.

He couldn't nod because he'd dislodge her grip on his horns and maybe make her lose her balance.

She grabbed his other horn, now holding him by both hands and shouted again, "Carnage is MINE! Do you hear me? Do you all hear me? I claim Carnage! He is Mine!"

From somewhere outside, they heard a familiar male voice respond, "Good gods, we all heard you. Keep it down!"

Carnage snorted a little, his form of laughter. She burst into uncontrollable giggles.

Finally getting control of herself, she asked softly, "Do you agree to be my male, Carnage?"

He couldn't look at her, because she held him by both horns, and he was practically bending over, so she could maintain her hold on him. He reached up and took her hands from his horns, holding them in his own, as he straightened to stand before her. He looked her in the eye, wanting her to think about this, to be sure.

He placed a hand on his own chest, "Gaaaahhhll" he said.

She thought about it for a moment, then it clicked, "Yes. Goyle. You are a Goyle. I am a human. Glad we got that straightened out."

Carolena tried to reach for his horn again, but in spite of her jumping a bit, couldn't quite reach them. "Lean down here," she instructed.

Dutifully, he leaned over. She reached up, grabbed one of his horns, spun on her heel and marched to her bedroom with him in tow.

<<<<<<<>>>>>>>

Outside, Destroy leaned back against the trunk of the tree he sat under. He'd been waiting for Carnage to leave, so he could knock on the door and ask Carolena to read him a little more of the story that she'd read earlier. He wanted to know what happened next, and patience wasn't one of his high-points. And since he'd decided to wait, he'd been witness to her claiming Carnage. He felt disappointed, but not entirely surprised. Besides, he thought as he relaxed a bit more, the claim wasn't complete. Carnage may still screw this up, and if he did, Destroy would be there to seize any opportunity that may present itself. He would not mind in the least having Carolena as his female. She was nice to him. And she liked to talk to him, and she could read to him every night. He put his hands behind his head and looked up at the stars, imagining what would happen next in the story. He couldn't wait until tomorrow evening — he hoped she'd read to them again.

<<<<<<<>>>>>>>

Carnage couldn't believe it; his Leena had chosen him. He'd tried to get her to consider Enthrall, not because he didn't want her, but because he believed Enthrall a better match for her than he could be.

He watched as she turned down the bed and climbed in. Patting the place beside her. "Come lay beside me, Carnage. I feel safest when you're here."

Carnage turned down the oil lamp on her dresser to a soft glow and slid into bed beside her. She immediately curled up against him. "Will you hold me, Carnage?"

He took her in his arms, arranging her body next to and on his. He sighed deeply, loving the feel of her in his arms.

Carolena draped one leg over Carnage's leg, her arm across his abdomen, her head on his chest. He lay perfectly still, allowing her to touch him at will. She stroked his chest; he maintained his control. She rubbed her leg against his; he rumbled just ever so slightly, but still maintained his control. She ran her fingertips down to his waistband, and lightly feathered her fingers across the button there, stroking the skin underneath. His hand shot up, trapping her fingers in his own.

She looked up at him, his eyes locking on her in the near darkness of the room. He didn't move, neither did she. They held their positions until she moved quickly, unexpectedly up his body to press her lips to his. Rather than close his eyes and enjoy, his eyes popped open, and he watched her until she, too, opened her eyes.

When she finally did, she sat back on her heels and asked, "Do you not want me?"

His forehead wrinkled as he realized that she thought he didn't want her; he struggled for a way to let her know. He reached out a hand, pushing her hair behind her ear, "Mine," he said quietly.

Carolena smiled, nodded her head, "Yes, yours."

He put a hand behind her head, pulling her slowly to him. He pressed his lips against hers, kissing her. He'd never kissed a woman before. He'd fucked, but never kissed. To him kissing was more intimate, more personal. You didn't have to look at a woman to fuck her, but you had to look at a woman to kiss her. You shared the same close space, you shared breath, every essence of who she was could be tasted in her kiss. He softly pressed his lips to hers again, and when she sighed in pleasure, he took the opportunity to slip his tongue out and trace her lower lip with just the tip. Her eyes got huge, and she opened her mouth even more, granting him entry. He was careful not to hurt her with his fangs, kissing her gently, but passionately. Soaking up every sensation his first kiss brought him.

Carolena leaned forward, pressing her breasts against his chest, and the length of the rest of her body against his. Carnage rumbled and traced the outline of her breast with his thumb. Tilting his head to kiss her again, which she eagerly allowed.

She rolled her hips against his leg in response to him stroking the outside of her breast, and he froze. She felt him pull back and stopped as well.

"What did I do wrong?" she whispered.

Carnage shook his head.

"I don't understand," Carolena told him.

How to tell her that he wanted to go slow, make sure that he was what she wanted, that was his problem. He didn't know how to make her understand without the words most others took for granted.

He scooted down in bed, keeping her in his arms.

He settled into the pillows, pulled her onto his chest, and closed his eyes.

Carolena watched him. Not understanding. She asked, "Are you angry with me?"

He opened his eyes and looked at her, shaking his head, no, a look of exasperation on his face.

"I thought that was what males liked," she said, embarrassed that she'd done something to displease him.

He placed his hand on her heart, then tapped her temple.

She looked at him confused.

He did it again, touched her heart, but this time he pointed at himself, then her temple.

Carolena watched him intently, trying to figure out what he wanted to say.

"I don't understand," she told him.

Carnage sighed, thinking of how to let her know. "Lllllooob' 'arnge," he told her.

She watched him, an inkling of understanding beginning to take shape.

He let go of Carolena, using his huge clawed hands, and made the shape of a heart with his fingers.

Carolena said, "Heart."

Carnage grinned, nodding his head yes.

Then he pointed at himself and said "'Arnge"

"Oh! 'Arnge! You! You're Carnage, 'Arnge, right?" she sat up excitedly.

Carnage smiled, nodding his head and made the shape of a heart with his hands again. Then he pointed to Carolena, made the shape of a heart and said, "'Arnge."

She understood. "You want me to love you first. Not just choose you because you're the best offered in this situation."

Carnage put his hands down and smiled sadly at her.

She looked at him for a moment longer, then said, "Just like I said the other night, I always dreamed of being adored and loved, not just marrying whomever my father chose for me because he thought they were the best choice."

Carnage nodded, repeatedly.

She met his eyes again, "Okay. I understand."

He brought her in close for another kiss that left them both breathless. And when he pulled back from their kiss, she surprised him by running her tongue up one of his fangs, and didn't that just make him shiver.

He closed his eyes to regain control, his cock now throbbing, and pressed her head to his chest, holding her tightly.

Carolena closed her eyes, smiling smugly, knowing full well the effect she had on her Gargoyle. She wondered how long he could hold out. It was sweet that he wanted her to love him, and she completely understood. But things had changed for her. She'd chosen Carnage because she truly wanted him. Now she just had to convince him that she truly wanted him; that she wasn't settling. Tomorrow, she'd begin convincing her male that she'd chosen him with her heart, not her head. Or so she thought.

Chapter 15

Carolena woke the next morning alone. Again. She huffed as she threw back the covers and started getting dressed. After she dressed, she went straight to the kitchen and poured herself a cup of coffee. Enthrall heard her puttering around the kitchen and came in to greet her.

"Good morning, Carolena. How did you sleep?" Enthrall asked.

"Very well, thank you. I always sleep well with Carnage beside me," she answered with a tone in her voice.

"Then, why are you irritated?" he asked, trying not to smile.

She turned on him, "Because I wake alone!" she said exasperatedly. "He always sneaks off during the night, so I wake alone. Why?" she asked. "Why does he keep doing this?" she demanded.

Enthrall's eyes roamed around the kitchen; he turned his head this way and that, considering her question before finally giving in and admitting, "I have no idea. If it were me, you'd have to pry me from your side. I don't know why he keeps leaving before you wake each morning."

"Hmpf," was the only response he got.

Carolena took her coffee and sat at the table. Enthrall went to the bread box and took out what was left of the last loaf he'd made, slicing off a large piece, and placing it on a plate with a big chunk of cheese and leftover piece of dried sausage. He placed the food on the table in front of her, "Have something to eat, Carolena. You'll feel better after your belly is full."

She didn't answer, but broke off a piece of cheese and placed it in her mouth.

"After you finish breakfast, why don't I show you around Whispers? I'll introduce you to some more people. We'll make a morning of it," Enthrall offered.

"Thank you, Enthrall. I'd appreciate it. But wait, I thought you were going into town again this morning," she said.

"I went earlier — you slept in this morning," he answered.

"Oh, well, okay. I'll hurry then, so we can get started," Carolena told him.

"No, no rush at all. Whenever you're done, we'll go," Enthrall said.

<<<<<<<>>>>>>>

An hour later and Carolena found herself the subject of much curiosity. Some people were very kind to her; others were more standoffish. Though most of the standoffish could probably be attributed to the killer glare Enthrall shot at everyone who didn't automatically greet her with a smile, or Destroy who followed along at a safe distance, determined to be included even if he was not acknowledged.

The children were especially welcoming of her, and when she asked permission of their parents before she spoke to their children, their parents warmed to her as well. She was genuinely interested in these people — they would apparently be her future. She relaxed, smiled easily, and laughed without a care.

Enthrall watched her, amazed that once she let her guard down and let her true self shine through, his people immediately responded. Carolena was a very special woman. She was good, pure, no ulterior motive, and his people saw that.

Destroy, who had followed for a while, grew impatient as the morning wore on. Gradually he joined Carolena and Enthrall as the three of them took a leisurely tour of Whispers and met any inhabitants that wanted to come out to greet them. One of their last stops was near a lone home actually built on stilts, standing over the water. Two children were playing in a circle drawn in the dirt about 20 feet from the water's edge. Carolena did as she had earlier. Before interacting with the kids, she asked their parents if she could speak with them. Their mother, Serafina, readily agreed. Their father, Simon, said nothing as he stood back watching her suspiciously, but neither did he attempt to stop her when she approached the kids and knelt down in the dirt to see what they were doing. Eagerly, they showed her what kept them so busy. They each had pieces of shell and sea glass. They were busily trying to assemble a "dirt" castle, using the pieces of shell and sea glass to decorate it. She asked if she could play, and they each generously took several of their precious decorations and placed them in front of her. The little boy, who was probably about 7 or 8, stood and with his bare foot erased the circle on the side that was nearest Carolena. He dropped down to his knees and used a small stick to redraw the edge of the circle, larger with room for Carolena to have her own space to build. She was startled, and her breath drew in sharply when he stretched to draw the circle nearer her, and she saw flaps of flesh on his neck just below his ear. When he turned to complete the circle on the other side, she saw that he had the same flaps of flesh on the opposite side of his neck as well. Her eyes flew up to Enthrall's, but instead she caught the eyes of their father. He smirked at her reaction and stepped closer as though to protect his children from her scorn. She dropped her eyes back to the children and composed herself, and even had a smile ready for the child when he looked up to tell her, "There, now the circle's big enough for all three of us to play."

"Thank you. It's very nice of you to let me play with you," she told him.

"You're welcome. It gets boring just playing with Serena," he told her.

"Serena?" she asked.

"Yeah," he pointed a dirty finger at the little girl, "my sister. I'm Seth."

"Well, it's very nice to meet you, Seth," Carolena said.

A small female voice cleared and when she turned, Serena, a little girl of about 5, was waiting for acknowledgment as well.

"And, Serena, what a beautiful name you have," Carolena complimented.

"Thank you. My mom and dad picked it," Serena said, going right back to carefully arranging piles of dirt and using her hands, a stick, even a cup to shape them before pressing the colored shells and glass into their sides.

Carolena sat on her bottom, no regard for her clothing at all, and dug her hands into the dirt. She was vaguely aware of Enthrall and the kids' parents visiting, but was truly enjoying herself and did not pay the adults much attention. Some time later, she sat back, as did Seth and Serena, satisfied with their creation. It was quite a large pile of dirt, accented here and there with twigs and small pieces of wood that Destroy had wandered here and there and brought back to them. He'd used a small piece of fabric torn from his own shirt to tie to one of the straighter twigs and fashion a flag of sorts for them to stick into the top of their "dirt castle." Carolena had noticed that Serena, also, had the flaps of skin in her neck just as Seth did. She said nothing, though. It didn't matter to her; they were just kids, regardless of their species. When they were completely done with their creation, she took another twig and wrote, "Castle SS" on the tallest tower they'd managed to get to remain intact.

Seth looked at it for a moment before asking, "What's that?"

"It's letters, they spell the name of your castle," Carolena answered.

"Oh," he said. He reached out and ran his finger over the shapes she'd made in the dirt. "What's its name?"

"It says, 'Castle SS,'" Carolena said. "S for Seth and S for Serena. So, Castle SS," Carolena explained.

"This one looks like a snake," Seth said. "It's kinda squiggly."

"Yes, it does, kind of. Those are the S's."

The children watched curiously as she wrote more shapes into the dirt.

"What's that?" Serena asked excitedly, crawling over to see what Carolena was doing.

"That's your name, Serena. See? S, E, R, E, N, A, Serena," Carolena said, smiling.

"What's mine look like?" Seth asked her as he also moved closer.

Carolena leaned closer to Seth and wrote his name in the dirt as well.

"There you go, S, E, T, H, Seth. That's your name," she said.

Each child jumped up and hurriedly searched for sticks; then, they sat down near their own names and began trying to copy the shapes she'd made in the dirt.

Carolena applauded their efforts and encouraged them until they got it right. "You should keep practicing until you get it perfect," she told them. "You're doing a great job!" she said, smiling.

"Can you show us more?" Seth asked.

"Well, yes, sure I can. If your mom and dad don't mind," Carolena said, pausing to look up at their parents who were speaking with Enthrall.

Their father looked up sharply and said, "I don't think they..."

But their mother cut him off, "Yes!" she said firmly. "You can show them any letters you want to show them. I don't know my letters," she turned to look at their father who stood, jaws clenched, watching his wife defy his wishes, "neither one of us does. And they can't go to schools — for one they're too far. And," she paused before continuing, "they're not like the other kids in school. Even the kids here don't play with 'em. So they haven't had much chance to learn things like letters and numbers." She rushed to assure Carolena and play up her children, "They're smart. Really smart, they just don't have anybody that can teach them," she finished.

Carolena looked back and forth from Serena to Seth, their faces hopeful, waiting for her answer to their mother. "I'm not a teacher, but I can read and write. One of the few things my father gave me was an excellent education. I'd be happy to teach them whatever I know. If it's alright with you, of course," Carolena told their mother.

Serafina's face split into a huge smile, "Really? Oh, thank you. That would mean ever so much to me. And I'll find a way to pay you for your services."

The kids were whooping and hollering, jumping around all excited.

Carolena laughed as she tried to speak over them, "Don't you dare! I do not want payment of any type. I'd be honored for you to allow me to teach them a little."

"Why would you do that?!" Simon snapped at her. "Why would you want to teach my kids anything? And for no money," he asked.

Carolena was speechless — she didn't understand why he was so against her teaching his kids. She stammered as she searched for the right words, "Because, they're kids. They're excited about learning. Why would I not?" she countered.

"They ain't just kids," Simon told her.

Carolena regarded the kids sitting with her in the dirt, now subdued and looking intently at their names where they'd been scribbled as they tried to duplicate her letters. "Yes," she said powerfully as she climbed to her feet, "Yes, they are. They are kids just like any other," she proclaimed as she took a few steps toward their father. "They're sweet, and funny, and kind. They're mischievous, and loving, and adventurous, and they want to learn. Why would you keep them from learning?" she demanded.

"They ain't human. They don't need human ways," he said flatly.

Carolena stood for a moment, not sure how to proceed, then she realized that he was prejudiced against humans. Maybe he'd been treated poorly as a child. Maybe he just hated humans.

"Mr. Simon, I don't honestly care what species they are. They're kids. When I look at them, when I speak to them; that's what I see — kids. If you have a problem with me because I'm human, that's one thing. But it has nothing to do with the fact that your children are indeed children. I know how to read and write. I love kids, ALL kids. And yours want to learn."

Carolena turned to Serafina, "I don't have a clear plan in mind, but I'd like to teach them. If you decide that it works for you, please let me know, and we'll work something out."

"I will, Carolena. Thank you," Serafina said as she shot dagger looks at her husband.

Carolena walked over to where Enthrall stood watching, allowing her to handle this on her own. He wanted his people to respect her, and she'd have to stand on her own two feet for that to happen.

"Are you ready?" Carolena asked him.

"I am." He turned to Simon and Serafina, "Thank you for visiting with us today. It has been a most interesting experience."

As Carolena and Enthrall walked away, back toward the north of the community where his home stood, she realized that Destroy was not with them. She turned around to find him squatting down near where she'd written the children's names, tracing his own finger over the letters she'd written.

"Goyle!" she shouted over her shoulder.

"What?!" He yelled back.

"We're leaving. Are you coming or not?" she asked without turning around.

He grinned, he liked that she was no longer afraid of him, "I'm coming."

As soon as they were out of earshot of the family, Carolena asked, "What are the marks on their necks, Enthrall?"

He smiled, surprised that she'd been able to wait as long as she had to ask, "They are called the Loire. The flaps of skin on their necks are gills. They are able to exist both in and out of the water. They're the only Loire that we have here. There are many legends surrounding them; no one knows for sure exactly what they are and aren't capable of, but they came here asking for sanctuary, and I gave it. They've been no trouble at all. They follow the rules and are always polite."

"Why does Simon have a problem with me teaching the kids?" Carolena asked.

"Simon has a problem with most people, regardless of who they are. He's intensely private, but he's a good husband and a good father. And, Carolena, make no mistake about it — he's a predator. Their species is predatory, though they mainly exist in the water. They can be dangerous on land as well."

"Maybe people have been mean to him. Maybe he wants to protect his family from whatever he's suffered."

Enthrall stopped walking and turned to face her, smiling, "Do you always try to find the good in everyone?"

She smiled back, "Most of the time."

They started walking again, "Could be, Carolena, I've never asked what he suffered through. If he wants me to know, he'll tell me. All I need to know is the kind of person he is now and that he wants the best for his kids and his wife."

Carolena raised her eyebrows at him, and he answered without her having to ask, "Yes, he does want the best for them. A place for them to grow up and be able to be themselves. Where they're safe from any type of danger because they are different. He may not trust you personally, but that doesn't mean that he doesn't want the best for his kids."

<<<<<<<>>>>>>>

Two days later Enthrall was proven right when Simon appeared in Enthrall's yard while they were having breakfast. Enthrall went out to greet him, "'Morning, Simon. How are you today?"

Simon stood with his kids, one on each side, holding their hands. "Good morning, Enthrall. I was hoping that maybe I could speak with Ms. Carolena."

"You realize she's under my protection. She is a member of our community now," Enthrall said calmly.

"Yes, I do. And I know that her male is Carnage, too. Nobody wants him riled up."

"Okay, then. Just a moment, I'll call her for you," Enthrall said.

Carolena had been listening, standing just inside the front door. Enthrall opened the door and came in, "Carolena, Simon wants to talk to you. Is that alright?" Enthrall asked.

"Of course. Do you think he's going to allow me to teach the kids?" she asked, hope in her eyes.

"There's only one way to find out," Enthrall answered.

Carolena stepped out onto the porch and smiled at the kids, but addressed their father. "Hello, Simon. Can I help you?"

"'Morning, Ms. Carolena. Yes, I think maybe you can." He shuffled his feet like he was uncomfortable.

"I'd like to apologize for my behavior at my place the other day. I'm very protective of my family, and I judged you to be like all the rest. My most sincere apologies if I offended you," he said as he raised his head to look her in the eye.

Carolena smiled, she went down the stairs and right up to Simon where he stood, clutching the hands of his children in his own. She extended her hand to him, waiting for him to take it. He released Seth's hand and took hers. Carolena shook his hand as a man would. "Thank you for your apology, Simon. But it's honestly not necessary. I admire any male who protects his family so fiercely."

Simon smiled shyly at her, "Thank you. Anyway, I was, we was, wondering if you would still be interested in teaching our kids. They really want to learn, and Sera and me was hoping that you'd still be interested."

Carolena looked down at the children, both with huge smiles on their faces, waiting for her answer.

"I'd be honored, Simon. Thank you for asking me, and for trusting me," Carolena told him.

Chapter 16

Carolena sat on the ground in front of Enthrall's home. She watched Seth and Serena diligently trying to recreate the letters she'd made for them in the dirt. It had been days since she'd seen Carnage. He came home most nights, and she knew this only because when he left each morning, he left a flower on the pillow next to her. She didn't remember him being there, though, and she was lonely without him. She missed him. He'd said he wanted her to love him, but he was never there to spend time with. How did he expect her to grow to love him, if he was never there? She had no doubt that she'd chosen the right male; her commitment to that never waivered. But the fact that he spent all his waking moments away from her, without explanation, was becoming very worrisome. And her heart hurt. She sat upright, her heart hurt! She did love him. He'd stolen her heart, then disappeared. "Damn him!" she whispered harshly to herself.

Both children stopped trying to write their alphabets in the dirt and watched her closely. She stood, stomped a couple of feet away, then seemed to remember that Seth and Serena were in her care today while she taught them to read and write. She hurried back to them, changing the subject and hoping they'd ignore her outburst.

"Let's see how you've done," Carolena said as she knelt beside them, checking their work. "Very good," she said, beaming at the children, "Very good indeed."

"Are you okay, Ms. Carolena?" Seth asked.

"Of course I am, why would you ask, Seth?" Carolena asked.

"Well, because you just damned somebody. And you was stomping your feet," he explained. Seth got to his own feet and looked around the yard. When he looked back to her, his eyes had changed colors, and he was hissing softly. "Who do you need damned, Ms. Carolena? Did somebody hurt you?" he asked protectively, still looking around the yard for whomever had upset her.

Carolena realized that he meant to protect her, "No one, Seth. Everything is okay, I promise. I was just a little irritated, but I'm fine now," she explained.

Seth glanced around the yard once more before saying, "Okay, if you're sure." Then he sat down and began to trace out his letters again.

Carolena looked around the yard herself, hoping for Carnage to appear. But time passed, and he didn't. She resolved to stay awake all night if she had to, so that she could confront him. She was tired of being an afterthought. If he didn't want her, she needed to know, now before she fell any deeper for him.

<<<<<<<>>>>>>>

Carnage worked for most of the day as he had the last several days, reassembling the home that he and Murder had moved piece by piece to where it now stood. Most of it was finished, but not all. They'd framed the entire thing, replaced the floor joists, and laid the floor. They'd reassembled the walls, and put the rafters in place for the roof, and replaced the tin on the roof. They had only to plaster the inside walls, and put a railing up to frame in the large platform they'd built it on. They'd built the platform in the same way one would a deck, then rebuilt the house right in the center of it. That left a good eighteen feet of deck in front of the house, about twelve behind the house, and there was ten feet of deck extending on both the left and right sides of the house. Carnage planned to build a set of stairs that would lead from the ground up to the deck, also with a railing on either side. This way the house was up off the ground, so no slithering creatures, or creepy crawlies to scare his Leena, and the house was up in the trees, so that it would be cooler, and the Eucalyptus scent more prevalent to keep the mosquitoes and other stinging and biting insects away from her. Tonight, they planned to install a water cistern, and connect pipes to bring the water to a tub, just like the one that Enthrall had. Carolena loved to soak in the bath, so he was going to make sure she had that same luxury in her own home. Murder had already installed a sink in the kitchen and a toilet and sink in the bathroom. The pipes had been run; he only needed to hook them up once the cistern was in place. The pipes for the toilet were already installed. Gravity would do its job, and he'd dug a deep hole in the ground some thirty feet from the house. The pipe leading from the toilet fed directly into the hole and into an additional cistern he'd buried in the ground to collect waste, then covered and filled the hole in. With just the two of them living there, the waste pit would take a long time to fill. When it did, he'd just dig another.

Before they'd roofed the house, Murder had brought the furniture in through the top. They had a bed, a table, chairs, a couch, two chests of drawers and a chifferobe to keep their clothes in. They'd installed cabinets and the wood burning stove in the kitchen, and shelves and cabinets in the bathroom for Carolena to store her linens. He'd already made arrangements for Enthrall to bring linens, towels, and anything he thought that Carolena would need in her own home. And Enthrall had made several trips to town over the last days bringing back as much as he could each time. Carnage smiled as he stood in the center of the living room, looking around at the home he'd created for his woman. He was very proud of it. He hoped she'd like it and want to live there with him.

Murder walked into the room breaking his thoughts, "Do you want to try to finish tonight? There's not much left. All the furniture is moved in — all we still have to do is connect the roof cistern. We could finish it tonight if we work all night."

Carnage nodded his agreement and then walked over to the wall. He rubbed his hand up and down it and looked back at Murder.

Murder spoke, "Yes, the walls, too. We need to plaster the walls. We might be able to finish it tonight. If not, definitely tomorrow."

Carnage grinned, "'Es!"

"Well, then, let's get to work. The sooner you get your female here and away from Enthrall and Destroy, the better," Murder said.

Carnage's brow furrowed. He wasn't sure why Murder thought it was a bad thing that she'd become friends with the other two men. She'd already told him she'd be friends with whomever she chose, and she'd already claimed him. He knew that she only wanted him, but Murder's words put suspicion in his heart. He'd have to watch Enthrall and Destroy closely. Maybe Murder saw something he didn't.

<<<<<<<>>>>>>>

Carolena was seated on the front steps, waiting for Carnage to arrive. It was dusk out and the sun had almost set. Simon had come for his kids earlier in the afternoon, and she'd been alone since then. Destroy was lurking, she had no doubt, but he didn't always make himself known until she settled with a book in her hands, or unless she started off on a walk. Then he'd be there, without fail, every time. She'd given up waiting for Carnage to come back to her each night, so she'd started reading the rest of The Beauty and The Beast to Destroy. He begged incessantly, and it seemed foolish to wait to finish it for a male who wasn't interested in being there to hear it. Most nights Enthrall would join them as well.

Enthrall had disappeared earlier in the afternoon while Seth and Serena were still there. He'd watched her giving them their lessons for a bit, excused himself and disappeared.

Now though, there was a male striding toward her through the gloaming, and she perked up, thinking it Carnage. But it wasn't. It was Enthrall. He was striding toward her with a package in his hands and a huge smile on his face. He knew that when he ghosted from one location to another it greatly unsettled her, so he tried to ghost to a location just out of sight and walk into the house whenever he could. She appreciated his effort, but it wasn't necessary — it was after all, his home, not hers.

She tried to quickly hide her disappointment that he wasn't Carnage and greeted him, "Hello, Enthrall."

"Hello, Carolena," he said as he came closer, holding the package out to her.

"What's this?" she asked, surprised.

"Open it," he said.

"For me?" she asked.

"Well, not exactly, but in a way of sorts," he answered.

Carolena watched him curiously as she tore the tissue paper wrapping and found inside three small slate boards and several boxes of chalk. She looked up at Enthrall, her mouth open in surprise, "I can't believe you did this!"

"It's nothing really, Carolena. I just saw you teaching the children earlier, writing in the dirt with sticks and decided that you needed better tools. So I went into town and bought these."

Enthrall was standing right beside her and she stood to wrap her arms around him, "Thank you, Enthrall. You are truly a good man," she said earnestly as she hugged him.

He chuckled sadly, "Maybe once, now I'm just a male, not really a man any longer."

"You're a good man, Enthrall. And thank you, so much! Seth and Serena will be so excited tomorrow!" Carolena said.

Enthrall stood there, letting her hug him for as long as she wanted, hugging her back, soaking in the contact. It was the first contact of any sort he'd had in a long while. He hungered so for any type of warmth. And when genuine and from a female he admired, even more so. Unfortunately, she pulled away all too soon, changing the subject as she rewrapped her slate boards.

"Do you know where Carnage is?" she asked hesitantly.

"Not exactly. Why?" he asked.

"I've not seen him in days," she answered.

"He comes back at night, I can scent that he's been here," Enthrall told her.

Carolena nodded, "Yes, he leaves me a flower on my bed pillow when he leaves. But he doesn't wake me. He doesn't talk to me. I never see him," she said sadly.

"You miss him," Enthrall said.

Carolena sighed deeply, turning to go up the steps and into the house, "Perhaps. He doesn't appear to have the same feeling though. Maybe I was wrong in thinking I knew how he felt for me."

Enthrall watched her go into his home, still talking as though he was right behind her. He looked around his yard, saw Destroy sitting high up in a huge tree just at the edge of the yard and held eye contact for just a moment. Destroy had heard her, and Destroy was just waiting for an opportunity to step in where Carnage was stupid enough to allow it.

Enthrall followed Carolena into the house.

She had placed the slate boards on the couch and was in the kitchen preparing dinner for them.

He took a seat at the table, "Carolena, don't count him out. I don't claim to understand Carnage. But you seem to. His absence is not without reason. Give him more credit than that."

Carolena continued making dinner, "I'm trying. I'm just lonely. I miss him."

"I'm sure he'll be here more often before you know it," Enthrall told her. He wanted to kick himself. She was doubting Carnage; he could have taken advantage of that and turned her attentions toward himself. But he didn't. Because he was indeed a good male. And because he'd seen the way she looked at Carnage — she'd never looked at him that way. His reverie was broken by her asking a question, apparently he'd not heard her the first time.

"If you'd rather not explain, that's fine, I was just curious," she said.

"I'm sorry, say again," he said.

"I said, if you're a Vampire..." she started.

"There is no if about it, I am Vampire," he told her, amused.

"Fine, as I was saying, if you're a Vampire, why do you eat regular food? Why do you not drink blood?" she asked.

He smiled at her, deciding to indulge her curiosity, "I do drink blood, just not as often as you'd think. And I eat regular food because I'm alive just like you are. I need the same sustenance you do. I just need living blood to supplement my own. I have sources nearby. When the need gets too great, I take what I must."

"You don't kill to take it?" she asked.

"Not any longer. I've learned control as I've aged," he told her, smiling when her head whipped around to regard him thoughtfully.

They enjoyed a quiet dinner, and later when she picked up her book to read, Destroy magically appeared at the front door. Enthrall looked to Carolena who nodded, smiling. Enthrall invited him in, and she read to them for a while. When she became tired, she took a bath and went to her room to wait for Carnage. She was not going to sleep this night until she'd spoken with him about his absences. She wanted him to be truthful with her.

Hours later she jerked awake on her bed where she'd fallen asleep while waiting for him to come to her. She looked around, still alone. Carolena got up and went to the living room, taking a seat on the couch, determined to wait for Carnage.

Chapter 17

The sunshine of the next morning woke her. Still, Carnage had not come. He'd stayed away all night. Surely that said something. Sadly, she made her way to her bedroom to dress and prepare for Seth and Serena to arrive as they did each morning now for their lessons. Her heart hurt. She hated this. And she was angry with herself for believing that a creature such as Carnage could ever be satisfied with her. He was amazing, handsome, strong, passionate; what could he possibly see in a simple human. She berated herself all the way to the breakfast table. Her state of mind was not missed by Enthrall, who silently placed a bowl of oats in front of her.

She picked up her spoon and mechanically began to eat, staring sightlessly ahead.

Enthrall watched as he ate his own breakfast, but could not contain his comments as he watched her hurt. "Do not assume what you are not sure of, Carolena."

She was silent for a moment before quietly answering, "I am trying not to."

The day went much the same as the previous days without Carnage. She taught the children, who always managed to make her smile. They had a picnic for lunch, and then she read to them from a book of fairy tales that Enthrall kept in his library. They loved hearing the stories almost as much as learning to write their letters.

Early afternoon brought Simon to pick them up, and this day he brought along several jars of fruits that Serafina had sent for her. She refused to accept payment, so Serafina had found a way around that, by sending preserved figs, peaches and cherries, which Carolena very happily accepted.

Enthrall took her to visit her Dragon tree, and afterward they made their way back home, intending to share a snack of the preserves that Serafina had gifted Carolena. Only there was not enough bread, so the afternoon turned into a bread making lesson.

The doors and windows to Enthrall's home were open to allow a breeze through to offset the heat from the wood burning stove they would use to bake their bread.

Enthrall cleaned the table well, then sprinkled a little flour on it to assist when they rolled out the dough. He brought out his bread bowl and handed it to Carolena. "Here, you will make it. You need to know how to make bread so that you can provide your own home with bread once you move out."

Carolena took the bowl from him, looking sadly at him. "I'm not sure where I'll be moving to. I may be here a little longer than I thought."

"Nonsense. You will be in your own home before you know it," he answered.

She said nothing, just looked at the bowl in her hands.

"But regardless, I would be honored if you would always consider this your home. You are always welcome here, no matter the reason. The bedroom you sleep in is always yours, Carolena," Enthrall told her.

Carolena smiled then, "Thank you, Enthrall."

Enthrall gave her a small bow and a smile. "Now, let us begin with our bread. Imagine! A female unable to cook!" he said tsking and grinning as he tried to raise her ire, distract her from her sad thoughts.

It worked, "I can cook! You know I cook, I've made dinner and lunch for us all, often!" she declared indignantly.

"Perhaps a little, but bread? Cakes? Are you able to make them? They are somewhat more difficult and do take a bit of expertise," he teased her.

Carolena raised her chin in the air defiantly, "No. I cannot make bread, but only because I've never tried. And I do not need to know how to make cakes, I prefer pies!"

"Ah, well, then we shall remedy that this day. Come, woman, let us make bread, we'll save the cakes for another day." Enthrall said, taking her by the hand and leading her to the kitchen counter top to start mixing the ingredients for the crusty French bread he loved so well.

Carolena grumbled, "I said I prefer pies."

"Yes, I am aware," Enthrall teased back, "We shall make cakes."

<<<<<<<>>>>>>>

Carnage and Murder had worked through the night, and most of the morning. Carolena's home was, for the most part complete. He still needed to do some caulking and he had no doubt she'd want to hang curtains in their windows and decorate it in the way a woman would, but it was livable. He'd installed the window that Enthrall had brought him to replace the one he'd broken. There were screens on all the windows, which allowed him to open them without letting insects in. He'd installed the windows in such a way as to create a cross breeze when he opened one at the front of the home and another at the back. He could open and close other windows to pull the breeze in any direction he chose — it was quite ingenious. He was exhausted, working from sun up to well into the night each night, and then last night's all nighter. But it was worth it. He'd be able to bring Carolena home today. He was thrilled. He'd be able to spend more time with her and win her heart. Taking one last look around, he was satisfied with the appearance of their home. He placed the handful of wild flowers in the mason jar in the middle of the kitchen table and walked out, closing the door behind himself.

A while later he came out of the woods into the clearing that Enthrall's home sat in. He could hear their voices and laughter as he came nearer. He paused to see what was happening.

Enthrall stood behind Carolena at his kitchen table. Her hands were working some kind of dough, and Enthrall was against her back, his hands with hers, helping to work the dough. His head was bent near Carolena's, and he was speaking softly to her. He dropped his head lower so that his lips were just at her ear and said, "That's it. Strong fingers, soft hands, caress the dough as you would a lover, strong yet gentle."

Carolena turned her head ever so slightly, their lips were centimeters apart, Enthrall stared into her eyes — and Carnage lost all control.

Roaring, charging the house, ripping the front door off its hinges as he rushed to get between Enthrall and Carolena. Somewhere in the back of his mind a little voice told him, "This! This is what Murder tried to warn you of! Fool! You left her alone, and she turned to another."

Enthrall and Carolena, startled by Carnage's sudden appearance and the tone thereof, jumped back, both of their hands covered with flour and bits of bread dough.

"Carnage!" Carolena said, "Look what you did to Enthrall's door!"

Carnage, his face a twist of anger, snarled at her as he stepped between Enthrall and Carolena.

Carnage placed Carolena behind him, and faced Enthrall directly. He did not fear Enthrall. He knew that he was physically the superior of the two and could win any confrontation; as long as Enthrall didn't start that damn shrill sound that he used to control the more animalistic of their people. If he did that, then everyone froze until he stopped.

"Control yourself, Carnage. Nothing has happened here," Enthrall said calmly.

Carnage snarled at him and shoved a hand in Carolena's direction.

Enthrall did not look away from Carnage, "I said, nothing happened here. Though it well could have and should have. You left her alone for so long she questioned you, your intentions and her choices. She has just begun to assimilate to a new world. You left her."

Carnage's face flashed to rage; he made a series of growls and flung an arm out in the direction of the home he just built.

Enthrall could guess his intention, and said, "I am aware. She is not."

Carolena put a hand on his arm, turning him toward her, "Why are you so angry?"

Carnage pointed a finger at Enthrall, "Traawwl!"

"Yes, he's Enthrall. He was only teaching me to make bread."

Carnage used two fingers of his right hand to tap his lips while he glared at Carolena.

Carolena shook her head, "There was no kiss. Nothing happened," she said almost sadly.

Carnage stared at her for a short time before spinning to pin Enthrall with a threat-filled glare. "MINE, Leenah!"

Enthrall watched him with a swirl of emotion on his face before finally responding, "Then perhaps you should actually make her a part of your life. Introduce her to your world, rather than leaving that to other males in her life."

Carnage roared a string of unintelligible sounds, and in one motion, turned, threw Carolena over his shoulder in spite of her protests, and stalked out of Enthrall's home.

Enthrall did not go after them. He knew beyond a shadow of a doubt that Carnage would not hurt Carolena, no matter how dangerous he was to everyone else. He adored Carolena. And he also knew that his presence at this particular time would only escalate the situation. Instead he took a deep breath, pressed his hand against his own lips in an effort to end the tingling that had started when he'd made the decision to kiss Carolena. He was actually grateful that Carnage had interrupted them. He didn't want to do anything that would endanger the easy friendship that he and Carolena had developed. But with her feeling slighted, her obvious affection for him, and his need for contact, it was almost too tempting not to explore. He sighed, rinsed his fingers off before toweling them dry and flouring them again, so he could finish making the loaves of bread they'd started.

<<<<<<<>>>>>>>

Carnage kept a steady pace in spite of Carolena dangling down his back, regularly beating at his back, and shouting threats of removing his manhood if he didn't put her down. The only response he gave was when she stopped fighting and just said softly, "Your shoulder is hurting my stomach."

He didn't miss a step, but swept her from his shoulder into his arms to carry her there instead. He did not look at her, did not even break stride. He was angry, and did not want to let that anger out on her. This was new for him. Normally, whatever emotion he experienced was let out into the world, anger being no exception. But with Carolena, he'd have to learn control. He'd been trying — this was the greatest trial yet. He'd much prefer to turn her over, spank her like an unruly child, and smash a few trees on the way to his new home.

He spared her a glance, and lifted his lip at her, displaying a huge fang. She lifted her lip at him and snarled back, crossing her arms across her chest in an act of defiance.

He was shocked, but not unpleasantly so. He couldn't smile though, because then she'd know his anger was dissipating. He instead popped her on the bottom, "Ssspaaann eww," he said.

She flinched in his arms, her mouth dropping open. "I don't think so! And if you do, you better not go to sleep. Because I will find something heavy to hit you with, Mister!"

"Hmpf," was the only reply she got.

Thirty minutes later Carnage slowed and stopped walking. He looked down at Carolena in his arms and waited for her to look back at him. She was staring at the tree tops, studiously ignoring him, though he carried her.

Since she wouldn't look down at him, or around, he turned so that her eyes would fall on the trees their home was built in the center of.

Slowly, she became aware of what she was seeing. She pulled herself more upright in his arms. "There's a house up there, in the middle of those trees!" she exclaimed, forgetting that she was angry with him.

"'Es," he said.

He knew the minute her eyes followed the line of the house down to the support beams and the two levels of stairs that led up to it. Her face lit up, and she struggled to be put on her feet.

He obliged her, setting her gently on her feet. She walked over to the support beams and ran her hands over one of them. Then walked around the outer edge of the home, looking up at the bottom of the deck it was mounted on.

"This is amazing! Who lives here? I've never seen anything like this. Can we go look inside?" she asked in rapid succession.

He walked over to the stairs and indicated that she should go first. She wasted no time in starting the climb to the top of them where she'd find the home in the trees. The climb was easy really, the stairs were only inches apart and spaced so that they were on a slight rise. About halfway up there was a landing where the stairs switched directions, then continued their rise. When they arrived at the top, there was a small wooden gate, whitewashed, with a hook and latch closure. Carnage reached out, flipping the catch and releasing the gate, which swung open gently.

Carolena looked up at him with a smile, delight in her eyes. She walked through the gate and onto the deck. She was like a child, going from the railing to the house and back to the railing again, trying to see everything she could from so high up in the trees, and peering through the windows at the same time. Finally, after her third trip back to the railing, she turned and almost stumbled into the little table that Carnage had placed on the front deck for them to sit and have breakfast or dinner at. It was the same table and chair that he'd had in his original space down near the edge of the swamp, only he'd added a chair so that they could both sit.

Carolena recognized the table. She walked over to it, running her fingertips across one of the chairs sitting there. "This is your table," she said, not waiting for an answer.

With her hand still on the chair, she looked at the house, then turned to him, "Is this your house?"

He shook his head, no.

She looked back at the house, then down at the table. She had no doubt this was Carnage's table. "Then whose house is it?" she asked him, looking directly in his eyes.

A slow smile spread onto his face, all his teeth eventually showing as his smile grew. He pointed a finger at her and said, "Leenah howwsh."

Her eyebrows shot up, "What?" she whispered.

He never stopped smiling, just pointed at the house then her, and back at the house again.

"Mine?" she asked, completely dumbfounded.

"'Es," he answered. He walked over to the door, opened it and stood back, as he waited for her to enter.

Carolena walked past him, still in shock and peered inside. She saw the larger kitchen table with four chairs, her sink, her stove. Her living room with a couch and two chairs, and hallway that lead to, where? She walked slowly through the house lightly dragging her fingertips along the tops of the furniture and walls in the hallway. The first door opened on a bathroom. There was a tub, very similar to the one that was in Enthrall's home. There was a toilet and a sink. She opened the cabinet and found folded towels and washcloths and a set of sheets for a bed.

She left the bathroom and went to the next door just a few steps further down the hall. She opened it expecting a bed, but it was empty. She looked at Carnage, who offered no explanation, just stood there silently watching her explore. He shrugged his massive shoulders, so she turned and went to the final door at the end of the hallway. She opened it, and there she found the bed piled high with pillows, a chest of drawers and a chifferobe. There was a soft rug on the floor beside the bed, and there was a mason jar filled with water and fresh picked wildflowers, just as there'd been in each room.

She spun in a circle, slowly taking in all the details of the room. She stopped when Carnage came back into view. "This is where you've been, isn't it? This is why you were gone from me all this time. You were here, building a home for us?"

Carnage smiled sadly, nodding his head yes.

Carolena looked around the room again, "And all the while I was whining about being alone. I feel like a terrible person." She turned to face him, taking the steps that separated them until she was right in front of him.
"I'm sorry I doubted you. I'm so sorry. I thought you wanted to keep me separate from your life. I thought you were having second thoughts." She looked down at her hands where she wrung them together near her waist, then up at him again, "Can you ever forgive me?"

Carnage understood. He'd have felt the same if she'd just kept disappearing with no explanation. In retrospect, perhaps he should have told her what he was up to, but he'd wanted to surprise her. He leaned down, took her chin gently in his fingers and brought her lips to his. Just before he pressed his lips to hers, he said firmly, "Miinne, Leenah."

Carolena nodded, her chin still in his grasp, tears in her eyes, "Yes, yours. And you're mine."

Carnage grinned, "'Es!"

Chapter 18

Carolena and Carnage spent the rest of the afternoon exploring their new home. He showed her all the little things he'd added just for her, and she let go of the hold she'd had on her emotions, all doubt of her Goyle now gone. Murder had stopped by to see how she liked it, and she was almost sure she'd seen a blush on his dark skin when she rushed over to hug him and kiss his cheek in thanks for helping Carnage build it for her. Murder explained about the Eucalyptus trees and the way they naturally warded off insects, especially mosquitoes, which was the reason that Carnage had chosen this location. She offered him a drink. Carnage had stocked their kitchen well with sarsaparilla root, but he declined. Shortly after Murder left, she caught Carnage yawning. "Why don't we take a nap?" she asked.

Carnage raised his eyebrows in answer.

"You've been working so much, and I didn't sleep well last night without you, it's our home, we can do whatever we like, so why don't we just take a nap?"

Carnage gave one single nod of his head and held his hand out for her to take. He led her down the hall to their bedroom, but she stopped him outside the room that was empty. "What is this room for, Carnage?"

He shyly looked away from her, but she didn't move, standing there, holding his hand waiting for his answer.

Finally, still looking away from her, he mimed rocking a baby in his arms. He did it so quickly that had she not been looking right at him, she may have missed it.

Her heart warmed, she'd not thought of it before, "Can we have children?" she asked.

Carnage shrugged, but was now at least looking right at her.

She took his answer to mean that he wasn't sure, but he'd planned for it, just in case. "Well, we'll find out then, won't we? I'd like very much to have children. And since I've claimed you, you're my only chance."

Carnage did blush, no doubt about the pinkish hue that flushed through his bluish grey cheeks. He reached out, took her hand again, and led her to their bedroom.

He propped the door open with a large sparkling stone. She recognized it, quartz. He'd found some quartz filled geodes and broken them open to show their sparkling insides. He'd placed one in each of the bedrooms and in the bathroom to act as a door stop. He turned down the bedsheets, pulled his shirt over his head, dropped his pants to the floor and climbed in.

Carolena stood where she was, frozen in place. She'd just seen her Carnage, completely naked, for the first time. He was…stunning. He was so perfect he appeared to be carved of marble, and parts of him were just as hard. She was no wilting flower, but neither was she very experienced in these things. Carolena looked at Carnage waiting for her in bed, and realized she did know one thing. He'd never hurt her, and that her body was calling out for him. Once she gave herself to him, they'd be bound, and no one would ever be able to come between them. Carolena held Carnage's eyes as she lifted her shirt up and off her body, dropping it to the floor. Then she unbuttoned her trousers and dropped them to the floor as well. Her breasts were not bound, so she stood there, clad only in her panties — her delicates Enthrall had called them.

Carnage's chest heaved while he watched his woman undress. This was it. He'd decided to hell with waiting. Enthrall wanted his female. Destroy was obsessed with his female. Too damn many males wanting what was his. He'd found her. He'd verbally claimed her. He loved her. And today, in their own home, he was making her his.

Carolena watched her male, her husband after today if she had her way, struggle to control himself as she slowly pushed her panties down her legs, tossing them a short distance with her toe, before approaching their bed and sliding in beside him.

Carnage watched her, his eyes huge, other parts of him — even more huge.

She knew he said he wanted her to love him first, but what he didn't understand was that she already did. Seated beside him, she reclined against the pillows and turned to him, "I love you, Carnage. I know you said you wanted to wait until you had my heart, but you already do. I'm all in, there is no going back for me. If you told me I could go back to my other life, right now, today — I'd stay here with you. I don't want to be anywhere else."

Carnage listened to her, focused on her words, her eyes as she said them. He kissed her lips gently, "Mmyyy lahb Leenah." He struggled to say.

Carolena lit up, "I love you, too. And can I just say, I love that you call me Leena."

Carnage pulled one of the pillows out from behind her back, causing her to lay back even further. He was no longer looking in her eyes; he was lost looking at her body, trailing a sharp claw softly across her breast. "Mine, Leenah," he whispered as he pulled the covers down to reveal even more of her body.

She didn't answer, just moaned her pleasure at his touch.

Carnage leaned over and dragged his tongue across her breast. He looked up to see if it was okay with her. Her eyes were flashing, and she was panting as she wrapped her hands around his horns and brought his face back to her breasts. "More," she begged.

He wasted no time, alternately lapping at her nipples and suckling them. When she purred and gave him more moans, he experimented and lightly grazed her breasts with his teeth. Her hips bucked up off the bed in response. He smiled to himself, being sure to discover all the things his mate loved best. He was a very big male, and when he opened his mouth fully, he found he could fit almost her entire breast in his mouth, tonguing it when he did. She held him tighter to her and whispered, "Yes! More, please!"

Carnage flung the covers off Carolena and suckled and kissed his way down her body. This was new for him as well.

He'd only ever flipped over a willing female and slammed into her from behind. He'd not ever taken his time to give a female pleasure, to take his own pleasure from the beauty of her body, the sounds she made while he pleasured her, the tastes, the scents. All were assaulting his senses in a way that he hoped never ended.

He nudged her legs apart and settled his body between them, looking at her most secret places. He ran his fingers through the soft hairs that hid her from his view, dropping a kiss on her pelvic bone before he pushed her legs back, to make her knees rest almost on her shoulders.

Carolena gasped when Carnage bent her almost in half, his hands pressed against the backs of her knees to keep her in place, then shouted nonsensically in response to his tongue running the length of her womanhood. Carnage raised his head and looked up the length of her body to look her in the eyes. She was panting, fire in her heavily hooded eyes, as she tried as best she could to lift her hips and return his attention to the place it was before. He smiled seductively, and while continuing to meet her eyes, he reached his tongue out toward her, just not quite making it to his desired target. He wiggled the end of his tongue as though it was not quite long enough. She huffed at him, "Carnage!" she begged breathlessly.

He watched her as he slowly lowered his head and again ran his tongue the length of her, top to bottom. She dropped her head back on the pillows and became one mass of sensation. All she knew were the places he was touching her, his hands behind her knees, her feet resting on his shoulders, his lips and tongue between her legs. He licked and suckled and quite accidentally found a special little piece of flesh that made her almost lunge out of his grasp when he suckled it.

His head popped up to look at her. When she lifted her head to see why he stopped, he asked, "Huurrrt?"

Carolena shook her head vigorously, "No, no hurt. Very good! Please, don't stop."

He grinned and went back to the little, round, firm piece of flesh he'd found at the top of her womanhood. He suckled it and ran his tongue over it while he had it pulled into his mouth. She shivered and moaned, goose flesh rising up on her skin, but she didn't push him away or tell him to stop, so he didn't. After a few moments more of this, she arched her back, said, "Oh, my God! Yes!" and screamed while holding him to her by his horns as she ground her soft folds into his mouth. He allowed her to ride his tongue and lips, loving the flow of satisfaction from her body. He slowly lapped at her, until her grip on his horns weakened. When she finally released him, he crawled up her body, kissing a path to her breasts again.

Carnage held himself above her, his body aligned with hers, slowly rubbing himself back and forth in her hot wetness. Carolena eventually came back to herself and looking down their bodies, took him in hand, and ran her fingers over him, from base to tip. He was huge, and she said as much, "So hard," she whispered.

Carnage nodded.

"Does it hurt?" she asked.

Carnage nodded harder.

A look of mischief came over her face and she smiled slyly, "Would it feel better if we put it — here?" she asked as she ran the head of his cock back and forth between her dripping folds.

Carnage closed his eyes, enjoying the sensation.

She stopped rubbing him back and forth.

His eyes popped open, and he glared at her.

She laughed, then asked, "Would it feel better?"

"'Esss!" he practically snarled at her.

She lined him up with her opening and pulling her legs up and over his waist, started to push.

Carnage thought he'd pass out at the pleasure racing up his spine from being held inside her. He slowly pulled his hips back and pushed a little further in. She was so tight, so tiny, that it was very slow going.

She moaned and reaching down, used her own hand to pull her folds a little further apart to try to accommodate him.

Carnage pulled back and pushed in again, this time pushing all the way, until he felt her telltale barrier. He pushed gently, and she caught her breath. Damn, this was going to hurt her. He couldn't hurt her. He'd heard that human women who had never had sex had a barrier that had to be broken, and it was painful for them. He just ever so slightly pushed again, and she whimpered. Nope, he wasn't going to hurt her.

He pulled out of her, sitting back on his heels, rubbing his own hand up and down the length of his cock. The glistening drop of precum proof that he wasn't that far away from satisfaction himself. But he still couldn't hurt her. He licked his lips, the taste of her still lingering. His claw brushed against his lip, and suddenly he knew what to do.

"Please don't stop. We can make this work," she said.

He nodded at her and pushed her legs up toward her chest again, laying down between her legs, his face just inches from her center. He opened his mouth and took all of her into his mouth, using his tongue, lips and teeth to work her into a frenzy once again. When she was panting and rocking her hips in response to his ministrations, he grasped her ankles one at a time with his right hand, bringing them to rest on his shoulders. Her feet pressed against his shoulders, letting him know that she was firmly planted there. Then he used his tongue to search through her swollen, pink flesh until he found that little rounded nub again. He suckled it, teethed it, tongued it and didn't let up until she started shivering again, her entire body tensing up. He slowly, carefully pressed a finger inside her. Her walls clamped down on it, and he had to try not to smile in satisfaction as he continued to tongue her to completion. He very slowly rubbed his finger inside her, in time to his tonguing until she tipped over the edge into ecstasy. And the very moment she did, he pushed his finger further inside her, using the tip of his claw to tear through the barrier keeping him from finally claiming his woman. Once the deed was done, his finger remained inside her, giving her something to cling to as she rode out her pleasure. When she calmed, and the clamp she had on his finger lessened, he slowly pulled it out of her and put it directly into his mouth where he looked her in the eye as he suckled it clean. He climbed back up her body and started all over. Only this time, he rubbed himself against her, and through her wetness, coating himself so that he wouldn't hurt her when he slid inside. Because this time he wasn't stopping. When she lifted her legs and wrapped them around his waist, he lined himself up and pushed. The head of his cock popped right inside. He waited for her to adjust and when she reached for his hips to pull him closer, he pushed a little further in. He moved slowly so as not to cause her discomfort, but gradually, he managed to push almost all the way inside. One more pull, and a push to go deeper, and he was fully seated inside her, pushed up against her tightly, her legs around his waist, one of his hands at the back of her head, wrapped in her hair, the other planted in the pillows beside her head, holding himself up. He rocked his hips experimentally, and she moaned. He paused, giving her time to adjust. Carolena surprised him. She used her legs to bring him in tighter; then, she whispered, "Why are you waiting? Don't hold back. I love you, the real you, give me you."

He didn't hesitate; he pulled back and pushed back in. She seemed to like it, so he did it again and again. Soon he was slamming himself inside her, his hand now at the top her head to prevent her head from banging into the headboard. Carolena held on for dear life, loving every sensation, every moan, every snarl that her Goyle emitted, or brought forth in her. She was meeting his thrusts, every single one with a thrust of her own. Finally, he adjusted his angle and just as her body clenched around him, Carolena calling out his name, he threw his head back, roaring, slamming his hips into hers, shoving his cock as deep as it could possibly reach, smashing into her cervix as he emptied himself into her. He held himself there, feeling his seed leaving his body, filling his female with all that he was.

Carolena wrapped her arms around Carnage, her legs still around his waist, luxuriating in the feel of his hot semen filling her womb. Slowly catching her breath as her heart rate returned to normal. The single most amazing day of her life, burning itself into her memory, into her womb. Once they'd caught their breath, Carnage released her hair and leaned back a little to be able to see her face. "Kay?" he asked.

Carolena nodded, then smiled at him seductively, "Yes, I'm more than okay, but…"

Carnage's eyebrows scrunched up; did he do something she didn't like? Or maybe he didn't do something she wanted. He raised his eyebrows, a question clear on his face.

Carolena giggled, then cupping his face in one of her hands said, "Can I have more, please?"

Carnage rumbled low in his chest, pulling slightly out of his female before slamming back in. Her skin again pimpled in gooseflesh, and she moaned her pleasure.

"Yes, just like that, harder, faster."

Carnage was only too happy to oblige. Neither got a nap, in fact, no rest at all until well into the wee hours of the morning.

Chapter 19

Enthrall carefully wrapped the loaves of bread in clean kitchen towels. He did the same with several jars of fig and peach preserves and placed them carefully in a basket, along with Carolena's clothes, for ease of carrying. He gathered the small slate boards, the boxes of chalk, and the book that Carolena had been reading to everyone. He ran his finger over the gilt image of the beast embracing his beauty on the cover of it. Carolena had indeed claimed her beast — of this he had no doubt. Enthrall took a deep breath, gathered everything he planned to take to her, and ghosted to the grove of Eucalyptus trees he knew Carnage had built their home in. Rather than just show up at their home uninvited, he'd decided to ghost close to it, then walk the rest of the way, more than sure that Carnage would be aware of his presence as he got closer. Before their home came into sight, he could hear Carolena's voice carrying clearly in the early morning light. Enthrall made sure to step heavily, to brush against the lower branches of the shrubbery, to be sure that his approach was noticed.

The stairs came into view, and he tilted his head up to take in the home that Carnage had made for her. He was truly impressed — Carnage had done well. His eyes took in all the details and followed the line of the stairs to the deck, where the little gate was closed. He was not surprised to find an annoyed Gargoyle looking back down at him.

"I've brought some things for you and Carolena," Enthrall said, slightly lifting the filled basket and the slate boards in his hands.

He could hear quick footsteps, then Carolena's face peered down at him over the railing surrounding their raised deck. "Enthrall! Good morning!"

"Good morn', Carolena. I've brought the rest of your things, the slate boards for the children and some jams and breads. I hope you don't mind me dropping in uninvited," Enthrall said.

Carnage growled deep in his chest at the same time Carolena said, "Of course not. Come on up."

Carolena didn't even look at Carnage, but tapped his shoulder lightly with the back of her hand, while saying quietly, "Hush, Carnage. He's brought my things and gifts, and he's asking respectfully for permission to visit."

Carnage continued to stare down over the railing, but did not make a move to invite Enthrall into their home. Carolena turned to him, "He's our friend, Carnage."

Carnage looked at her for only a moment longer before deciding that it would be best to invite Enthrall versus raising the ire of his newly claimed mate. After all, they were actually bound now, no one could take her from him. Carnage stepped to the gate, unlatched the little catch, and pushed the gate open, indicating to Enthrall that he should come up.

Enthrall smiled, bowed slightly, and started up the stairs as he said, "Thank you, Carnage."

Enthrall stepped through the gate and onto the deck that supported Carnage and Carolena's home. Before he could say anything to either, Carnage whispered, "Mine," as he walked past him at the gate.

Enthrall did not hesitate to answer swiftly, "Absolutely." Then he addressed them both, "Thank you so much for welcoming me into your home. I knew Carnage was making a place for you, but I had no idea how wonderful it was. You've done a great job, Carnage."

"Hasn't he, though?" Carolena said, looking around the deck and the trees surrounding their home.

"He has indeed," Enthrall answered. "Here, I've brought your things and some bread and goodies. I've also brought 'La Belle et la Bete.' I thought surely you'd like to have it."

"Oh, I can't take your book! It's part of your library," Carolena told him.

"Please, it is my gift to you. I'd be honored if you'd accept it — as a housewarming gift," Enthrall said sincerely.

Carnage had snatched the book from Enthrall's hand as he'd held it out to Carolena and was running his hands over the cover as though it was a very precious thing to him. He loved the book, he loved when Carolena read to him, and he loved the story. He'd not yet found out how the story ended, but he loved that the beast and the beautiful girl were meant for each other; just like he and his Carolena. At least he hoped that was how the story would unfold.

Carnage grinned and held the book up to show Carolena. Carolena laughed and spoke to Enthrall, "Well, then I'll accept it." She indicated Carnage, "Obviously I'm not the only one who loves the story."

Enthrall chuckled at the sight of the huge, imposing Goyle cradling the book in his hands as he grinned like a child. "You are most welcome. Both of you."

Carnage clapped Enthrall on the back and indicated the table with his chin.

"Thank you, Carnage. I'd be most pleased to join you," Enthrall said.

Carnage waved toward the table with one hand and walked away, disappearing through their front door only to emerge a moment later with another chair. He placed it at the table where Carolena and Enthrall were laying out one of the loaves of bread and the preserves. They each took their seat, and Carolena tore off pieces of bread and spooned out fig preserves onto the small plates beside the slices of cheese already on the table. One plate was shared by Carnage and Carolena; the other was placed before Enthrall.

"I can see that congratulations are in order. I am happy for you both," Enthrall said, a huge smile gracing his face.

Carolena looked at Enthrall, confused.

Enthrall smiled, trying to let her know he knew they'd finalized their claim without being too bold and embarrassing her. "You've, ah, completed your claim. You are officially a couple. Congratulations."

Carnage grinned happily around his mouthful of bread and preserves.

Carolena blushed slightly, and looking at Carnage, smiled as she said, "Thank you, Enthrall."

After they'd enjoyed their breakfast, Carolena asked excitedly, "Would you like to see our house?!"

"I would, very much so," he answered.

Carnage followed them through the house as Carolena excitedly pulled Enthrall from room to room chattering about all the things Carnage had put in their home for her.

Enthrall looked over his shoulder a time or two to see Carnage grinning ear-to-ear, beaming with pride at pleasing his female so well.

It wasn't long before they heard little voices chattering and exclaiming at the house up in the trees, followed by a more masculine voice, "Hey! You have company down here! The least you could do is provide us with a way to tell you we're waiting!"

Enthrall shook his head. Carnage let out a soft grumble that sounded much like an ugghhh. Carolena chided them, "Now, be nice. He's our friend, too."

Carnage raised his eyebrow at her.

"Well, he is. He's trying. You just don't understand him. Give him a chance. Come on, let's go invite him in," Carolena said.

Carolena rose from the couch to go outside with Carnage following. When they got outside and looked down to see their visitor, Carolena exclaimed, "Oh! It's Seth and Serena, too! Hi, babies! Hello, Simon! Come on up!" she unlatched the gate and held it open as she waited at the top of the stairs for them to finish their run up to the top.

Destroy, who was the owner of the voice that had announced their arrival, fell into step behind Simon and his kids as they climbed the steps toward Carolena. "I'm down here, too. Not one word of greeting for me," he mumbled.

"Destroy, you know I'm happy to see you. You are always welcome," Carolena told him.

Carnage immediately started shaking his head, his eyes squinting, his mouth screwed into a scowl.

"Stop that!" Carolena scolded him, "Destroy is my friend."

Carnage remembered what Carolena had told him about trying to control her friends and decided that now was not the time to push the issue. He'd just have to make sure that he and Destroy came to an understanding later.

"This is just the best house ever!" Serena cried out as she ran full speed toward Carolena waiting at the top. Seth was a bit less enthusiastic as he followed his sister up the stairs, "Could have told us you was moving."

"Were moving, Seth. Could have told us you were moving," Carolena corrected. She addressed their father, "Simon, I'm sorry I wasn't there for the children's lessons this morning. I was surprised with our new home last night, and the move to here was so sudden that I didn't even think to let you know. I'm very happy you found us, though. Please, come in, join us on the deck."

"Thank you, Miss Carolena. I understand. Thank you for inviting us up." He looked around the outside of the home, the deck, the trees. "This is very nice. Carnage sure provided for you well. He must have thought of everything."

Carnage inclined his head to the male and offered his hand to shake. Simon looked at him momentarily, surprised, before taking Carnage's hand in his own and shaking it briefly.

Destroy, being Destroy, couldn't just be complimentary, "Yes, well, if he'd truly thought of everything, he'd have made some sort of way for visitors to signal they are waiting. And to be sure you're safe, he'd have made a pulley system to raise and lower the bottom set of stairs to keep anybody from just walking up them if you don't want them to." He swung the little waist high gate closed behind himself, "This is not any protection. More a formality."

Carnage growled softly in response. Enthrall chuckled, having no doubt that Destroy had been waiting for Carnage to move Carolena in so that he could offer criticisms about anything he could find to criticize.

"You still gonna teach us, Miss Carolena?" Seth asked, somewhat of a pout still in his voice.

"Of course I am. I'm just going to teach you here, now," she answered.

Seth looked around the deck, seeing only three chairs at the very small table. Carolena followed his eyes, "We are going to have our lessons inside at the kitchen table. And my husband will make us benches, so we can have our lessons out here when the weather is nice," she explained.

"Inside? Really? We get to go inside?" Serena excitedly asked, already running full speed for the front door. She burst inside the house with Carolena and Seth on her heels. Carolena paused at the door, "Simon, won't you please come in? Come see where your kids will be so that you'll know they are safe while in my care."

"Thank you, Miss Carolena. Well, Mrs., I guess it is now," he said respectfully.

After the kids, Simon, and Carolena went inside, Enthrall and Destroy were left on the deck with Carnage. Destroy looked at Carnage, "Husband?"

Carnage smiled back proudly, all his teeth on full display, his eyes sparkling with happiness. He pointed his thumb at himself, "Hsshbnn." Then he pointed at the door that Carolena and her guests had disappeared through, "Miiinnne."

Destroy thought about further irritating his fellow Goyle, but decided that Carolena was having such a nice morning, obviously very happy showing off her home, and very calmly referring to Carnage as her husband, that he would not ruin her day. She was truly his friend. And regardless of what anybody else thought of him he would not hurt her, or upset her. So instead he just said, "I am aware." He walked over to the door, pulling it open and calling inside, "May I enter, Carolena?"

To which she responded, "Of course, come on in!"

Enthrall looked at Carnage and rubbing his chin said, "You know, while irritating, he is not completely wrong. We could install a bell at the gate, with a rope at the bottom of the stairs that will ring the bell up top to announce someone's arrival. We could also alter the stairs. Install a pulley system at the middle landing, that would allow the bottom half to be raised off the ground and lowered as desired. If we put a wheel at the top with a counter weight, it could be easily raised and lowered by Carolena, herself, if she so desired."

Carnage thought about what Enthrall said and after a few moments of consideration agreed. "'Es," he said, nodding his head and walking through the gate to look at the landing and decide the best way to make the changes. He stopped at the gate, patting the post the gate was mounted to, and looking to Enthrall, his eyebrow raised in question.

"Yes, that's a good place for the bell. Let's figure out all we'll need, and what we don't have here, I'll make a trip into town for later in the week."

Chapter 20

Abraham boarded the train headed south; his extremely poor temper apparent to all he encountered. He'd fired the private investigator he'd hired, and true to his word, was on his way to find his only daughter himself. He'd repeatedly found during the course of his life, if he wanted something done, and he wanted it done right, he had to do it himself. Very few held themselves to the standards that he did, and their results were usually just barely passable at best. He sat back in his seat, irritation suffusing his face again. His daughter was again causing him an inconvenience. He'd hired her caregivers and tutors in her youth to provide her with the best of everything, just as he'd promised. And he'd hired women for these positions since her mother was gone, thinking the female influence something she'd need. But perhaps he should have stayed a little more abreast of what she was taught. She had her head filled with fantasies, legends, false impressions of what a woman should be, could do. A good woman knew her place, and all thoughts of adventure were left where they belonged — with the men of the world. When he found her, and make no mistake, he would find her, he was bringing her back and marrying her off to the first capable man he found. He was done. His responsibility to his dear dead wife finished. The girl was grown. He no longer needed to see to her welfare, keep her in line. Let her husband, whoever the man happened to be, see to that. He wanted nothing further to do with her, his duty finished once he rescued her from whatever trouble she'd managed to submerge herself into this time.

    He sat back, looking out of the window, waiting for departure. There was a nagging little voice at the back of his head. Wondering why the men he'd hired to keep an eye on her had not responded to his attempts to contact them. He'd paid them handsomely. He'd expected them to keep an eye on her. Protect her while she "oversaw" his investments. He knew full well that this trip was her attempt to prove that she was capable of making her own decisions, making her own way. He sneered, obviously she was wrong, because here he was disrupting his life to find her and force her to begin her own as any respectable woman should — as the quiet, demure, serving wife of the man her father chose for her.

<<<<<<<<>>>>>>>

Carolena sat on the bench her husband built for her, her feet up on the railing as she sipped her tea and enjoyed the early morning birds chirping around her. She smiled, her husband, her Carnage. She loved her Goyle, loved her home, loved her life. She had good friends, she had love. She was happy. In the weeks since they'd moved into their new home, she'd been approached by two other families asking if she would teach their children, too. Of course, she'd said yes. So now, she had a job that enabled her to contribute to her new community as well. Carnage had built her several benches on the front deck, and it was there that she taught her kids. Seth, Serena, and now Deaumanique' and Anton. She wasn't sure what Deaumanique' was. She was a pretty little girl, delicate looking with dark hair and black eyes fringed with long thick lashes. Unless she was angry or particularly challenged, then those black pupils would turn blood red in their centers, and her skin would flush with a reddish hue.

The other child, Anton, was very laid back. He was a very self-assured little boy with a great sense of humor. He was always smiling, joking, and found humor in almost everything.

He was not the slightest bit put out by Seth, Serena or Deaumanique'. She would almost have thought him human, except for the way he was not at all intimidated by the others. The only clue she had to his nature was that when his father dropped him off on his first day, he told him firmly in the thick Cajun accent they both spoke in, "Anton, we don't be bitin', no! You understand Papa'?"

Anton had dutifully nodded his head, "Ya, Papa'. I understand. No bitin'."

"If you do," Anton's Papa had gone on to say, "you won't be coming back. And Mrs. Carolena's husband, he's gonna hurt you bad, yeah."

Anton had looked from his papa to Carnage, who raised an eyebrow at him, and back again to his papa. "I won't be bitin' here, Papa'. Promise," he'd declared as he raised his little hand to cross his heart.

Assured that his son wouldn't bite anyone, "Okay, 'den, enjoy your schooling, boy. I'll be back 'dis afternoon to collect you. Don't you come on your own, no."

Anton was already running to join the other kids as he called over his shoulder, "I won't, Papa'."

She still wondered at his origins; what could he be that his father felt the need to warn him not to bite?

Carnage came out onto the deck to join her on her bench. He sat quietly behind her, nuzzling her neck just behind her ear, sending shivers down her spine.

"I love when you do that," she said to him.

He hummed at her and did it again. They'd had a late night of lovemaking and were both well and truly sated. Still enjoying the afterglow of their passionate loving this morning. Since their first night in their new home, they'd spent each night and every available moment wrapped in each other's arms. They were both very happy, exactly where they wanted to be. Their lives had taken on an easy predictability that suited them both just fine. Each evening after dinner, it was only a matter of time until Destroy showed up, ringing the bell they'd installed to announce company down below incessantly, until finally Carnage could take it no more and stomped over to the side of the deck where the stairs were located to snarl down, "Coooommmmmmme!" Destroy would flap his leathery wings and bring himself aloft to drop heavily down on their deck. "Carolena! I am here," he'd call out, "let the reading commence."

And she would, she'd settle wherever she felt like that evening, with Carnage next to her at her feet looking up at her lovingly, and Destroy sitting near enough to make Carnage uncomfortable, but not near enough to actually set him off. Occasionally Enthrall would join them, but sometimes not.

It was the same book, 'La Belle et la Bete.' She'd read the entire story twice. But yet, all three males seemed to never tire of it. She believed that it was because they saw themselves in the role of the beast, unworthy of love, yet craving it, needing it so, the only thing that would set them free. She honestly believed that Enthrall and Destroy both craved a "beauty" of their own. Carnage had made his opinion of the book perfectly clear. The first time she'd finished it, saying the end. He'd taken it reverently from her hands, running his huge fingers over the gilt cover. He'd pointed to the girl on the cover and then to Carolena. Then pointed to the beast embossed there and then himself.

She'd smiled and taken his face in her hands, kissing him gently. "You think we are beauty and the beast?"

He'd smiled at her and nodded.

"Well, then, I'm truly lucky. You are the most beautiful beast, my Carnage." She'd kissed him then, whispering of loving him.

Destroy stood, "Must you go on like this? It's a perfectly good story, and you ruin the ending with all this emotion!" he grumbled as he stood, spreading his wings and taking to the air. Only a moment passed before his voice could be heard just above them, "I shall return tomorrow, that we may start again," he said haughtily. Then in a more sincere voice, "Thank you, Carolena."

This morning, though, it was Enthrall who joined them unexpectedly. But instead of dropping in unannounced, he politely rang the bell and waited for an invitation to come up.

Carolena started to rise to see who rang the bell, but Carnage tightened his arms and said, "Trraawl."

So she settled back against Carnage and called out, "Come up, Enthrall! Join us!"

A moment later and he was standing in front of them, his hands holding new slate boards and chalk for the additional children that Carolena had taken on, his face troubled. "Good morn', Carolena, Carnage."

"Morning, Enthrall," she said, rising to her feet to take the boards from him, "Are you okay? You seem upset."

Enthrall ran his hand through his hair and looked from one to the other of them. "No. I'm not okay. I've just come from town. Carolena, you have to go."

Silence answered his declaration, but as soon as his words sank in, Carnage jumped to his feet, standing chest-to-chest with Enthrall.

Enthrall gave him no time to posture; he stepped back and around Carnage. "There is word in town of a man, a human man, who says that if you do not make yourself known, he will burn the entire swamp to the ground to find you."

Carolena listened to Enthrall with her heart in her throat, her mind whirling, "Oh my God, my father. It must be. Why? Why would he even threaten that? Can anyone do that?" she asked, nearing panic.

"It is said that he bought the rights to all the land from the town to the water. It's thousands of acres, Carolena, but he bought it. Said that whoever was hiding his daughter would be the cause of the destruction. Return her to him now, or he'd forever change the land as we know it. And if that didn't produce you, he'd systematically begin burning the town."

Carnage was in a fury, snarling, rumbling, his fangs on full display, his fists clenching and unclinching. "Nooooo, goooo," he said.

Carolena made the few steps to Carnage, wrapping her arms around his waist. "I'm not leaving you, Carnage. Calm, it'll be okay."

She turned back to Enthrall, "Surely something can be done. I'll go speak to him. I'll take care of it — I don't want to leave." Her eyes filled with tears, and her voice hitched, "This is my home. I don't want to go."

"Carolena, he's not alone. He's got another man with him. He's claiming he's your betrothed."

Carolena's mouth fell open — she was stunned, "I don't have a betrothed. I'm already given. I'm Carnage's. And he's mine." She was clearly flustered.

"I know, but short of killing them and everyone in town to keep them from looking for them, I don't know what else to do. You're going to have to go. You have to make them believe that you've survived on your own somehow. We can't have them coming in here looking for you. We can't have them destroy our home, Carolena. If it means you must go in order to save each of us, then you must go," Enthrall told her, pain evident in his voice.

Carnage darted forward, grabbed Enthrall, and threw him over the railing, roaring his rage non-stop.

Carolena, in a daze, peered over the edge, seeing Enthrall safely standing on the ground, looking back up at her. "As soon as he arrived in town this morning, he told everyone in the store, and he's posted it around for all to see. If you're not found and brought to him before Wednesday, he'll start burning the swamps. He's even offered a cash reward for your return. There will be humans wandering the swamp looking for you."

"No!" she almost begged, "They can't come here! They'll find us. They'll find out about us."

"Exactly," Enthrall answered.

"But, won't they be afraid? Won't your glamour keep them away?" she asked.

"Most, hopefully. But it will do nothing against the fire he threatens," Enthrall said sadly.

The constant roar and rage of Carnage as he stomped back and forth across their deck drew Enthrall's attention. He hated this. He hated hurting Carolena and Carnage. But he couldn't think of anything else to do. He'd have just killed the man and been done with it, but it was too late. He'd involved the entire town, offered rewards if she was found, and threats to burn their town to the ground if his daughter wasn't delivered to him. If he was killed now, too many would look for him. The only thing he could think of was to return Carolena to her father. He explained just this to Carolena, having to raise his voice louder and louder to be heard over Carnage's fury. Finally, there was nothing left to say.

"Talk to Carnage, Carolena. Make him understand," Enthrall told her.

When Carolena said nothing, just continued peering down at him, he said, "Think about it; make a decision. Let me know what you decide. I'll let the children know there will be no school for a while." Enthrall turned to walk away, but stopped, looking back at her. "I'm sorry, Carolena. I'm so sorry. I don't want you to leave, either. But I've got to put my people first. There are far too many of us to relocate quickly. If he makes good on his threats, many would be left exposed. Humans would make sport of killing those that are unable to protect themselves properly. I'd kill as many aggressors as I could, as would most of our warrior class males, but we would lose innocent lives. And when the news spread of what the humans found living just outside of their town, swamps and forests all over the world would be burned, supernaturals the world over sought out and murdered, or at the very least, hunted without end. We cannot allow that, Carolena."

Carolena said nothing, just watched as he turned and walked away, but she knew in her bones he was absolutely right. She would have to give up her happiness, her life, her new family, in order to ensure the safety of the same.

Chapter 21

The next day found Carolena standing in front of Enthrall's home. Carnage was with her, and she was flanked by the families of the children she'd become teacher, friend and mentor to.

She'd spent the night before and most of the morning trying to make Carnage understand that she had to go in order to protect him, Enthrall and all their people. Enthrall had been right — no human should have ever been allowed here. At least not one with ties still in the human world. She honestly didn't believe that her father would care if she went missing or not. He'd never been interested in her or anything she did as long as she left him alone. Yet here he was, threatening to destroy all she loved and held dear if she didn't come back to him. She couldn't let that happen. She looked around at the innocent beings surrounding her. Thought of those in other places, that she'd never meet, who had no idea that her decision today may hold sway over their very future existence. So she had to go. Carnage had his arms around her, his front plastered to her back. She'd given him strict instructions that he was to behave himself. He could not destroy anything or hurt anyone, and he was to keep their home nice and neat, because she'd be back. One way or another, she'd find a way back to him that would leave no one looking for her or threatening her people or their community again. He was nearly uncontrollable, but when she told him that if he broke his promise, she'd never come back, he sobered immediately, and begrudgingly nodded his agreement.

So now they stood, everyone but her, quiet, listening to her words as she told Enthrall that she'd go to her father. That she'd walk away from those she loved in order to save them. Carolena stepped away from Carnage to move closer to the porch where Enthrall stood at the base of his steps. Destroy stood nearby, his face a growing mask of anger, watching it all develop. He stalked over to Carnage, snarling at him. "You're just letting her leave?"

Carnage yanked his eyes from his woman and glared at Destroy, giving his own head one sharp shake to indicate no.

"Well, I don't see you doing a damn thing to stop her! You're just letting her leave us! What kind of male are you?!" he shouted at Carnage.

Enthrall, hearing Destroy's outburst, and seeing Carnage struggling not to lose control as per the instruction of his Carolena, got between them, fast, leaving Carolena standing some feet away nearer his home.

"Destroy! Leave us! Now!" Enthrall bellowed.

"NO! Somebody has to stop her from leaving us! How can you just let her go?" he demanded.

"Do you think I want her to leave? Do you? I love her as much as you do, as much as any of us do! But this is a matter of her going back to where she belongs, or risk losing everything we've worked for. Our entire community and everyone in it. There is no choice! It's the best fix for the problem, Destroy."

Destroy stood there seething. And Carnage...he was lost, crushed, standing there watching his Carolena, his life, preparing to leave him. The only thing holding him together was her promise that she'd return once it was safe to do so — as long as he behaved. And he was hell bent on behaving, because the one thing he'd have, the only thing that mattered, was his Carolena. He'd behave, and he'd wait, and she'd come back. She'd promised.

Destroy, distraught at what he considered his only friend leaving him, snarled at Carnage, "You aren't even fighting for her! She'll never come back to you! She should have been mine!" and took to the air.

Carnage was growling, a low, constant growl. Carolena hurried over to him, "Carnage, love, don't pay any attention to Destroy. He's upset, so he's lashing out."

Carnage didn't look down at her; he was staring at the place in the sky that Destroy had disappeared into. Carolena patted his chest, then reached up and grasped his jaw, forcing his eyes down to hers.

"I will be back, Carnage. I promise you. If it's the last thing I do, I'm coming back to you. Please wait for me," she begged on a sob.

He nodded, his own eyes filling with tears as he swept her up in his arms, burying his face in her neck, burrowing his nose into her hair, filling his lungs with the scent that was uniquely her.

Finally she wriggled a bit to let him know to put her down. She turned and faced Enthrall, "So, do you need to wipe my memory or something?"

In spite of the sadness permeating the group gathered there, he laughed, though sadly, "No. If I could do that, I'd have done it to begin with, and you'd be off living your life already."

She said, "I thought I was doing just that." Then, "So, now what?"

"So now, I take you to Bobby's house. If the animals haven't carried them away by now, we bury their bodies, and leave you there. If no one comes for you in a day or two, you start walking. When you get to town, you tell them the story about Bobby and his brothers keeping you there, just as it was in the beginning. Only you tell them that they turned on one another, fighting over you. Bobby was killed by his brothers; then, they fought, killing each other."

"But, wait, aren't they still alive? Won't you have to kill them?" she asked, not wanting anyone to die because of her, not even them.

Carnage looked at Enthrall over her head; Enthrall looked at Carolena, "No, they are not. They have paid for their crimes against one of our own. Their bodies have surely decayed enough to prevent any type of proper investigation. We'll dig a shallow grave if they are able to be found. You say you did the best you could to bury their bodies. You did not try to go to town because you were afraid to walk through the swamps alone. If you have to walk to town, when you arrive, tell them your food was gone. You had no choice but to finally head to town. You shouldn't have to walk alone, though. I'll go into town, I'll mention to one of the men in the saloon that I'd heard Bobby speaking about his new lady the last time he was in there. That will make them start thinking — they'll go there to look for you."

Carolena, her brow wrinkled, surprised at learning that they'd been dead for some time now, just nodded, "Okay."

"It's time, Carolena. We must go," Enthrall told her.

She nodded, Seth and Serena, and even Anton hugging her about the legs and waist, Serena crying openly, "I don't want you to go."

Seth had glassy eyes, but was managing to hold back his tears, his mouth set firm. Anton smiled sadly at her, "You coming back?" he asked quietly.

"Yes," she told him. "I'm going to be back — I just don't know when," she answered.

She hugged the children and looked around, trying to find Deaumanique'. A little red-skinned girl with long black hair and piercing black eyes with red pinpoint pupils waved sadly from the shelter of her mother's skirts. She realized that the child must be Deaumanique'. She must be very upset to have had her skin turn red. She waved goodbye to the child and turned to Carnage. He let out a mournful wail, crushing her to him, his chest heaving as he tried to deal with her walking away from him.

"I love you, Carnage. Don't ever forget that," she told him, tears streaming down her face.

It took every ounce of strength she had, that Enthrall had, to break Carnage's hold on her. Once out of his arms, she turned and locked eyes with him as Enthrall took her in his own arms and ghosted her away. The last thing she saw and heard of her husband was his pain-filled roar and him dropping to his knees as she disappeared.

<<<<<<<>>>>>>

Suddenly she was standing in front of Bobby's shack. The stench filled her nostrils at once. Enthrall said quietly, "You realize that you may never be able to find your way back to us? It may never be safe, and even if it is one day, I keep a glamour around the swamp to keep humans away. You are human. And I will be strengthening that glamour as soon as I return."

"I know," she answered, her voice breaking.

Enthrall kissed her forehead and said, "Do not look toward the cabin. I'll take care of the bodies. Just give me a moment."

Not more than 10 minutes later, Enthrall was walking back to her, calling to her, "I've moved two of the bodies. The third is missing. I'll bury them in the woods just inside the tree line; then, I'll dig them back up and make it look like an animal has done it." He held up a hand and popped his sharpened nails out, "These clawing at the dirt should do it."

She had turned to watch him after he told her that the bodies had been moved. "I brought a chair out here for you to sit. Ill take care of the bodies out back, now."

A little later and he was back, "Okay, all done. The pile of cans and jars in the garbage pile at the back of the house will make anyone believe that you'd been surviving on the little bit that was left here."

Carolena merely sat, watching Enthrall.

"Carolena? You alright?" Enthrall asked.

She nodded slowly, her eyes filling with tears.

Enthrall said nothing, just watched her, not knowing what to say, what to do.

Then she spoke, "I've never been happy, 'til now. 'Til Carnage and you and your people. And now, because a man who has resented me all my life decides he has to save face, I have to leave you all behind."

He felt such sorrow, watching her crumbling under the stress of leaving all she loved, "It'll be okay, Carolena."

"No!" she shouted. "No, it won't," she sobbed. "You've just finished confirming what I already suspected. Even if I'm able to come back, I may never be able to make my way back here again. This is goodbye. If my father never allows me to leave his control again, I'll never see any of you." She sobbed for a moment or two, trying to catch her breath, "It's even safer if I never return, even if I can."

"I didn't say you couldn't, Carolena, just that it would be difficult," Enthrall said.

She nodded, but didn't meet his eyes. Staring off into the distance she said quietly, "Just go. Go back to Whispers."

Enthrall took a step toward her, but she turned her head even further away, so he stopped. He watched her for only a moment more before he turned and walked toward the edge of the swamps.

She called after him when he was nearest the edge, "Take care of Carnage. Don't let him lose himself. Make him live."

Enthrall turned to look at her one last time, "I promise." Then he was gone, disappearing before her eyes as she watched him.

<<<<<<<>>>>>>>

Enthrall stood on the outskirts of town. He always walked into town from the opposite direction of the swamps just in case anyone got curious of where he came from. He started his walk, composing himself as he went, his own sorrow at making Carolena leave them a palpable thing. But he'd truly had no choice; her father had threatened their very home. She had to return to him, or the man would destroy everything in his quest to find her. He had to protect Whispers and all who depended on him for their safety.

He stepped into the saloon and took a seat at the bar, listening to all the conversations around him. Determining who to drop his bit of information to. Finally, he found what he'd waited for. Two young men, sitting at a table in the corner, talking about what they'd do with the money they'd get, if only they'd be lucky enough to find the missing girl.

One of them stood, approaching the bar, and Enthrall struck up a conversation with the bartender. "You know, if I were looking for a missing girl, I think I'd start at the last place she was seen."

The bartender glanced up to see if Enthrall was speaking to him. He'd seen Enthrall come in from time to time, kept to himself, but always tipped well. "Well, yes, I would, too," he answered. "But that there's the problem. She wasn't seen no where last. Just disappeared from the boarding house. No trace."

"Really? Well, I'd heard that Bobby had come to pick her up early one morning. I hear that the lady from the boarding house knows it and just doesn't want to say because she doesn't want to be held responsible if Bobby has hurt the girl," Enthrall said, leading them easily.

The young man never said a word, but paid for the two beers he'd ordered and went back to his table, talking in hushed tones to his friend. Not two minutes later, they stood and hurried out the door.

Enthrall breathed deeply, his bait cast and taken. He laid a few coins more than was needed on the bar top to pay for his drink and turned to leave, saying under his breath, "Be safe, Carolena. Be well."

He walked out of the saloon and instead of walking back out of town as he usually did, he went around the back of the saloon, looked around to be sure he was alone, and ghosted back home.

Chapter 22

Carolena sat on one of the wooden stumps that Bobby and his brothers had placed in the yard around their fire pit as a chair. It had been a couple of hours since Enthrall had left her there. She'd cried, sobbed, and raged at having to leave her home and her husband. But she knew if she didn't go to her father, he'd stop at nothing to find her. And she couldn't have the people she'd come to love in danger because of her father's pride. She'd vowed to herself that she'd be back and soon. But first, she had to do this. She thought about the bodies buried out back. It was unsettling being here with only dead bodies. She wondered when they'd had time to kill the brothers, then all of a sudden she knew; it was the evening they left her alone when she was napping. The same day that Murder had come to protect her from Destroy. The same day that both Enthrall and Carnage had come home covered in blood. They'd been out avenging her, making sure that she'd never be threatened by the brothers again. She smiled sadly, knowing that they loved her that much, to ensure her safety by any means necessary, and that she'd have to give up that love in order to protect them. Life wasn't fair, and it was most certainly cruel.

She paused in her thoughts, thinking she heard something. But when she listened, there was nothing there. She got up, going inside to get one of the old tin cups, so she could scoop some rainwater out of the catch basin they had out front. She grabbed the cup from the table top inside and walked back out the open door, straight into the chest of a young man who was as startled as she was.

Carolena bounced off his chest, "Oh!!! I'm sorry, I didn't know anyone was here!"

"No ma'am, I'm sorry! Begging your pardon. Are you Carolena?" the young man asked.

"Yes, I am. How did you know my name?" she asked, feigning ignorance.

"Everybody knows your name. The whole town's looking for you. Your daddy has everybody out and about — even offering a reward for the ones that finds you," he explained.

"Oh, thank goodness! I've been so frightened. I didn't know my way back and wasn't sure what to do. I've been alone here for, oh, I don't even know how long." She offered a token sniffle and tipped her forehead toward the young man's chest. "I was so scared. They, they hurt me. Then they fought. I did the best I could. I mean I couldn't just leave them here in front of the house. They'd attract wild animals, so I took them around back."

"Took who around back?" the other man asked.

"Bobby and both of his brothers. They fought. And now I'm here all alone. I can hear the animals out there at night, but I just couldn't make myself go back there and see them," Carolena said, sniffling.

The man closest to her, the one her forehead now rested against, patted her shoulders, "It's okay now, Miss. We found you. You're going to be safe and good as new in no time. My name is Frank; this here is my friend, Mark. We're going to get you back to town and to your Pa. Everything is going to be just fine."

Carolena nodded, not looking up at either man, mumbled, "Thank you."

"I'll go check around back," Mark said.

Frank nodded, still standing there, soothing the young woman they'd found. Before Mark went around back of the little shack, he exchanged a triumphant smile with Frank — their payday had arrived. They'd be rewarded handsomely for finding this girl.

Carnage watched from the trees, fighting his instinct to rip apart the man now touching his Carolena. He had to be strong — he had to endure. But he also had to make sure she was safe, and no one would try to hurt her before she made it to her father. If someone tried, he planned to bury them right underneath Bobby's brothers. He shifted in the tree and focused on the men who'd "found" his love. They seemed to be okay. They were checking her for injuries and didn't seem to be taking advantage. He'd follow them as far as the cover of trees would allow to make sure before he'd finally be forced to return to his home. He'd wait in his home for his mate to return, and that's all he planned on doing until she returned to him. As he watched and waited, movement across the way caught his eye; he peered closer and smiled. Enthrall. Enthrall was doing exactly the same thing he was, watching over Carolena.

As both deadly creatures of the night watched, Carolena was given fresh water. The first man, Frank, checked her to make sure she was okay, and then they started on their trek toward town. Carnage felt much better about the men with her when he heard one say, "You'll be fine, Miss. If you get tired, let me know, and we'll rest for a bit. Stay between myself and Mark, that way you won't step on snakes or walk into spiders or nothing. There are some scary things out here in these swamps. You have to be careful."

Carolena looked around at the surrounding areas, "Yes, I'm sure there are. I'll be very careful."

Carnage followed until the lack of trees prevented him from going any further. When he was stopped, shrouded by heavy shrubbery, straining to catch even the slightest little glimpse of Carolena, he felt a hand on his shoulder. He turned, knowing exactly who'd be standing there. Enthrall. Enthrall had followed him as he'd followed Carolena. "I've got it from here — I'll watch over her until she's with her father."

Carnage nodded, and Enthrall ghosted away.

<<<<<<<>>>>>>

"They've found her, Mr. Ashlar!"

Abraham Ashlar sat at a table in the town's saloon calmly eating his lunch. He placed his fork and knife on the outer edges of his plate, removing the napkin from the neck of his buttoned shirt as he sat back to regard the small group of people who were assembling before him. He wasn't particularly excited, but the gentleman sitting across from him was.

"Is she well?" Abraham asked in a droll tone.

"She seems very tired, and a little shaky, but she's walking on her own, sir," one man answered.

Abraham turned to the gentleman seated with him, who had not stopped eating and was still busily shoveling steak into his mouth. "If she has been violated, you are still responsible for her. This does not nullify our agreement, Norris."

Norris stopped chewing only momentarily, "No, sir. It does not. She'll still service me. Still perform the duties a good wife should. Maybe even better than if she'd had no experience at all. Does not change a thing." He promptly shoved another piece of meat into his still masticating mouth and returned his full attention to his meal.

Abraham stood, "Show me," he said to the small group of people assembled at his table awaiting his response.

He followed them out of the doors of the saloon and onto the small wooden banquette that lined the main street of the little town. There they waited for the two men and one small woman to make their way up the street to them. Once Carolena reached the banquette her father stood on, watching her approach, she looked up at him, making no move to go to him, no move to show affection at all. "Father," she said by way of greeting.

"Carolena," he answered, looking her over from head to toe. His nose lifted in disgust, "You're dirty."

"Yes, sir. I am. I've been taken against my will and kept in the swamps. There was no place to bathe, and no where to go for help when I was left alone. I apologize for my appearance," she said.

"Yes, well, perhaps you could rectify it. Go to the rooms I've secured, make yourself presentable, and try not to make a nuisance of yourself. We have four days before the train returns for us. Do not forget your place," he said as he turned to go back inside.

Carolena was not surprised at his lack of concern for her. He'd never been concerned for her. He was obsessed with his work, his money, his holdings and his reputation — what others thought of him. She had a thought, "Father!" she called out. He stopped and turned back to her, one eyebrow raised.

"These two gentlemen found me, saved me and have been very kind and considerate as they escorted me to town. I promised them that you'd be so thankful to have me safe and returned to you that you'd pay them twice the reward you originally offered."

Abraham glared at her; she smiled sweetly back. "I assumed that you'd be overjoyed to have your only daughter returned to you and offered a reward for my safe return. Was I mistaken? Did I speak out of turn?" she asked coyly.

Abraham's eye began to twitch, "No. You are not mistaken. I will, of course, give them double the reward. How thoughtful of you to want to see to their reward personally."

"Yes, I thought so, too," she said.

Abraham went back to his place at the lunch table, "The sooner you take this woman off my hands, the better!" he snapped at Norris.

Norris sat back in his chair, rubbing his hands over his full stomach, wiping his mouth with the back of his hand, "She'll be taken in hand soon enough. Don't you worry about that," he said to Abraham.

"See that she is, but do not make a scene. And you be sure to treat her properly. Public opinion is very important to my position. Do not behave unseemly in any way that others will be aware of."

"Yes, sir. I understand," Norris answered. "When do I get my money?" he asked.

Abraham looked up from his plate sharply, "When you have her under control, and I am no longer burdened with her."

Abraham glared at Norris for a good while before he slowly returned to his meal. Norris only signaled the barkeep, "You got anything sweet? And I don't mean just food," he said, winking.

Carolena turned off the water in the bathroom she stood in. She stepped into the water and sat down, allowing the warmth of the water to soak into her skin. Her heart hurt, her soul mourning. She pulled her legs up, allowing herself to sink down into the water and submerge her head. Eyes closed, she held her breath and stayed there for as long as she could before coming up for a breath. Water sloshed all over the floor. She sputtered with the water she'd inhaled when she spied a man standing over her as she rose from beneath the bath water.

"Don't choke or nothing. If you die, I don't get paid," he said.

"Who are you? Get out! You have no right here! Father?! Father?!?!?" she called out rather loudly.

"Quit your caterwauling! He's not here. Besides, I belong here, just came to take a look at what I signed up for." He smashed his lips together as though he was disappointed, had hoped for more. "Doesn't matter really, you all feel the same when you spread your legs," he said. Then already bored with looking at her body, "I'm your betrothed. You will be my wife, you will learn to behave, and you will learn not to order me about if you know what's good for you. If not, you might not be too happy. Not my problem though, you'll learn your place, be a good, quiet wife and perform your wifely duties just as I demand, or you'll be punished."

"You will not strike me! You will not marry me! You will not touch me!" Carolena shouted at him.

Norris laughed evilly, "Done deal, sweet. Already a done deal. As soon as we get back to your father's home, we will be married. And you will be mine. And I will do whatever it takes to keep you in line."

Carolena, her hands covering her body strategically, watched him as he spoke, listened to his words and had no doubt that this was the man that her father had decided was best for her. He was a big man by human standards, but compared to Carnage he was small. He had big hands, was big limbed and had a cruel look in his eye. She had no doubt that he'd have no problem exerting any type of violence he thought he could get away with in order to secure her cooperation. And she'd never tolerate his touch. Only Carnage would ever touch her. She already found her husband, her mate. And no one would ever take his place.

"I don't want you. I will never accept you or your touch. Look elsewhere for your future, and leave my bathroom!" she shouted at him.

He looked her over, her nude body on full display in the bath, as she tried in vain to shield the special places of herself. She was small, but not too small. She had curves, and it looked like she had soft skin. Her hair was brown, which was not exactly his favorite. He preferred blondes, tall, leggy blondes that knew how to take a spanking and how to drop to their knees when he commanded. This one, the one he'd agreed to marry in exchange for financial security and a job with her father's company, was definitely not his type. "Look, I don't care if you like me or not. I have more than enough women who appreciate me. And just to be clear, I will continue to spend as much time with them as I like. You, on the other hand, will learn to please me. You will learn to take instruction, and you will learn your place. Period. You'll like it, or you'll pretend you do. I don't care which. I've got a contract with your father, and if I have to whip your ass daily to keep you in line, I'll start my mornings with it and end my days with it. I have no problem with that. And if you want to wear bruises on your wedding day, I'm good with that, too. But for now, get your ass out of the bath, dry your mousy hair, and get to your father's room. He is waiting."

Chapter 23

Carolena waited until she heard the door slam and jumped from the bath. She dried hurriedly and threw on the same clothes that she'd been wearing when she was "found." She toweled her hair dry as best she could and tied it back out of her way; then, she hurried to her fathers room just down the hall. Not because the brutish man her father had chosen for her had told her to, but because she was outraged and planned to make her feelings well known. She was not going to just settle for this. She knocked on the door, waiting for his invitation to enter.

"Come," her father's voice called out.

Carolena opened the door and let herself in the room. She recognized the cherry-scented tobacco he smoked in his pipe, and as she walked further into the room, was not surprised to find him seated and enjoying a drink and a smoke with the man that had invaded her bath.

Norris smiled, rising from his seat, "Well, now. She is a pretty one, isn't she?" he said to her father.

"Oh, no, don't you play that with me!" she shouted at him, "Father, this man just let himself into my bath. He stood over me as I sat in the tub and lectured me on what I will and will not do. He said I may wear bruises on my wedding day if I choose, but I will be married."

Her father pressed his lips together, and said quietly to Norris, "I told you not to make a scene."

"I didn't. But I have a right to see what I've signed on for," Norris answered.

Abraham looked Norris in the eye, "I need a man who can handle her, not another soul that I need to handle."

Norris inclined his head one single time.

Abraham glanced back at his daughter, "May I introduce Norris Sheffield, Carolena. I have hand-picked this man to be your husband. He is strong; he will make a good husband and addition to our family and our business."

"I will not marry him!" Carolena shot out.

"You will," Abraham said in a steely voice. "You agreed that you would come here for whatever little adventure you had in mind. If it didn't play out well, you would return home and marry the man of my choosing. It didn't play out well — I had to come rescue you."

"You did not rescue me. Frank and Mark did," she snapped.

"At my behest!" Abraham shouted. "Enough, Carolena! You will return home with us on the morrow. You will marry and become the woman your mother planned for you to be. You will do your duty."

"I will not," Carolena said quietly, more in control now.

"You will!" Abraham shot back, "and this very attitude is the reason Norris was chosen. He will keep you in line. A strong man is needed to keep a spirited woman in line and keep her knowing her place. Best you figure that out sooner, than later."

Then he seemed to notice her clothes. His nose scrunched up at the scent of the dirty clothes. "What are you wearing? Did you not just cleanse yourself?"

"I did. Then I put my clothes back on," she said stubbornly.

"Return to your room at once and redress yourself. You smell," Abraham told her disdainfully.

"I will not, and I do not care," she answered.

Abraham watched her, grappling with his own self-control. How he'd have loved to leave the stubborn girl wherever it was that she'd been found. But again, his promise to his dear, dead wife rang in the back of his head. "You will. Or I will have your betrothed dress you," he countered.

Carolena took a step back, "You wouldn't!" she rushed out.

Abraham, tired of her insolence, answered, "Try me."

Twenty minutes later Carolena was dressed in some of the clothes that she'd left at the boarding house. They apparently had been collected by her father, or his people, and placed in her room. She declined his offer to join them at dinner by saying she was tired and still not feeling herself after her ordeal. It had actually been easier for her that neither asked her details about her "ordeal." She didn't have to lie or make up any details, nor did she have to relive the time she had actually spent with Bobby. Thankful for small reprieves, she lay down on her bed and closed her eyes. She'd locked her door securely and placed a chair under the doorknob to keep anyone from surprising her while she slept. She wrapped her own arms about herself, pretending they were Carnage's, and cried herself to sleep, unsure how she'd manage to get out of this and back to Carnage, but with no doubt in her mind that she would find a way.

The morning found her seated on the train, her father and Norris seated behind and beside her. She sat with her head leaning on the window, staring out into the gloomy, grey morning waiting for the train to take them back home, well, to her father's home. There, they thought her future would begin. She knew that either she would run away and disappear into the city, to eventually make her way back to Carnage, or she'd die trying. She really hoped she didn't die. She'd promised Carnage that she'd come back to him, and she didn't want to have lied to him. She didn't want him to spend his whole life waiting for her to come back if she was dead and in the ground.

Lost in thought, staring into nothing, she didn't notice the mist that had begun to swirl around the rails and the platform of the train stop.

"Will you look at that?" Norris said to her father. "Never seen anything like it, fog actually looks purplish."

Abraham peered out of the window, "It does indeed. Perhaps it's a reflection of the black of the locomotive making it appear that shade. So many uncivilized things in this part of the country... I cannot wait to get back home where proper folk live," he finished condescendingly.

Carolena watched the purplish swirling mist as it seemed to caress the train car she sat in. She wished that it would come to life and take her away. Little did she know just how close she was to her wish coming true.

Carolena heard the whistle blow, her tears spilled over, and she'd have sworn she saw the mist swirl up to meet the window she leaned against as the train began to pull out of the station.

<<<<<<<>>>>>>>

More than a week later, Carolena looked around the bedroom she grew up in. All of her childhood things were still here, just where she left them. The entire third floor of her father's mansion had been reserved for her, her nannies, her tutors. Even her playroom was up here. He'd had a back staircase installed, so they could go up and down the staircase without disturbing him when he was home. She'd loved it outside and spent many a day playing on the estate, but like most kids, ran inside and out, often. It annoyed him tremendously.

She didn't even take her clothes off. As soon as the servants left her bags inside her door, she closed and locked it, and went straight to the door that opened on the back staircase. She pulled it open, planning to go down those stairs and out of his house forever. She'd leave her clothes on a river bank and jump into the river. She was a strong swimmer. She'd come out the other side, everyone would think she'd died, and she'd make her way back to Carnage in any way she had to. But she was not prepared for the brick wall that greeted her at the opening of that door. Her father had walled up her access to the staircase. Why would he do that? It was obvious that her rooms were not kept. They were dusty and stale smelling, but walling up a perfectly good staircase?? It made no sense. Frustrated, she stalked around her room wracking her brain for a way to get out of the house without being noticed. Waiting until she was married, then running, was not an option. She could not chance having to endure Norris' touch. She had to run beforehand. There was a knock at the door. She called out, "Go away. I'm resting!"

A feminine voice called back, "Apologies, miss. I was told to bring you dinner."

"Just a moment, please," she called back. She didn't know the woman, but she was starving and was thankful that she'd not have to venture downstairs to find something to eat.

Carolena opened the door and found a girl not much older than she was standing there holding a tray. "Hello," Carolena said.

The girl curtsied and dipped her head, "Where should I place it, miss?"

"On the table over there, please. And, stop calling me miss. I'm not any older than you are."

"I'll try, miss. I mean, I'll try. But it's part of my job," the girl explained.

"Well, if it's just you and me, please don't say it, just call me Carolena," Carolena smiled at the girl.

The girl nodded, having put her tray down, but wouldn't look up to meet Carolena's eyes.

"What is your name?" Carolena asked.

"I'm Rowan," she answered.

"I don't remember you; are you new? Have you worked for my father long?" Carolena asked.

Rowan shook her head, "I've only been here a short while. My father owes a great debt to yours, so they agreed that I would live here and work for him until the debt is paid."

Carolena couldn't believe her ears — she even shook her head a few times, "Are you telling me that you have no choice? Your father traded you to mine for his debt?" she asked incredulously.

"It's not as bad as it sounds. I have a warm place to sleep, and I get regular meals, and in return I clean, cook, keep the house as he likes it. He does not demand anything else of me."

Still Carolena was flabbergasted, "For how long?!" she asked.

Rowan shrugged her shoulders, "Until he decides that my father's debt is paid."

"And what does your mother think?" Carolena demanded.

"She thinks that as long as Mr. Ashlar requires nothing more than housekeeping, I should be thankful," Rowan said, still looking down.

"What is wrong with people?!" Carolena cried out. "How can you be thankful for working off your father's debt as an indentured slave? It's ludicrous!"

"Miss..." Rowan started, but a look from Carolena had her correcting herself, "Carolena, we are immigrants. We cannot always find work. There are some days we don't have enough to eat. There was a while that we had no where to sleep. No safe places. This is a good place for me. I work and in turn I get fed. My father's debt gradually decreases, and my parents no longer have to support me. It is not the worst of situations."

Carolena watched Rowan trying to justify her position. She noticed that the girl was dark-skinned, she had lovely golden eyes and naturally red lips. A waterfall of long black hair fell gloriously down her back, and the most unique accent spilled from her lips each time she spoke. "I am not judging you, Rowan. Good, honest work is never anything to be ashamed of. I just think you should be paid rather than work for free so that your father's debt is paid."

Rowan nodded, "I understand. But it is the way of things."

Carolena asked, "Where are you from?"

"Romania, miss," Rowan answered, then quickly, "I mean, Carolena."

Her father's voice carried up the stairs, "Rowan! Where are you, girl? We are awaiting our dinner!"

"I must go," she curtsied, "enjoy your meal, Carolena," she said as she turned, hurrying from the room.

Carolena locked the door behind her, then seated herself to have her meal. After she ate, she hurried to the window, thoughts of possibly using it as a means of escape playing through her mind. She threw the latch and tried to force it open, but it wouldn't budge. She adjusted her grip and tried again, to no avail. Carolena leaned against the window and finally saw why she'd had no luck forcing the window open — it had been nailed shut from the outside. There was no hope of escaping from her bedroom. She'd have to wait until after the rest of the house was asleep, then she'd try to sneak away. She sat on the edge of her bed, a tear escaping her eye. The depression overtook her again, and she laid down once more. Sleep quickly came, and she was comforted with dreams of Carnage, Enthrall, and even Destroy. She dreamt of the Dragon tree and of a purple swirling mist as it gathered around the legs of a huge black Goyle that she immediately recognized as Murder. His eyes watched her closely as he said, "We are coming, Carolena. Hold on."

    Carolena came awake hours later to a pounding on her door. "Wake, woman! Open this damn door, post haste! Do not ever lock yourself away from me again!" a drunken Norris slurred at her from the other side of her very solid, very locked door.

    "Go away!" she yelled back at him.

    "Open this door now! I will know my wife this night! Make yourself ready this moment!" he demanded. Suddenly he hit the door so hard that it shook. She slipped out of bed and ran to the corner of the room, not having anywhere else to go since her father had walled in the back staircase. The battering of the door continued. He must have been slamming a chair or some such thing into it to make the racket he was making. She cowered in the corner, her hands over her ears, praying the heavy, wooden door would hold against his assault, when just as suddenly as the battering and screaming started, it stopped. Not another sound. It was just gone. Carolena did not move. She stayed where she was for fear he may hear her moving around and start after her again.

    She sat there, her head on her knees, praying for Norris to go away and stay away. She felt a sensation as though she was not alone — someone was watching her. She raised her head, prepared to flee, and her mouth dropped open when she found herself surrounded, engulfed even, in the same purple mist from the train station. There was no sound, but serenity suffused her very being. Carolena stood, watching the purple mist caress her arms, and hands. "What are you?" she whispered to the mist. There was no answer, but slowly it left her, dissipating beneath the still-standing door of her bedroom.

Chapter 24

Lore placed Murder in the hall just behind Norris as he pounded on Carolena's door demanding entry, then allowed the mist that was himself to drift under the door and into her room, completely undetected by the drunken man. He went straight to Carolena, where she sat huddled in the corner, surrounding her, soothing her.

Out in the hallway Murder did not hesitate. He wrapped his arm around the throat of the drunken man yelling threats to Carolena through the locked bedroom door. Norris, startled and drunken, tried to brush the arm away, shuffling his steps, "Let go o' me!"

Murder forcefully turned Norris to face him. Taking a special pleasure in the terror that he saw in the worthless human's eyes. Murder smiled, displaying his full set of teeth, especially his fangs, tilted his head to the side as a confused animal would, and said quietly, "She is not yours."

Norris opened his mouth to scream, but quickly Murder jammed the heel of his hand into the bottom of the man's chin to shove his mouth closed. Then he opened his huge hand and encompassed Norris' entire face, claws digging in firmly and painfully at his hairline, temples, and jaw. "You will not have her — ever."

The purple mist once more appeared from beneath the still closed bedroom door and moved down the hall. Murder snarled, "Quiet," into Norris' face and silently followed the mist, with Norris in tow, as it lead the way to Abraham's office.

They descended both sets of stairs to the main floor. Once there, the mist moved down a hallway and slipped under the door. Murder came to a stop outside the office door and said to the quickly sobering man, "Open the door."

Norris whimpered, reaching out to turn the doorknob.

Abraham, seated at his desk inside, jumped to his feet at the sight of Norris in the huge, black monster's grip.

"What evil is this?!" he shouted, and started spewing a constant stream of prayer as he crossed himself repeatedly, backing up against the wall.

Murder laughed, the rich, deep laughter of a male completely submerged in evil, "Save your prayers, old man. Words cannot save you now."

The purplish mist hovering at knee level in the room began to swirl, and gather, shaping and reshaping until it finally took the shape of man.

Abraham, praying louder, turned and snatched the slender golden crucifix off the wall, holding it out toward them as though to ward them off.

Lore shook his head, tsked, reached out and snatched it from Abraham, "Do you think that a pitiful piece of metal can banish us? It has not even been blessed," he snarled in his spectral, echoing voice as he kissed it and shoved it back at Abraham.

Murder shook the man he still held by the face, "This! This was found pounding on your daughter's bedroom door. Demanding entry to know what is his."

Abraham sputtered, "But, she is his betrothed."

The look of disgust that overtook Murder's face was enough to have Abraham changing gears. He immediately turned on Norris, "But nonetheless, I told you to respect her and not to do anything untoward! At least wait until the wedding!"

Murder, shaking his head in disbelief, "So all is well as long as he waits until you see them properly married to rape your daughter?"

Abraham, still pressing himself against the wall, his eyes flicking between the specter and the monster standing in his office, replied stupidly, "If they are married, it is not rape. It is the duty of the wife to service her husband. Keep him satisfied that he may keep her happy."

Murder shoved Norris away from him, causing Norris' body to slam into the left wall of the office, as Murder stalked to Abraham, "You do not deserve a daughter such as Carolena. She is good, she is kind. She loves honestly and loyally. You should be kissing her boots!" he shouted as he caught Abraham up by the throat.

Lore watched the entire thing with an amused look on his face, as much of it as anyone could see anyway as it flickered in and out of focus.

"What? What do you want from me? It is yours, only say the word!" then on a sob, "Release me, demon, that I may see another day."

Lore snickered, "Murder, perhaps we should take him up on his offer of getting what we want from him. Go, bring Carolena to us."

Murder released Abraham, shoving him back toward the wall he was previously cowered against, "I shall return shortly," he said to Lore as he left the room to return to Carolena's door. Once he arrived there, he knocked softly. She did not answer. He knocked again, and called out, "Carolena. Open the door."

Carolena still hiding inside her room did not answer, though the familiar voice had her peeking from her hiding place, now inside the chifferobe.

"Carolena, open the door, we've come for you. You need not fear any longer," Murder said, trying to make his voice soothing.

Carolena's heart soared, that was Murder, she had no doubt that was Murder's voice! She jumped from the chifferobe and ran to the door, pausing before she opened it to whisper, "Murder?"

"Yes, little Carolena, it is I. Open the door, you are under my protection, no harm will come to you," he promised.

Carolena wasted no time; she shoved the chair from under the doorknob and out of her way. She unlocked her door and flung it open. On seeing that Murder was indeed standing in wait for her outside her door, she flung herself into his arms, sobbing.

Murder caught her as she launched herself at him, "All is well, shh, no tears now, all is well."

She lifted her head from his shoulder and through her tears begged, "Please, tell me, how is Carnage? Is he well?"

Murder loved that this little human loved his friend so. He smiled at her gently, "He hurts, but he will be very well when we return you to him. Fear not — it will not be much longer."

Carolena nodded and laid her head back on his shoulder as she tried to regain control of her emotions.

Murder spoke to her as he walked them downstairs, "Your father has offered to give us anything in exchange for his life. Lore asked me to bring you to your father's office. I'm not sure what he plans, but we shall soon come to know."

"Will you kill him?" she asked, her voice still shaking with relief to be once again under Murder's protection.

"I think not, though I'd love the task to be completed by my own hand. What kind of father has such complete disdain for his own daughter as he has?" Murder hissed.

Carolena, having adjusted herself more comfortably in his arms and now rode curled against him, shrugged, "He has never been a father to me. He's never even liked me, much less loved me. It's just how it's always been."

Murder walked into the office, Carolena sheltered in his arms, her own arms wrapped about his neck.

Abraham took one look at his daughter resting comfortably in the arms of the "demon" and spat, "You know this creature? You cavort with demons?! Shame on your soul, girl! Shame to your very name! I knew you were not worthy of your mother's life. How she could waste her last breaths extracting promises from me to protect and see to your happiness is bewildering to me! Evil even in your first minutes of life, you stole her life from me and even her last moments!"

Carolena listened to his words, realizing for the first time why he hated her so, "You blame me for her death. That's why you've hated me all this time."

"Your very existence stole her from me. Now I see you as you are; you are a demon yourself! Thankful I am that she did not live to see your evil come to fruition."

She wriggled to be let down so Murder did so, while whispering, "Do not go too close to him." She didn't hear him, she was intent on her father. "Are you out of your mind? I was a newborn babe. How could I steal her life? How could I possibly steal her last minutes from you?"

Abraham's face skewed up in disgust, "She wanted you — even before conception she begged me for a child. I could deny her nothing, so I gave her a child. Then everything was about you, the baby will need, the baby will want, the baby, the baby, the baby! Then you came, and with your birth, you caused so much bleeding that her life slipped from her. And even then she was still yammering about you!! Keep the baby healthy, keep my Carolena happy. Promise me, on our love, promise me." He looked at Carolena with such resentment that Murder stepped forward to stand as one with her against her demented, bitter father.

Abraham continued, "So I promised her. I promised her that I'd look after you. That you'd be healthy, happy. Then she passed away from me, not once saying that she loved me, that she'd wait for me. I've done my duty — I've fulfilled my promise. Giving your hand in marriage to a man strong enough to keep you in line was the last of my responsibilities. I was finally to be free to mourn my wife, to live the remainder of my life without a constant reminder of the person who stole my love from me."

Carolena watched him, dumbfounded at his words.

Murder placed his hands on her shoulders and pulled her toward him, "You are well, Carolena. You do not need this male in your life."

Carolena nodded her head, "I know. And now I know that my mother loved me and wanted me. I don't need him."

She turned into Murder's chest and stood there, letting him hold her.

Her father shouted in disgust, "He is a demon! Do you have no shame?!"

Carolena turned, "He is no demon, Abraham. He is a Gargoyle. And he is more honorable and kind than you ever dreamed of being."

Lore had watched all this and was becoming quite antsy. He was not the type to stay in one place for very long. His mists wandered and drifted wherever they pleased, usually in search of his soul. Here, in this office, they'd been contained in this form for too long, and he was feeling the need to surge from this place. Thankfully, his time here was almost at an end.

Norris, where he lay at Lore's feet, began to stir. Coming to and running a hand up his own face in response to feeling the blood running down his face. He pulled his hand away and stared at the blood now staining it, then jerked his head up sharply to look around the room. On seeing the Gargoyle that had held him by the face and the specter now standing over him were real and not a figment of his drunken mind, he began shrieking incessantly.

Murder, wincing, stepped over to him quickly, "Stop that shrieking!" he snarled in his face as he leaned over and snatched him up off the ground. "Now! This instant! Silence!"

Norris, afraid of the creature holding him up off the floor, stopped shrieking.

Murder sighed, "Thank the gods, what a horribly pitiful sound." Then he faced Norris, "Do not worry, I will not kill you. Your soul is not mine to take. It is, however, of interest to my friend here."

Lore smiled sinisterly, placing his hand on the top of the man's head, where the soft spot would be for a new born. Lore looked him in the eye; Lore's complete lack of sanity very clear. "Do you know that this very spot on your head is the last place that the gods touch you? This is where your body is sealed after your soul takes up residence. It would be much easier if it were still soft, but...since it's not, I shall just crack it a bit. You don't mind, do you?" Lore, with inhuman strength, unequaled in any, grasped the man's head in one hand and squeezed until it cracked. Norris screamed, pain and fear the only thought in his conscious mind. Lore smiled and said, "Hush, now, it won't take long. Besides, you have it coming. A lifetime of wrong doing begets... hmm, Murder? What is it that a lifetime of wrong begets?"

Norris, shivering, going into shock, blood streaming from the puncture wounds Murder left on his face, and blood streaming from his nose, whispered, "Forgiveness?"

Lore laughed maniacally, "Oh, no, no, no! Not even close. A lifetime of wrong doing gets you — me." With the hand still in place on his skull, Lore crushed it even more, inhaling as though a sweeter scent he'd never smelled. He kept his hand over the top of Norris's head, smiling and licking his lips as the man slowly dropped to his knees, then prone on the floor, obviously nothing more than a lifeless body.

Carolena did not see this. Murder had turned her to face him, holding her tightly against his chest to keep her from witnessing what Lore had done to Norris.

Lore, finished with his snack, turned to Abraham, "I could eat your soul as well."

"Lore, we need otherwise, my friend," Murder said.

Carolena tensed, remembering that Lore was the Ancient that Destroy had warned her against.

"You are completely safe here. We both came for you. Trust me," Murder said to her.

Carolena nodded, but pulled away from his hold enough to look on Lore, the Ancient.

Lore smiled at her, not disingenuously, though there was still a hint of insanity to it.

She smiled shakily back at the purplish tinted form of mist man standing there, then she realized, "You're the mist!"

Lore smiled again at her, "For now, child, but in truth I am many things. Do not fear, I will not hurt you."

Then he remembered that they still had business before they could leave this place. He called out to her father, "Abraham!"

Abraham, visibly trembling, answered, "Please, do not take my poor, pitiful life. Spare me, and as I promised, anything you wish is yours."

"Ah, yes, I do remember that now. Here is what will happen; you will release any claim you have on Carolena, legal, familial, anything. You will sign over to her all lands you hold in

Louisiana. You will sign over all rights to her, to her holdings and will never come for her again. If you do, you will meet the same fate as your friend here." Lore prodded Norris where he lay on the floor, with a misty toe.

Abraham looked at the "specter," shocked — he never expected to have to sign over any of his holdings.

Lore approached him menacingly, "Or, I could just as easily devour your soul now. Then Carolena will be safe and happy in the arms of her love again."

Abraham latched onto the last bit of what Lore said, "Carolena is happy? She has a love?"

Lore watched him as only one of the most insane can, intensely, unsettlingly so, "She does. We have come to liberate her. And destroy all that stand in the way of her happiness," he said as he flitted his hand about.

Murder, ready to leave, asked, "What shall it be? Your soul, or your land? The contract we demand not only deeds your land to Carolena evermore, it also states that you never utter her name, or mention that you've seen us. You agree to those things, and you may live awhile longer. You speak of us, or any of this, and you certainly will not."

"Those things are not written into this contract — it is merely an agreement between myself and Norris!" Abraham said.

Lore laughed maniacally, "Stupid, stupid man. Look again."

Abraham picked up the contract on his desk and perused it briefly. He looked up at the creatures and his daughter standing in his office. "How did you do this? It's completely different from the one I'd scripted."

Lore waved his hands about the room as he strolled casually toward Abraham, "'Tis mere child's play. But make no mistake, little man. I see things. I hear things. I will always know your thoughts. Do not test me — you will lose."

"You can't possibly know my thoughts—" Abraham started.

Lore cut him off, "The reason you wish to know that she is happy is because you believe your dear, dead Clara is waiting, watching, and because of that you must make it so, or risk disappointing her. You want only to be rid of your child, free to wallow in your own misery and memories of your wife. You knew that Norris was not a good man, but cared not because at least he'd beat Carolena into submission, you'd no longer have to deal with her, and some of her beatings might at least make up for having to bear her presence all these years."

Abraham opened his mouth to speak, but again Lore interrupted him, "Oh, and you scald your flesh each night in your bath, because you can hardly keep your thoughts from taking the beautiful Rowan to your bed. Which is not a good idea in and of itself — she belongs to another, just like the demon there," he confided, thumbing his hand toward Murder. "Regardless, in an effort to rid the sin from your body, you take scalding baths. But still, each day, you take yourself in hand as you think of the girl. Pity, your dear, dead Clara knows those thoughts as well."

Abraham resembled a fish — his mouth bobbing opened and closed at Lore's words.

"What shall it be, Abraham, your soul or your lands and your daughter? Either way I win," Lore danced about the room, "win/win, win/win, choose what you will, but I shall win!" he sang to an erratic tune.

Carolena could not watch much more; her father was cruel and unfeeling. He was demented with bitterness at best, but he was her father, and at one time her mother had loved him, she supposed.

"Abraham," Carolena said, "Perhaps you should just sign the document. Otherwise, he may think you disagreeable and revoke the offer."

Abraham snapped his eyes up to look at his daughter, then taking pen in hand scribbled his name across the bottom.

"Fine! Begone, all of you! Leave me in peace to await my fair Clara's company once again!"

Lore, still dancing and humming, danced closer to Abraham, snatched up Abraham's hand and raked a razor sharp claw across his finger, slicing his skin. Lore very easily held the man's hand in his own, allowing Abraham's blood to drip onto his signature on the contract, then pressed Abraham's fingers into it to leave his fingerprint there.

"Ah-hah!" Lore shouted happily, "Signed in blood! Irreversible, it is done! It is sealing and binding. Say it! Say it, Abraham!"

Abraham, horrified, said nothing, clutching his bleeding finger and staring at the paper before him.

"Say it!!!!!" Lore demanded.

Carolena quietly said, "Abraham, we will be gone, but not until you agree."

Quickly, he said, "It is done."

Lore raised both hands toward the ceiling, "Yes!"

Abraham shoved the document at Carolena, "Be gone from my life, my home, everything. You are happy, you are well. I have fulfilled my promise. I have kept my word to my Clara. Go!!!"

Murder took Carolena by the hand, leading her out into the hallway, the deed to the land in Louisiana, the swamp, now her swamp, held tight in her other hand. She walked with Murder, looking back one time at her father, "What will become of him?"

"As long as he does not try to come after you, or speak of us, nothing. He will live his lonely, miserable existence a bitter shell of a human. Do not feel badly for him — it is his only wish."

Carolena nodded as Murder pulled her closer to him for a hug.

Her thoughts turning to Carnage, she whispered, "How will we get back?"

"Lore will take us. I will hold you in my arms, and he'll transport me as I hold you," Murder explained.

Carolena nodded, closed her eyes and waited for Lore to join them.

Lore moved toward the door to join Murder and Carolena and transport them home. But he couldn't resist one parting shot at the miserable excuse for a human father. He faced the man once more and said in a voice of all seriousness, all manner of insanity gone, "Your Clara? She is very disappointed in you. She has mourned all these years the love you denied her precious daughter. Now that she knows her daughter is safe, loved, and happy — she watches no longer. She waits not for you. She is done with you," Lore lifted his hand, brought the fingers of that hand together and flicked them as though flicking powder into the air, "Done," he repeated.

Then his form dissipated, he misted from the room, and surrounded his friend and Carolena. Slowly they faded away. The last thing Carolena heard was Murder telling her to keep her eyes closed, she did not want to see the things they must travel through to return home. The horrors encountered in the dimensions that Lore traveled in could permanently scar anyone, most certainly a human female. He lifted her into his arms again, she adjusted herself, pressed her face against his neck, her arms around him and held on tight. He held her just as tightly, trusting Lore to bring them both home safely.

Chapter 25

Carnage stood suddenly, paced down the hallway, opening each door, peering inside and then continuing on to the next. Then he'd go back to the living room and sit again. Wringing his hands, looking around, mumbling to himself, appearing completely unaware that his friends were there with him. Enthrall was there, as was Destroy. But he barely noticed them. His rage was barely contained. He was on the brink of losing all self-control. It had been two weeks since he'd last seen his Carolena, and two weeks since he'd gone to Murder and Lore begging for help. He'd offered Lore anything he wanted in order to have Carolena back at his side. He didn't care what Lore wanted; he'd get it for him, as long as they brought his Carolena back.

Murder had answered his call when he walked aimlessly around the deepest, darkest parts of the swamp, screaming for Lore at the top of his lungs. One moment he was alone, calling over and over again. The next Murder stood in front of him. He'd been so relieved to see the male that he'd embraced him, his hands grasping at Murder's shoulders as he tried desperately to tell him what happened, "Leenah!" he croaked out in a broken voice.

Murder clasped him back, "I know. I heard. I'm so sorry, Carnage."

Carnage slapped his own chest, "Mine, Leenah!" He threw his arm out indicating 'away.' "Bing haaohm."

Then he dropped to his knees on the wet, mushy, ground, "Peeez. Leenah!!!!"

Murder watched his friend, knowing full well what he asked for. He wasn't sure if Lore would help or not. And if he did, he wasn't sure that Carnage would be willing to pay whatever Lore asked in payment. He didn't have time to ponder it though, as the purplish mist began swirling in the distance.

Moments later, Lore had pulled enough of the mist together to form a face, and it hovered there slightly above and beside where Murder stood, looking down at Carnage, begging for their intervention.

Lore regarded Carnage for only a moment longer, "You wish me to return your female to you," he said, a statement, not a question.

Carnage nodded vigorously.

"What if she does not wish to come back to you?" Lore asked.

Carnage hadn't thought of that. Perhaps after being home, she would not want to live in Whispers any longer. He thought about it for a moment, knowing she'd told him how her father didn't care what happened to her as long as she left him alone. How he'd tried to marry her off to any man that would have her, so he didn't have to look after her again. How unhappy she'd be if she were forced to live her life on someone else's terms. He knew then, he wanted her happy, no matter what that was.

Carnage looked up at Lore, "Feeee Leenah," he said slowly.

Murder translated in case Lore didn't understand, which he, of course, did, "He said, 'Free Carolena'."

Lore smiled, "Stand up, Carnage. There is no need for your pleas. You've just told me all I wanted to know. You love her. Your request is genuine, not selfish. I know you want her, but even if you cannot have her, you want her free to make her own choices."

Carnage, having risen to his feet, nodded, agreeing.

"There will be a price," Lore warned.

Carnage nodded again, spreading his arms out from his sides, his hands held palms up, indicating, 'anything, it's yours.'

"Very well, we will go for your Carolena. We will bring her back. But at some point in time, I will require your payment. You will not want to disappoint me when the time comes," Lore warned again.

Carnage nodded again.

"Go home, wait for us there. We will return soon," Lore said, just as the misty face dissipated as did all trace of the purplish mist.

Carnage turned his attention to Murder who was still standing there.

Murder said, "He will not ask for your life, nor your woman, but make no mistake; at some point he will ask for repayment of this favor."

Carnage nodded.

"Go home, try to calm yourself, we'll be in touch," Murder told him, just before he unfurled his huge black wings and took to the sky. He could already feel Lore calling for him — their mission was already beginning.

Enthrall sat at Carnage's kitchen table, watching the big Goyle wander aimlessly around his home. Opening and closing doors, peering inside each room before going to the next, completely out of sorts now that Carolena was gone. Destroy spent his time between sitting on the deck outside and flying back to Enthrall's home, hoping that Carolena would be there, having made her way back to them. For once, Destroy was not the smart ass they expected him to be. He was missing Carolena also and resented that she had to leave them.

Carnage had not told anyone that he'd made a deal with Lore to bring her home. Only he knew the reason he kept going to each room, opening doors and peering in, was that he was waiting for her to appear. He was waiting for Lore to bring her home, and he wasn't quite sure how that would happen. He wasn't sure if Lore would just send her there and she'd appear somehow, or if they'd walked out of the trees and she'd call to him, or if they'd both materialize out of thin air, or if perhaps Murder would bring her home. So he was not leaving his home, and he got up often to see if she was there yet, checking any room she may have been deposited in. Lore was insane from years of loneliness. There was no rhyme or reason to his thought patterns, but once he gave his word, he always came through. There was no one older, no one more knowledgeable, no one stronger, no one more capable. They'd be here, he had no doubt — at some point they'd be here.

The bell outside rang, signaling someone waiting below. He jumped up and almost mowed both Enthrall and Destroy over in an effort to get outside to the railing to be the first to see her, if it was her.

His heart sank as he peered over the edge to find Seth there, waiting, red wild flowers in hand.

"Hello, Mr. Carnage. I was hoping Miss Carolena was home." He looked down at the flowers in his hand as he said, "We miss her."

He looked back up at Carnage, and now Enthrall and Destroy were looking down at him as well. Carnage shook his head.

Enthrall answered for him, "No, Seth. She had to return to her family. We hope, though, that she'll be back one day soon."

The child nodded, his hands still clasping the flowers, "I brought these for her. Can you keep them for her until she comes back?"

Clearly Seth didn't grasp that it may be a very, very long time until she rejoined them, if she rejoined them at all.

Enthrall said, "Carnage, can we lower the staircase, so Seth can bring his flowers up?"

Carnage just shrugged, his head hanging low. He didn't care. It shouldn't have taken this long. What if when Lore had found her, she'd not wanted to leave. What if her father had hurt her, and she was no longer? His chest heaved with the pain of it. He turned to walk away from the railing, going inside to throw himself into his and Carolena's bed and surround himself in her scent, but froze. Still as stone, not even breathing, he stood there.

Enthrall made to go behind him to turn the wheel that lowered the bottom half of the staircase at the same time that Carnage turned to go inside. But Carnage had stopped so suddenly that Enthrall ran into him. He bounced off Carnage, then looked at the Goyle to apologize, but found Carnage frozen in place, staring straight ahead. Enthrall followed his line of vision, then froze himself.

Destroy, realizing something was off, followed their line of sight as well and let off a whoop, shocking them all.

There, on the deck, not six feet from them, was a swirling purple mist, and within that mist was the flickering image of Murder, and cradled in Murder's arms, was Carolena.

Carnage let out a wail that could be heard the swamp over. Enthrall, for only the second time in hundreds of years, crossed himself and sent up a prayer of thanks.

Carnage, still frozen in place, watched as Lore took on the shape of a man, releasing Murder and Carolena from his shroud of mist. Murder placed Carolena on her feet, holding onto her as she steadied herself. Then she looked around, realizing that she was home. She turned swiftly and saw him standing there, flanked by Enthrall and Destroy, watching her.

She took a step toward him, holding her arms out, "Carnage?"

Her voice, it was all he needed to snap him out of his immobile state. He rushed to her, sweeping her into his arms, cradling her against him as he dropped to his knees, both of them sobbing. Carnage, saying over and over again, "Mine," and Carolena nodding, and saying, "Yes, and you're mine."

They were allowed only moments alone before Enthrall and Destroy joined them, patting Carnage on the back, hugging Carolena as best they could with her still firmly entrenched in Carnage's arms — there was no way that he'd be letting her go anytime soon.

Seth had heard the commotion and decided to climb up to see what was happening. He was almost sure that he'd heard Miss Carolena's voice. As soon as he saw her, he screeched in happiness and threw himself into the mix, trying to hug her as well. She opened her arms and invited him to their group hug.

Carnage realized that Murder and Lore stood there still, watching. He stood, placing Carolena on her feet, but maintaining touch at all times, his arm around her, holding her close.

He formed a fist and pounded it over his own chest, over his own heart.

Lore gave a short, shallow little bow.

Murder said, "You are most welcome, my friend."

Lore said to Murder, "This. This is what I search for, long for. This is my torture. I know not how much longer I can bear it," he whispered.

Murder spoke quietly to Lore, "We will find your soul, Lore. We will not stop searching until we find her."

"My mind leaves me. I have nothing to hold to. I may not last that long," Lore confided.

Enthrall spoke, "Lore, Murder, I had no idea that you'd gone after Carolena. Thank you. How can we repay you?"

Lore looked from Enthrall to Carnage, "He has already made a binding agreement. There is no need for you to become indebted as well."

Enthrall was drawn up short, "What did you promise, Carnage?"

Carnage, his smile beaming from his face, shrugged his shoulders before wrapping Carolena in his huge arms again.

"You don't know? You didn't ask?" Enthrall said.

Carnage shook his head, though he was still smiling when he looked down at the woman in his arms, tightly holding onto him. It didn't really matter, as long as she was at his side; it didn't matter what Lore wanted, he'd happily give it.

Lore watched for a moment longer before saying, "It is time I took my leave."

Carolena stepped free of Carnage's arm's, walking quickly to where Murder and Lore stood just a few feet away, "Thank you, both, so much! I can never express how much I appreciate both of you."

"You are very welcome, sweet Carolena," Murder said, embracing her.

"Anytime you ever need anything, just ask. I'm always here for either of you," she said.

"Thank you," Murder said, "Just keep this male happy, and I've been more than repaid," he said, indicating Carnage, who had followed her and was standing at her heels impatiently waiting for his opportunity to get her back into the safety of his arms.

Then she spoke to Lore, "Lore, thank you. Thank you for soothing me, thank you for protecting me. Thank you for bringing me back home."

A purplish wispy hand reached out caressing her face, "You are most welcome, child. Be happy, love well."

"Will you come back to visit me? I don't know what you eat, or even if you eat, but you are welcome to come see me whenever you like. Will you?" she begged. "And you, too, Murder."

A high pitched, lilting laughter met her words, "You cannot and do not want to feed me what I eat. I will, however, with your invitation, come for a few kind words from time-to-time," Lore said.

"As will I," Murder said.

Carnage could take it no longer. He wrapped his arms around Carolena and held her closely to him, his front to her back. She held his arms as his arms held her. He rested his chin on the top of her head, smiling as Lore dissipated to loose mist and surrounded Murder, and they gradually faded away.

Lore's voice echoed, "I shall be in touch, Carnage," as they completely disappeared.

Carnage called out, "'Es!" in answer.

Destroy said, "Carolena! You cannot possibly invite him into your home; he's an Ancient! He's dangerous! He's evil! I warned you about him!"

She laughed easily, completely happy to be home among her family and the people she loved, "He is no more dangerous than I. He is my friend, as are you."

Seth had almost crushed the flowers in his hands, but still he held them out to her, "I'm your friend, too?" he asked.

"Yes, you are," she answered.

"I'm going to tell Serena that we have school tomorrow! She'll be so excited!" he said, as he ran back to the spot where he'd climbed over the railing, intending to climb back down.

Enthrall said, "Perhaps you could tell her that school will be next week. Give our Carolena a few days to rest, yes?"

"Okay, I'll tell her next week, and the other kids, too," he called over his shoulder as he threw his leg over the side of the railing to climb back down.

Destroy still wasn't convinced that Lore was safe, "But…"

"Do not be so judgmental, Destroy. If you'd endured all he has, you would not have the presence of mind that he still does. Be kind," she chided Destroy.

Enthrall, intrigued at just how much she knew of Lore's background, asked, "Did he tell you of his circumstance?"

"Not exactly, but on our journey home, certain feelings, inferences, emotions could be felt. Some of it was very confusing, but some things were very clear. He suffers. He's lonely. He's made choices that caused him to be punished, and he rebelled against that punishment, making bad decisions determined to become as bad as he'd been perceived, but he is not bad, not truly. There is a tiny spark of good there, just waiting for the chance to surge forth."

Enthrall nodded, thinking on her words.

"Oh, here! Please put this away for now. We must go into town and file it with a judge and make sure that everyone knows that this is my land, no one is welcome here without express permission from me," Carolena said, holding the signed document out to Enthrall.

Enthrall reached for the document, confused, "I don't understand, what is it?"

"It's a deed to all the land from town to the water's edge and beyond. The swamp, it's mine. Lore made my father sign it over to me and seal it in blood and his fingerprints. No one will ever threaten Whispers again."

Enthrall couldn't believe it; he was speechless, unrolling the document and glancing over it quickly. "Carolena, I don't know what to say."

"Say thank you, say you'll take care of all the legalities for me, letting people know that this is now private property," she answered.

He looked up at her, and she smiled at him, "Your Whispers is safe forever, Enthrall. It's yours."

He pulled her in for a hug, "Thank you, Carolena," he whispered in a husky voice, rife with emotion.

"You are very welcome, Enthrall," she answered.

Carnage, impatient to be alone with Carolena, simply picked her up and walked away from their friends on the deck. Once he got her inside, he closed and locked the door and went about pulling all the shades down over the windows.

Enthrall burst out laughing, "Fine! We can take a hint! We will see you in a few days. Welcome home, Carolena. None of us was the same without you."

"Thank you!" she called back.

Epilogue, Eighteen months later

A chubby little cherub of a girl with slate blue eyes and silver hair laughed a full belly laugh as only a young child can, as she sat in the grass in front of her Uncle Enthrall's home, playing with the purple mist that swirled in and out of her grasp. Lifting her hair and swishing it back and forth. She'd throw the ball as far as her little arms would let her, and the mist would gently roll it back to her and tickle her belly. She'd dissolve into peals of laughter and throw it again.

Her laughter made the adults on the porch smile and chuckle as well. Carnage stood and went down the stairs toward her.

She looked up and saw him coming. She happily started kicking her chubby little legs and reaching up to him, "Papapapapapa!"

He made kissy sounds at her and picked her up, tossing her over his head and catching her.

Lore lifted the ball and made it appear to float in the air, tossing it around, bobbling it. She squealed and reached for the ball. Lore's mist swirled, and his form became visible, "Lily, did you show Papa what I taught you?"

Lily was only 10 months old, but she was very intelligent and understood more than some adults. She held her little hands out in front of her, squeezed them together, brought them to her mouth and blew on them. Purple mist immediately floated out of the other side of her clasped hands.

She squealed excitedly and waved her hands in the mist to make it float away, then clapped her hands, proud of herself.

Carnage smiled, and adjusting her in the crook of his arm, clapped his own hands and said, "Aaayyyy Leelee!"

Lily grinned and called, "Ama!"

Carolena answered, smiling, "I saw you, sweet girl! You are so smart! Uncle Lore is going to have his hands full when you get a little older."

Enthrall said, "Lore, you better watch it, you're teaching her all your tricks; she'll end up as powerful as you are."

"That was my plan all along — you should all be very nice to her," he teased back, not even a trace of his insanity present.

Destroy sat with Enthrall and Carolena watching the Ancient playing with Lily. He'd come around quite a bit since it had been announced that Lore would be Lily's godfather, but still was hesitant to trust him. It seemed no one knew exactly his entire story, and the fact that he could eat souls was very disturbing to Destroy — though no one else seemed to mind too much — so he still kept his distance, but he no longer actively avoided the Ancient. He couldn't if he wanted to be around Carolena and Lily; Lore was always near them. He watched the little girl as she played with her father and Lore — they all adored her.

He'd been there the day that Lore had materialized at Carnage and Carolena's house, announcing that he'd come to collect the debt that Carnage owed him for rescuing Carolena.

Carnage had stood and faced Lore, waiting to see what payment he'd have to pay.

Lore had looked from Carolena to Carnage, then announced, "I want your child."

Carnage roared, as did Destroy who jumped to his feet, also roaring.

Carolena had stared, open-mouthed, before finally recovering and saying, "What?! We have no child! And if we did, I certainly wouldn't ever give my child away. Shame on you for inferring that we would!"

"You will not have her baby!" Destroy had seconded "What kind of monster are you?!"

"A better one than you!" Lore had hissed at Destroy, causing him to take a step back.

Then Lore spoke to Carolena, "You misunderstand, Carolena. I wish to have access to your child, I want to teach her all the things I know. I wish to guide her and make her untouchable by any she does not choose. I wish to make her strong, independent. I shall mentor her! And I don't wish to have her torn from me later. I want to be a part of her life."

Carolena knew Lore and understood what he wanted. Few knew the full scope of his loneliness, but she did. She'd felt it firsthand as he'd brought her and Murder back to Whispers. And most of Whispers' inhabitants steered clear of him, thought him evil incarnate. He was evil, to a degree, but he was good, too. And he knew that most would not allow him near their children. So he was demanding entrance into her child's life as payment on the debt that Carnage owed him, that way, they'd have no choice but to include him. He wouldn't be alone anymore. He'd be a part of their family.

"Is this the debt you planned on collecting when you made Carnage promise to repay you for your efforts?" she asked.

Lore's image smiled, then swirled into a frown, before smiling again, "I knew not what to ask for. Only that it is good to have others indebted to you. But now, with your little one on the way, I wish to be involved. I am tired, child. So tired. And I'm losing my hold on sanity — I have been too long alone and searching. I have love to give, so much love. And power, more power than any one being should have. Your child will not fear me; she hasn't been taught to. Let me be a part of her life. I will make her stronger and more powerful than any other but me. It is my repayment. I am owed whatever I choose, and I choose this."

Carnage had stopped snarling, and listened, understanding. Carolena had spoken of some of the things she'd felt and heard whilst in the dimension that Lore moved in, and he'd brought his love back to him. He no longer feared Lore. Carolena stood and took Carnage's hand, "I have no problem with you being involved with our child's life, with our lives. But there is one thing that could prevent that for a while."

"What is that?" Lore asked.

"I'm not pregnant, as of yet there is no child. But as soon as we are, if we ever are, you are welcome to be his or her godfather. The one responsible for her if anything should ever happen to us. The one to help us guide her and protect her."

Lore smiled slyly, "Do I have your word on that?"

"Of course, you do."

Lore approached them, held out a hand, and placed it on Carolena's belly, "Here rests your daughter. She was there when I brought you back from your father's home, and she is there now. She is strong, stubborn, lively."

Carolena's smile dropped, she looked down at her stomach. Carnage brushed Lore's hand away, placing his own there. He lifted Carolena and stood her on the couch, kneeling to be face-to-face with her stomach, "Mine," he whispered, touching her belly reverently.

"No," she said.

Carnage looked up at her.

"Ours," Carolena said, as a huge smile beamed from her lips.

"Oorrrs," he repeated.

Destroy watched the little girl playing with her father and godfather for a while longer, then rose and started off toward the trees.

"Do not wander far, Gargoyle," Lore's voice called out.

Destroy turned and watched the mist still playing with Lily, "I may go wherever I choose!" he shot back in true Destroy fashion.

"Yes, you may. But if you wander too far, you may not be here when she needs us. I'll have to take another; you will miss your chance."

"When who needs us? You speak in riddles, just say what you mean!" Destroy shouted, before turning and continuing on his path.

He didn't make it very far before he heard Lore ask conversationally, "Carolena, do you remember the little gypsy you met at your father's home?"

Carolena, standing to go into Enthrall's home to get drinks and snacks for everyone, thought about it for a moment, "You mean Rowan? Yes, yes I remember her."

"I shall go for her soon — she belongs among us," Lore answered, before again allowing his mist to dissipate and tickle the child.

Destroy stalked back over to where his friends all visited, watching the mist swirl around the ground, "Who is Rowan? Why does she belong here? What does she look like?"

No one answered him, but Lore's maniacal laughter rang clearly in the yard and among the surrounding trees.

Destroy knew better than to beg Lore for information. He'd end up owing the Ancient a debt, so instead he changed direction and followed Carolena into Enthrall's house, "Carolena! Who is Rowan?"

"She is a servant in my father's home," she answered.

"Why is she coming here?" Destroy persisted.

Laughing at his sudden interest in the girl he'd never met, she told him, "I'm not sure she is, and if she does, I do not know why!"

"But Lore said she was! What does she look like? He said she's a gypsy, is she a 'put a curse on you gypsy?'"

Exasperated with all his questions, she faced him, "I don't know, Destroy! Go ask Lore."

"Well, at least tell me if she can read, can she read?" he demanded.

She put down the tray she'd just lifted, filled with glasses of sarsaparilla tea, "Destroy! I have no idea. Go ask Lore."

"Damn!" he swore under his breath. He really didn't want to ask Lore. He had no doubt he'd end up promising the Ancient a repayment and be in debt to him. He did not want to owe him a favor — he still didn't fully trust him. He stomped out of the house, looking for Lore. Instead he found Enthrall and Carnage sitting on the porch, Carnage holding Lily.

"Where is Lore?" Destroy asked.

"He said he had business to attend to, kissed Lily and left," Enthrall answered.

Carolena came out onto the porch and placed the tray on the table.

Lily reached for Enthrall who very happily lifted the girl from her Papa's lap and sat her on his own lap, letting her dip her fingers in his tea and suck them clean.

Carolena sat on Carnage's lap. He kissed her lips, "Lahb, Leenah."

"I love you, too, Carnage. Thank you for bringing me home with you," she answered, kissing his brow.

Destroy threw his hands up in the air and snarled, "Arrrgghhhhh!" before he started out in the direction of the deepest swamp, "Lore!" he shouted loudly. A few moments later, he repeated it, "Lore!"

He could be heard mumbling, "I'm going to regret this, I have absolutely no doubt," as he marched through the trees, and they lost sight of him.

"This is going to be interesting," Enthrall said.

"Indeed it will," Carolena agreed. "I can't wait to see how this plays out. Lore just loves to provoke him."

They all laughed.

Carolena looked around herself, smiling, thinking of how very different her life in Whispers started out, right there in front of Enthrall's home. She'd thought she would lose her life, become a prisoner here. Nothing could be further from the truth. She'd found love here, had a husband, a daughter, and close friends. Her life was sweeter than she ever thought it could be.

She sent up a silent little thank you to her mother for giving her life, for giving her the chance to be where she was, loved by whom she loved.

Life was good.

From The Author

Thank you for purchasing this book. I hope that my stories make you smile and give you a small escape from the daily same ole/same ole. I write for me, simply for the joy of it, but if someone else also smiles as a result, even better. Your support is greatly appreciated. If you liked this story, please remember to leave a review wherever you bought it, so that more people can find my books. Each review is important, no matter how short or long it may be.

See you in the pages of the next one!

Sandra R Neeley

Other books by this author:

Avaleigh's Boys series, books 1 - 5 (so far)

I'm Not A Dragon's Mate!

Bane's Heart

Kaid's Queen

Maverik's Ashes

Bam's Ever

About the Author

My name is Sandra R Neeley. I write Paranormal Romance with a small town feel. Why, you may ask? Romance, because who doesn't love a good romance, and Paranormal because, well — normal is highly overrated, so Paranormal it is. I'm 54, I have two kids, one 32 and one 12 (yes, God does have a sense of humor), one grandchild, one husband, and a menagerie of animals. I love to cook, I am a voracious reader, though since I started writing, I don't get as much time to read as I once did. I am a homebody and prefer my writing/reading time to a crowd. I have had stories and fictional characters wandering around in my head for as long as I can remember. I'm a Self-Published Author, and I like it that way because I can decide what and when to write. I am by no means a formal, polished, properly structured individual and neither are my stories. But people seem to love the easy emotion and small town feel that naturally flows from them. A bit of a warning though, there are some "triggers" in them that some people should avoid. I'm a firm believer that you cannot have light without the dark. You cannot fully embrace the joy and elation that my people eventually find if you do not bear witness to their darkest hours as well. So please read the warnings supplied with each of the synopses about my books before you buy them.

You can find me at any of these places:

authorsandrarneeley@gmail.com
https://www.sneeleywrites.com
https://www.sneeleywrites.com/contact
https://www.sneeleywrites.com/blog
https://www.facebook.com/authorsandrarneeley/

https://www.facebook.com/groups/755782837922866/
https://www.amazon.com/Sandra-R-Neeley/e/B01M65OZ1J/
https://twitter.com/sneeleywrites
https://www.instagram.com/sneeleywrites/
https://www.goodreads.com/author/show/15986167.Sandra_R_Neeley
https://www.bookbub.com/authors/sandra-r-neeley

Stop by to say Hi, and sign up to be included in updates on current and future projects.

Printed in Great Britain
by Amazon